School for Hawaiian Girls

Georgia Ka'apuni McMillen

THE PERMANENT PRESS
Sag Harbor, New York 11963

Copyright © 2005 by Georgia Ka'apuni McMillen

Library of Congress Cataloging-in-Publication Data

McMillen, Georgia.
  School for Hawaiian girls : a novel / by Georgia Ka'apuni McMillen.
     p.   cm.
  ISBN 1-57962-193-7 (alk. paper)
   1. Teenage girls—Crimes against—Fiction. 2. Brothers and sisters—Fiction. 3. Poor
families—Fiction. 4. Revenge—Fiction. 5. Hawaii—Fiction. I. Title.

PS3613.C58545S36 2005
813'.6—dc22

First paperback printing July 2009   2005048899

Printed in The United States of America.

THE PERMANENT PRESS
4170 Noyac Road
Sag Harbor, NY 11963

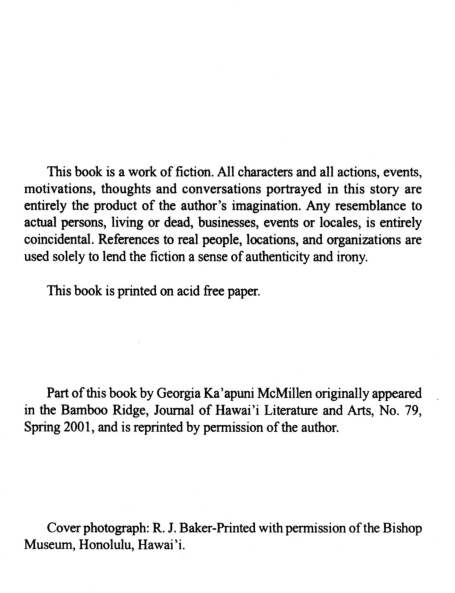

Part of this book by Georgia Ka'apuni McMillen originally appeared in the Bamboo Ridge, Journal of Hawai'i Literature and Arts, No. 79, Spring 2001, and is reprinted by permission of the author.

Cover photograph: R. J. Baker-Printed with permission of the Bishop Museum, Honolulu, Hawai'i.

Thanks

I am fortunate to have family and friends who never doubted this project's merits, or my capacity to see it through. My list of thanks is long and begins with my parents, Francis and Rosemarie. My thanks also to Cressida Connolly, and Martin and Judith Shepard.

1922, Kohala
Sam

Patience was hard to take straight on, her and her squash-nose, fat-lip face. Which was why I kept our meetings secret. Besides it was no one's business what we did in private. Let's keep our afternoons special, I told her.

On the days she carried the lunch pot down to the church ladies, I would wait for her outside the gate, the School for Hawaiian Girls at the top of the valley. Patience always acted surprised to see me, then she would scold me. Then she would say she couldn't come with me, but that girl was game—100 percent. Like last week when I pretended I was the plantation *luna* and she was the new girl, fresh off the boat from Manila. Only knew how to say yes, no and good morning.

That Friday I was waiting for her outside the gate, on the road going down to the church. The wind blew off Kohala Mountain and down through the valley. The trees creaked. I smelled the lunch they were cooking in the school kitchen and my stomach twisted. I crawled through the wrought-iron gate and ran across the schoolyard to the classroom building. Inside the open window, the lady with blue hair was walking up and down the desk rows, her hands behind her back. "Small, neat stitches, girls," she said. "You want to be proud to wear your handiwork."

There was Patience, holding the needle and thread up to her face because that was how blind she was.

"*Ei nei,*" I said.

She looked up, her right eye going left, the left eye going right. I could never tell what she was looking at.

"*I* need some handiwork."

One of the girls started laughing.

"*Hūi,* where's my lunch?"

The blue-haired lady walked to the window clapping her hands. "Who's there?"

Quick, I ran back to the gate, crawled through and hid behind the mock orange until I heard the kitchen door open and footsteps. I looked— it was my sister Lydie, taking her long steps across the school yard, the lunch pot hanging from her arm. I waited for her to close the gate before jumping out, "Who made you the delivery girl?"

"You! I almost dropped this." She shifted the pot to her other hand. "Where's Patience?"

Lydie walked ahead. "You're supposed to meet her in the forest after school."

"Patience's giving me orders now?"

Catching up with her, I lifted the pot lid. "Stew! How you knew that's what I wanted?"

She pulled away, gravy spilling on her skirt. "I'm gonna kick you."

"Patience always gives me a helping."

Lydie stopped. "Do I look like Patience?"

Nope, not by a long shot. Patience looked like the dead fish me and Gramps found the day before at sunset. My sister Lydie looked like the sunset—the curve of her forehead, the color of her skin. And it was funny how that went in our family. We all had the same features—me, Lydie, and my other sister Bernie. Only on me and Bernie they looked like shit. Our skin was black, our hair too frizzy—and on Bernie, one eye was round, the other *pākē*.

Lydie walked to the bridge over the stream, in the valley the old-timers called *Ka'īlio*. The Dog. She put down the lunch pot and pulled out of her pocket an envelope stuffed with dollar bills.

"Who gave you that?" I asked, but I knew. Every Friday the head-mistress gave Patience the lunch and money for the church ladies.

"Mind your own business," Lydie said.

"How about a loan?" I said, watching her count the bills. I could've told her: there was always ten. "I pay you back with interest. After this weekend, I'm gonna be rich."

"After this weekend, you're gonna be in jail—you keep it up."

"Nobody knows."

"Everybody knows because you can't keep your big mouth shut."

One month before, I'd found Sheriff Pua's stills in Pololū and started pouring off a little each day. That Saturday, I was selling the booze at the cock fight.

"How'd you like a rich brother?" I jabbed her with my elbow.

She shoved me back.

"Lydie, I get one question."

"You *have a* question," she said.

"How come they let *you* take down the lunch?"

"I'm late." Lydie picked up the pot.

"Church ladies not gonna starve."

Lydie crossed the bridge.

"Ei nei. What's the big secret?"

A year ago it was the baby in her belly. When the gossips in Kapa'au and Hāwī began sniffing the air, trying to find out if the Māhukona rumors were true, Mama made plans to get rid of Lydie. She told me and Gramps to take Lydie through the sugarcane field down to Keawa'eli Bay, then by canoe to Māhukona Harbor where she would catch the Maui-bound steamer. There someone named Gladys on Maui, Mama had said, would take care of Lydie until the baby was born.

"Least let me carry the lunch pot," I said, following her.

"If Mama sees you up here, you're in trouble."

"Ho! Make me laugh," I said. "What else's new?"

We walked to the bend in the road. From there, we could see the church further down, the whitewashed walls, the green bell tower and the meeting hall. After building the church, the missionaries had named it Light in the Darkness. Then they renamed the whole valley because they couldn't keep their church in a place called The Dog—some kind of Christian bad luck with dogs, pigs, rats and spiders. You name it, the missionaries had a problem with it.

I heard the trade winds blowing through the forest. They'd begun in March; now it was late April. Plus, on the Big Island up in Kohala, we had a wind called *Inuwai,* Drinking Water. I heard it rolling in from Kai'ōpihi.

So did Lydie. She lifted her chin and *Inuwai* washed over her face. Now I saw that her eyes were red. "Tell me," I said. "What's going on?"

"I'm running away, Sam. I need to find Angelina."

"Who?"

"I'm the mother and that's the name I choose. The Maui lady said I could come and visit."

"Don't sound like you going to visit."

"I'm taking her back," Lydie said.

So that's it. "Anybody knows what you up to?"

"Charlie does."

That *lōlō*—the one who got Lydie in trouble in the first place.

"He's waiting with a canoe at Keawa'eli."

"What? He's paddling you across the channel?"

"He's taking me to Māhukona. I'm catching the steamer for Maui."

"You catching the steamer?" I said. "What about that dumb Hawaiian?" Listen, my sister Lydie could've had any boy in the District. I even saw the plantation manager's son looking at her. But she chose

Charlie Moku, who could only talk about fish and fishing. Didn't even own a pair of shoes.

"As soon as he's saved enough, he's coming too," she said.

"And how you got your fare in the first place? What you gonna live on when you get there?"

"Gramps gave me his coins last night."

"You joking, right? His money's not even American." Most were English coins.

"Some are," Lydie said.

"Don't go today," I said. "I'll give you what I make tomorrow night. Then go next week." The steamer left for Maui every Friday.

"I've got enough," she said.

"You got shit. You don't even have extra clothes."

"Everything's in my schoolbag. I hid it in the cane field this morning."

We heard the church ladies laughing in the meeting hall. Lydie picked up the lunch pot. "Promise you won't tell, Sam."

"Write me as soon as you get there," I said. But either Mama picked up the mail or my other sister Bernie—Mama's spy.

"Don't write," I said. "I'm gonna meet you on Maui next Friday."

"Really?" It was the first time I'd seen her come close to smiling in a year.

"And I'm walking you down to Keawa'eli," I said. "It's about time Charlie Moku heard from me."

"Then forget it. I don't want your help." Lydie began walking to the meeting hall, but inside something fell. It rolled around and around on its rim, the church ladies whooping. Lydie waited, then walked in the door.

"Finally!" I heard them say.

I ran around the meeting hall to the kitchen in the back. Ho! It smelled good in there. Through the screen door I saw the cakes for Sunday cooling by the oven. The church ladies wouldn't miss one or two. I tried to open the screen door, but the hinges squeaked. One of the church ladies heard and looked back through the kitchen.

Mama was president of the Christian League, the club for Hawaiian women. She sat with the ladies at the round table in the middle of the meeting room. Above the table, they had hung blue and red ribbons from the ceiling light. Mama led them in a prayer, then dished out the stew. Now I saw Lydie, crawling on her hands and knees picking up blue and red ribbon scraps. "Lydie," I tried to whisper.

She turned her back to me.

Then a church lady pointed to the other side of the room. Now Lydie was crawling on the floor over there—and I didn't like this. She had a one-hour walk through the sugarcane field to Keawa'eli. Then a three-hour paddle down the coast to Māhukona—if the wind was at their backs. If Charlie Moku paddled his canoe as hard as he fucked my sister.

They made Lydie eat lunch with them. When they finished, Mama walked into the kitchen carrying the empty plates. "Lydia," she said, standing at the sink. "Bring in the lunch pot."

Lydie carried it into the kitchen. "You don't have to."

"Of course we have to wash it. Just look at you, gravy down your skirt." Mama washed the pot once, then twice, then she put it on the rack. Lydie grabbed it and started walking out. "What will I do with you?" Mama said, holding out the dishtowel.

Lydie began drying, but Mama grabbed the pot and towel out of Lydie's hands and did it herself—wiping and wiping. Finally she gave the pot to Lydie. "After school I want you to help finish the decorations for Reverend's birthday," she said.

"But—"

"I told Bernice to wait for you."

In the main room, a church lady said, "Lydia, play us something." There was a piano against the wall.

"Play some of that colored music," another said. It was Patience's Aunty Louise. She put her hands on her hips—wide as bookshelves.

"Reverend's down at the manse today," another said. Lydie sat at the piano and found the rhythm with her left hand, the melody with her right.

"Stop this!"

Ho! Mama even made me jump.

"Suppose Reverend heard?" Mama said, walking across the wood floor to the piano, still holding the dish towel. "Does this look like a dance hall?"

Lydie left the piano and walked to the door carrying the empty lunch pot. Aunty Louise handed her the bag of ribbon scraps. "The dressmaking class can use them."

"Play from the hymnal," Mama told Lydie.

"But I'm late," Lydie said, walking out.

"Lydia!"

"Let her go," Aunty Louise said.

Amen and about time.

"The money," another lady said.

Mama walked back to the kitchen, "I'll get it later."

Quick, I ran to the front of the church, across the road and into the forest. I reached the clearing before Lydie. When she saw me she said, "I told you to leave me alone."

"You told me to wait for Patience here."

She pulled the envelope with the money out of her pocket and wrote on it, 'Please return to the School for Hawaiian Girls.' She put the envelope in the lunch pot, and the lunch pot at the edge of the clearing.

"Keep the money," I said. "You gonna need it."

"I can't."

"Why not give it to Mama in the first place?"

"I forgot."

"Oh yeah? You weren't thinking of keeping it?"

"Stop arguing with me!"

Fine. I wasn't gonna argue. I wasn't gonna follow her. I let Lydie walk away, while I got comfortable. But my empty stomach started moaning and I heard a voice: Psss. I looked around. I heard it again.

Uh oh. That lunch pot filled with money was calling me. What else could I do? Better if I took the money home for safekeeping. Suppose someone found it before the school girls? Suppose the girls didn't return it? I knew them. Some were worse than me.

Then I heard branches snapping. The clearing dropped off into a gulch. Down in the gulch I saw someone running, his red shirt flashing through the green leaves. On Friday afternoons all the boys came up to the forest to meet the girls. I whistled my whistle, but the red shirt didn't stop—and I didn't like that. Not like I was king of the mountain, but all the boys knew me and would've stopped.

And whoever he was, he was too early. The school didn't let out until 3:00. By then the school would be wondering what happened to Lydie, and Mama would be telling Bernie to go and find her. By then, Lydie would be sitting in a canoe, Charlie Moku paddling like crazy so she didn't miss the steamer.

And that made me think about her plan. It was the dumbest thing I'd heard all year. Far as I was concerned, Lydie had no plan, except that she was going to Maui and praying for a miracle. On top of that, she had no money except the thirteen-dollar fare. Better if I caught up with her and gave her the ten dollars from the lunch pot—might as well. I wasn't doing anything the next couple of hours except listening to my stomach grumble. I ran down the path, then grabbed an overhead branch to keep from falling into Government Road—empty in the middle of the day. Across the road lay the field, the sugarcane standing as high as our house. The white-fringed cane tassels waved against the blue sky.

Next to the field someone had left his horse. Her coat was brushed and shiny, and the saddle was polished. I crossed the road and she looked up from the patch of grass she was munching. "Who left you out here all alone?" I said and ran my hand along her smooth, brown neck.

In the nearby field the cane tassels bowed. I called to Lydie, "Wait up."

I followed the irrigation ditch into the field. "I got something for you—to help find the baby."

I ran along the ditch and out onto the cane-haul road. The road cut through the field, all the way down to the sugar mill at Keawa'eli. There was Lydie, walking down the middle. The midday sun turned her black hair red, and her faded skirt bright white. "Wait," I said, running to her.

She put her hands on her hips and threw her head back. "Go away!"

"Let me go with you."

Her voice changed. "Will you?"

"Next week, after the cock fight. We go together."

"Don't you see? If I wait, I won't go."

"Then here." I gave her the ten dollars.

"You stole the church money."

"No, it's my money."

She crossed her arms over her chest, "Prove it."

"Take it. You going with nothing."

She walked on.

"Fine. Beg for food." I followed her to the rock outcropping beside the cane-haul road. She climbed up the rock.

"Lydie," I called up to her. "You got any water?" I was so thirsty I was ready to drink from the irrigation ditch.

She didn't answer.

I climbed up, "Lydie?"

She lay belly-down, her arm shoved in a crevice. "My bag's gone," she said, sitting up.

"Got any water?"

Lydie climbed down, "My fare. Gramps's coins." She leaned against the rock, "The blanket I made for the baby."

Then *Inuwai* rolled in, blowing in sets of three gusts. The first swept over the field. The second blew over the cane-haul road and sent the dust swirling. The third swept over Lydie's face. She pushed herself away from the dead rock. "I'm going anyway."

"Lydie..." I loved her so much.

"I don't need the bag."

She was braver than all of us put together.

"Give me the ten dollars," Lydie said.

Shucks.

"Hurry. I'm late."

I gave her the church money.

"What else you got? I need it, Sam."

I emptied my pocket. There was another eight dollars and thirty cents.

"Where'd you get this? Why didn't you offer it before?"

Business was business. There would be operating expenses tomorrow night.

"And you'll come next Friday?" she said.

"How will I find you?"

"Charlie will know." She began running down the cane-haul road, then stopped and turned. "Sam! Don't tell anyone."

Then, just inside the field, the tassels bowed and there was the flash of red cloth again. At the edge of the road I looked into the sugarcane, but I didn't see anything.

I knew what it was. My eyes were playing tricks on me. My stomach was behind the whole thing—pissed off because I didn't feed it since breakfast.

Now I heard the school bell. I ran back to Government Road. The horse was still there. "Why don't you come home with me?" I said, walking toward her.

Two of the school girls stepped out of the forest on the other side of the road.

"They let you out early?" I said.

"Better hurry, Sam," one said. "Patience is waiting for you."

Patience was blabbing about us?

I ran up the forest path. Four girls stood in the clearing, along with Eddie-Boy Kauka—his arm slung around two of the girls' shoulders. That greedy dog.

I saw Patience walking down the path to the clearing. I ducked behind a bush. She walked into the clearing, over to the lunch pot still sitting at the edge. "Has anyone seen Lydie?" she said.

The girls shook their heads, and Eddie-Boy just stared at her. He was like me that way. He didn't like answering anyone's questions.

"She was supposed to take this to the meeting hall," Patience said. Then she looked up, her cross-eyes going every which way. "Has anyone seen Sam Kaluhi?"

Eddie-Boy choked, then laughed. "That's who you meeting?"

That did it for me. It was one thing that Patience was cross-eyed. Then she made me wait all day. And now, on top of all of that, she let everyone know my private business with her. A girl had to know her place. A girl had to keep a secret. Especially girls like Patience.

1985, Kohala
Moani

No one plans on a career in the kayak business. After graduating from college I was supposed to work for my uncle, owner of Sam's Hideaways. He'd promised to make me a VP in one of his hotels. Instead, I went to the swap-meet and saw a pair of used kayaks, fifty dollars for both. I bought them, baptized them off Diamond Head and began exploring.

A week later a couple on their honeymoon said they would pay me for a ride. I told them, "You don't have to pay me."

The next day I met two businessmen who were playing hooky from their convention. They said the honeymooners had recommended me, and asked if I would take them for a ride too. They offered me twenty-five dollars and spent the afternoon taking pictures of each other in the kayak.

Oh. So that was it. They wanted to go home to Des Moines and show the brother-in-law their he-man vacation—while he hauled his brats around Disneyland.

I told Uncle thanks anyway. He called me a *lōlō*, but I didn't care. I had figured out a way to have fun and get paid. I didn't see what was so dumb about that.

I dubbed my company Lost Paradise, and began taking tourists on daylong kayak excursions from Waikīkī to Hanauma Bay. They wanted snorkel gear and lunch? My motto from the beginning was: Whatever the customer wants. As long as he was willing to pay. By the end of the year, I had bought a fleet of twenty single-man kayaks for trips to Hanauma Bay, Mākaha and Waimea Bay.

I bought eight tandem kayaks, hired two full-time guides and designed five-day kayaking trips on the neighbor islands. From April to August we took groups of twelve down the Nāpali Coast to Kalalau Valley on Kaua'i, along the Hāmākua Coast on the Big Island, and along Moloka'i's backside, from Hālawa Bay to St. Philomena's at Kalaupapa.

I served fresh banana pancakes for breakfast, grilled salmon steaks for dinner. I promised would-be clients, '...*an unforgettable outdoor adventure to the hidden Hawai'i of yesteryear.*' That's what I wrote for our brochure. My lawyer wrote "ironclad" liability disclaimers. My accountant found an insurance company willing to provide "excess."

I wore shorts and a sports bra to work, netted a six-figure income and bought my own condo in Honolulu. Besides all that, I knew I was doing something right at the end of my trips, what with the teary-eyed hugs at the airport. My clients always promised to keep in touch. A year later I got wedding pictures from people I couldn't remember, and Christmas cards featuring cross-eyed babies fresh from the birth canal. I tacked them to the bulletin board at the office. I got referrals from France. Saudi Arabia. You name it, I was out there. Global.

But how long can a girl paddle kayak for a living?

It was a key question we all had to ask ourselves. I was strong. I probably had years of paddling left in my shoulders and back. But thirty-seven years of age wasn't twenty-seven. And in no time I would be forty-seven. It was time to start thinking about the long run. That was why we found ourselves on the Big Island, the week before our first-of-the-season Moloka'i launch. As soon as we turned off the smooth black highway onto the valley road leading up to the old school, I knew it would work. The feel of the gravel and dirt road beneath the car tires told me so.

Take the road less traveled.

I was already writing the hotel brochure in my head.

We drove up the valley road past an old church, then around the bend in the road. There was a rain puddle beneath a giant banyan tree. I drove through it and the bounce startled my sister Pu, asleep against the car window. She sat up, opened her eyes, then closed them again. Sweat trickled down her cheek. The real estate agent had told me the sale included the school, church and surrounding fifteen acres, which stretched from the school down past the highway and into the fallow sugarcane field. He said the stream and valley were originally named after a dog. Not good.

14

Then the missionaries built a church, the agent had said—Light of the Holy Something—and renamed the valley after the church. Even worse.

Tourism and religion didn't mix. People flew to Hawai'i to romp around half-naked and drink mai-tais. My clients at Lost Paradise were no different; they just thought they were because they did their romping wearing sports gear and paddling a kayak.

We drove to a stone bridge. I liked that. It was quaint and cute. Then I heard goats bleating. I stopped the car on the bridge and rolled down the window. It was guava season, and the smell of rotting fruit filled the car. The goats scrambled up the embankment next to the stream. Another negative. They crapped by the stream and polluted the water. I could hear my lawyer now: Polluted water you knew about? My God, Moani. This's worse exposure than kayaking.

We drove across the bridge covering the stream. It needed more water and landscaping. The school buildings were hidden behind a high wall of mock orange hedging. Nice. My guests would be tired after the long drive up the coast from the Kona airport. They would be wondering where the hotel was. I would give them clues, borders of white ginger as they turned off the highway. Geranium pots at the bend in the road. Benches beside the bridge. A gravel path down to the stream.

We drove through two stone pillars, up to the back of a three-story building. Another hedge of mock orange surrounded the building, covering the first floor windows. I parked the car. "We're here, Pu."

She sat up, blinking.

"Remember the school I told you about?"

"I'm hun-gry."

"We'll get lunch after we look around."

She stepped out of the car, the back of her t-shirt wet. She swayed in the midday sunlight, holding onto the car door handle.

"Shut the door, Pu."

"Are there more cheese crackers?"

"You already ate three packs on the plane," I said, stepping onto the back porch.

"That was a long time ago."

"No more snacks," I said.

"If we were at my work? If we were at my work, it would be snack time now." Pu worked at Island Cares, which gave her a morning coffee & donut break and an afternoon chip & soda snack.

"They give you guys too much junk," I said, walking across the length of the back porch. It sounded solid. There was a door, but it was locked. "They were supposed to leave it open for me. Let's walk around to the front."

Pu followed, her ankles swollen. "Today? Today they gonna have cake. Today's my boyfriend's birthday."

"I thought you guys broke up?"

"He said I could still have cake."

There was a mango tree beside the building, rotting mangos on the ground. Pu picked up one.

"No, Pu. They're rotten."

She raised it to her mouth.

"Pu, I said no."

She bit it.

I knocked it out of her hand, but she looked for another.

"Don't you dare, Pu. It'll make you sick. It's full of worms."

She eyed me, leaning down.

"Look," I said, pointing at the swarming flies. I reached for her sticky hand. "I warned you about this trip, Pu."

She was supposed to be at work, but that morning, fifteen minutes after I had put her in the elevator, our concierge Victor had called me. "Ah, you know your sister's down here? Look like she not going out."

The Ko'olau Mountains stood behind Honolulu, our building next to the mountains. The mornings were always wet, the wind blowing rain showers off the mountain cliffs. I looked over the *lanai* railing. Twenty-three stories below the monkeypod trees were nodding in the wind.

In the lobby I found Pu sitting on the bench next to the fake waterfall. "Hey, Pu. What's happening?"

"Wall sing, Matilda, wall sing Matilda..."

"Pu, you'll be late."

"Wall sing Matilda with me-eeee..."

"Pu, it's time to go to work." Monday to Friday, eight to three-thirty.

She stopped singing and looked out the glass doors, "Lots of wind, Moani."

I stepped into the breezeway. There was a misty rain—no different from any other morning. "What if I get your wind-breaker?" I told her.

"I come with you."

"No, no," I said. "I'll be right back." Once Pu was in the apartment, she would go to the toilet again, drink water again, check her backpack and lunch box again.

16

But up on the twenty-third floor the second elevator opened to Pu. "I beat you, Moani."

"Pu, I told you to wait."

She thought about this, then, "No you di-dn't."

I ignored the howling wind whipping over the *lanai* and zipped Pu into the windbreaker. Down in the lobby she told me, "I don't want to go outside."

"Come on. You'll be late, and I have to leave soon too." It was already 8:00. My flight for the Big Island left at 9:00.

She shook her head.

"They're depending on you at Island Cares," I said. Just then, the misty rain turned into a downpour.

"Ho!" Victor, the concierge said. "Look at it coming down from the mountain."

"It's just a passing shower," I told Pu. "No big deal."

But at the door, Pu wouldn't budge. "Too windy."

"Come on, Pu. Don't you want to see your boyfriend?" For weeks she had been telling me about the latest retard at Island Cares.

"We broke up."

"Pu, you're making me late." I pulled her hand through the open door, but she began wailing. I realized Victor was staring at me.

Back in the apartment, I tried calling Pu's babysitter, Gina. She wasn't home.

"All right, Pu. You win."

"We're going down to the pool now?" she said.

"Pu, is this a game so you can go swimming?"

"I can swim, Moani."

"Pu, are you faking it to go swimming?"

"We going down to the pool now?"

"No, Pu," I said. "We're going to the Big Island."

SHE LET ME pull her up the front porch steps to the door of the old school. I pushed open the door, and we walked in. Fresh air followed, sending the dust swirling. I swallowed a mouthful, the residue settling on my tongue. Light from the grimy windows fell across the wood floor. The real estate agent had told me that the school closed sometime in the 1920s. I looked over the room and imagined desk chairs scraping across the wood floor and the school girls walking to the door.

"It smells in here," Pu said.

"Mildew." I waved my hand in front of my face.

"Mil-dew," Pu said, waving her hand in front of her face.

I walked to one of the closed doors off the center room. It was locked. So were the other doors. I walked to the windows overlooking the front porch. "Help me, Pu," I said, tugging at one of the windows, dust flying.

"It's dirty here, Moani."

The window wouldn't budge. I tried another. They were all stuck.

Beyond the front porch there was an overgrown field that stretched to a line of trees. On the other side of the trees, I could see the old church tower. I had already asked the agent if the owner would break up the parcel. I wanted to buy the school and church, but not the entire 15 acres.

"Isn't this nice, Pu?" I imagined a carpet of manicured grass on the field. My guests would take off their shoes and walk barefoot across it, while it was snowing blizzards back home in Chicago. I would hire someone to play guitar during dinner.

"You said we gonna get lunch," Pu said.

"Soon."

"Does someone live here?" she said.

"I don't think so."

"But there's chairs."

"Desks, Pu. Old desks." Someone had pushed them along a wall. And there was a rattan sofa, the cushion fabric in tatters. It looked infested. "Don't sit on anything," I told her.

Pu left me and touched the back of the sofa, the bamboo wrap uncoiling and gray. She held up her dusty fingertips, "Dir-ty."

I walked across the room, listening to the solid wood floor. I needed to return with an engineer.

Then, a high piano note sliced through the air. I turned to find Pu standing in front of a piano in the corner. The white keys had yellowed; the black keys had grayed.

"Don't do that," I said.

She hit the piano key again.

"I told you not to touch anything."

"No you di-dn't."

"OK, I'm telling you now. Don't touch anything."

"But—" Pu hit the same key again and again. "It's not right—right, Moani?"

"It needs to be tuned." It was beyond tuning. I would stack it with the other furniture and burn it.

"If you buy this place, will we get the piano too?"

"Pu, you can't play."

She stared at me, and her teeth chattered.

"Cut it out, Pu."

She closed her mouth, but her jaw continued to jump. I had seen others at Island Cares do the same thing. "You could show me how to play," she said.

"I can't play."

"If you learned? If you learned, then you could teach me how to play."

"Right, Pu. I'm taking piano lessons." I walked to the bottom of the staircase. "Let's go upstairs." I began climbing. More solid wood. I liked that too. Then there was another high piano note. "Pu. I told you no."

She stared at the piano keys.

"I'm going upstairs," I said, expecting her to follow. On the landing I looked over the nicked floor, imagining mint green carpet, with the same background color in the rooms, but adding a floral motif. Each room would be distinct. The Hibiscus Room. The Ginger Room.

Off the landing at the top of the stairs I pulled on a window, but it was stuck. I tried two doors, but they wouldn't budge. Then there was another piano note, low and flat. I leaned over the dusty banister, "Hey. Cool it with the piano already."

"Mo-a-ni, I'm hun-gry."

"You're getting fat, Pu." It was my fault. To get her in the bathtub the night before, I had promised chocolate-chip ice cream. To get her to bed, I had promised waffles in the morning.

I tried another door. It opened. Inside the room were two metal bed frames and a tattered curtain hanging over a closet. Outside the room in the hallway again, I looked for the bathroom. At the end of the hall there was a half-open door. I pushed it open, and it hit the back wall. Chips of paint fell on the floor. Inside, was a bathtub on claw feet, a sink and a toilet. The toilet tank hung on the wall near the ceiling, a rusted chain hanging from the tank. I pulled it, and brown water filled the bowl, then spilled over the side. I tapped the floor with my foot. It sounded dull and dense. Rotten.

Back at the staircase landing I listened for Pu. "Hey, what's going on down there?"

She didn't answer.

"I'm going up to the third floor."

A piano chord rang out.

"What did I say, Pu?"

Nothing.

"All right, I'm going up."

The staircase narrowed and the steps were steeper. On the third floor landing I faced two hallways on either side. I walked to the right, pushing open a door. The hinges squeaked. The room was smaller than the one I entered on the second floor. I would have to knock out walls, combine two rooms to make one. Build private baths for each.

I heard footsteps outside the bedroom. "In here, Pu." I stepped out of the bedroom into the empty hallway. "Where're you at?"

She surprised me, walking around on her own. Usually I had to ease her into everything. Seven years ago I began moving her out of St. Teresa's Home for Women, at first just driving her to the new condo each night. The first week we sat on the couch and watched TV, then I drove her back to St. Teresa's. The next week I showed her my bedroom. The third week I made dinner, but she wouldn't eat because, she said, she could only eat at St. Teresa's.

The fifth week we sat on the new mattress in her bedroom.

"I can't sleep here," she told me.

"Why not?"

"The nuns won't know where I am."

"I told them," I said. "From now on you're living with me."

"But I live there. I don't live here."

"I want you to stay with me now. It'll be better with me."

Her teeth chattered. She looked over the new mattress. "But you never wanted me before. How come you want me now?"

After Pu moved in with me, I found a job for her at Island Cares. I couldn't believe her brain still worked after being stuck in St. Teresa's for 18 years. They made her go to church at 5:00 every morning, then dumped her in the day room the rest of the time. There, an old nun sat at a piano and banged out Christmas carols in June, The Battle Hymn of the Republic, Irish folk songs and nursery rhymes.

But Pu surprised me.

At Island Cares she began weaving place mats, pot holders and coasters from *hala* leaves, a 'Made in Hawaii' label on the package. I bought them by the carton, complimentary gifts to my Lost Paradise clients.

We opened her own savings account where she deposited her paycheck. I taught her how to catch the bus to Island Cares, then to Lost Paradise's office, and from there home. We rehearsed the route, which was what Island Cares recommended. Preparation, repetition and more repetition.

"If someone's hassling you, what do you say, Pu?"

"Say, 'No thank you'."

"Suppose they insist, Pu?"

"Blow my whistle." She blew the silver whistle I had bought her and ran it along the chain around her neck where she wore a copy of the condo key. Uncle got her a free bus pass, but she wouldn't use it. "That's for cripples and retards," she had told me.

I THOUGHT I heard the floor creaking in the next room on the third floor. "Pu?"

No answer.

"Puanani?" I looked down the hallway. All the doors were closed. I listened, but only heard the wind blowing through the attic. "I'm going back downstairs," I said.

On the second floor landing I called up to her on the third floor, "Hello?"

Nothing.

"We're leaving soon. Going to the store."

Still no answer.

"Time for soda and chips."

But there wasn't a sound.

Back on the first floor I saw Pu standing out on the porch, leaning against the railing.

"Pu, I thought you were upstairs."

"Yo soy un hombre sincero..."

"Weren't you upstairs?"

"De donde crece las palmas..."

"Thought I heard footsteps upstairs," I said.

"I heard mu-sic."

"Do you like it here?" I asked.

She turned her face left to right, her new hair extensions brushing the sides of her cheeks.

"Why not, Pu?"

"Look," she showed me a piano key. The ivory was cracked and yellow.

"Pu, that doesn't belong to us."

"Whose is it?"

The owners were in Japan, the agent had told me. They wanted to unload the property. "You won't find another deal like this one," he had said.

I turned from the lawn, back to the open door. "If we clean this place up, paint it, bet it would look pretty nice." To the right, there was a separate building the agent called the dining hall. "Let's look."

"You said we going to the store."

"When we're done here. First, I need to look at that building too."

I shut the front doors, looking for locks—already acting like I owned the place. If I sold Lost Paradise, I could cover the purchase price, but I didn't have the funds to renovate, landscape and decorate. I needed to hire an advertising firm to market the place. I needed to hire a staff to run the place. I needed to cover the first three years' operating costs.

This problem led to Uncle, who had offered capital when I started Lost Paradise. I turned down his money, never wanting to share my business with anyone, especially not Uncle. If I accepted it, he would demand control. That was why he was rich, and everyone hated him.

"Come on, Pu." I stepped off the porch.

She wouldn't budge, her chin dropping and her lips pouting. "You said we're going to the store." Her chin started trembling.

"Pu, think I can buy this place without inspecting it?"

She nodded, "Yes, because you decided to buy it already."

"How do you know?"

"I can tell."

"So, you're a mind reader now?"

"Yeah."

I stepped back on the porch and reached for her hand. "We are going to the store. But first, we're looking at that building." I pointed to the dining hall. "Besides, I need to know what you think of this place."

She looked up. "I already told you."

"Think you might like living here?" I said. Ultimately, I wanted to leave Honolulu, move to the Big Island and run the hotel. I hadn't told Pu the plan yet.

"You lie, cause you a liar. You a goddamn liar."

"Hey. Since when did we talk like this?"

She dropped her chin, "You talk like that."

"I've never said that in front of you."

She covered her ears with her hands, "Liar, liar, liar."

"Come on, Pu."

"Holy, holy, holy..."

"Just one more building." I grabbed one hand from her ear, but she yanked it back.

"Lord God almighty..."

1922, Kohala
Sam

Mama walked into our kitchen, kiss-ass Bernie following behind her. "Where is Lydia?" she said, looking at the stove. The empty pots and pans. "Why isn't dinner started?"

"'S'what I like know," I said.

"That *is* what you *want* to know," Mama said. Then she asked Bernie, "Did she tell you anything?"

Ho! I wanted to laugh. Since when did anyone tell my sister Bernie anything?

By then, I figured Lydie had already boarded the Maui steamer. There was Charlie Moku waving and blubbering to her from the dock. I couldn't decide whether he needed a slap in the face, or a kick in the balls. Probably both.

Sunset came. Night time came.

In my mind's eye, I saw Lydie sitting on the deck of the Maui-bound steamer, seasick. The engine was loud. The sea spray was soaking her skirt, the gravy stain starting to smell. I should've given her my jacket.

At 7:00, Gramps told Mama he wanted to go out and start looking for her. I looked at him: You know the plan. Didn't you give her your coins? But I could never figure Gramps. One day he was beating the crap out of me; the next day he was singing to Kohala Mountain.

At 7:30 he told Mama he was walking up to the manse to use Reverend Christian's telephone.

"Wait," Mama said. "Just a little while more."

Poor Mama. She was so scared everyone was gonna find out what everyone knew already: that Lydie got knocked-up. Throw in that Papa died a drunk, and it turned out we were just another Hawaiian family, limping along like a three-leg dog. No better than anyone else.

"No. No more waiting," Gramps said. "She's in trouble. I feel it." That was Gramps, always sniffing the air. He never trusted what he saw. He never believed what you told him.

Me and Gramps walked up to the manse where Reverend Christian lived. Gramps stood at the front door, his hat in his hands: *Knock. Knock.*

Reverend Christian's daughter was headmistress at the girls' school. She opened the front door, her face as plain as a board. She made my cross-eyed Patience look like a blossom. "The Reverend has retired for the evening," she said through the screen door. "If you like, make an appointment for next week."

"Our Lydia did not come home," Gramps said. "We use the telephone. Go call Sheriff Pua."

Sarah pushed open the screen door when she heard that Lydie—the *punahele*, the favorite—was missing. "Why didn't you say so?" she said, letting us in. "She didn't come back from lunch."

Gramps called Sheriff Pua, who said to meet him on Government Road. Now, with Sheriff Pua in the show, it was time to look at my options. Under option one, I could honor my promise to Lydie and keep my mouth shut about her plans. Under option two, I could rat on her.

I decided to keep my mouth shut, at least until I went to Maui next week and helped Lydie find her baby. Even better, until next year. By then, I figured no one would separate mother from child. So that was what I did: I kept my mouth shut.

We rode in Reverend Christian's new car, Sarah and him sitting up front, me and Gramps sitting in the back. I couldn't get used to seeing Reverend Christian drive. The car seemed so modern; he seemed so old.

He drove down to our house where we picked up Mama and Bernie, then we all drove up the valley road to the girls' school. Sarah said the last time she saw Lydie was in the school kitchen. Mama said the last time she saw Lydie was at the meeting hall. I knew that—saw the whole thing from the kitchen door earlier that day.

Some of the girls like Patience came from Kona, Ka'u and Hilo, and boarded in rooms on the second and third floor. They all came down to the front gate when they heard us—Patience too. I broke off a mock orange bloom for her. Why not? The night was warm, and Patience didn't look too bad in the lantern light. But listen to this: she turned away, like anybody else was giving her flowers.

"*Ei nei*," I said to her. "I get one question."

"Where were you?" she said.

"How come Lydie was the delivery girl?"

"She needed to see your mother."

"And something else—what did Lydie give you so she could leave school today?"

"I did it as a favor."

"Just curious."

"Not everyone's like you, Sam."

We walked down the road and over the bridge. The boarders followed, until Sarah Christian noticed them behind us. She clapped her hands then said, "Back to your rooms, girls."

Come on, Sarah. The moon was rising. The stars were shining.

"You'll hear about it in the morning," she told them. "I'm sure Lydia's safe and sound."

At the edge of the road, Reverend Christian held his lantern high, like he was expecting to find Lydie sitting in the dark, her hands folded in her lap and waiting to be found.

Mama walked beside Bernie muttering her prayers. Nothing pissed me off more. We couldn't eat, drink or sleep without Mama throwing in some kind of amen—and all for nothing. Nine of her babies were buried on the hillside, Papa next to them.

We reached Government Road. There was Sheriff Pua and his deputies, plus boy scouts, plus guys I didn't know. Some rode on horseback, and everyone held lanterns. Sheriff Pua held a piece of blue ribbon. "Julia," he said to Mama. "Do you recognize this?"

Mama nodded, "I gave it to Lydia."

"We found it near the irrigation ditch," he said.

So everyone began walking down the irrigation ditch trail.

"Look," one of the boy scouts said. He ran to another piece of ribbon in the dirt, where the ditch trail met the cane-haul road.

But hold on. What was Charlie Moku doing here? Hanging around behind the search party? He should've been paddling up the coast from Māhukona—it took twice as long against the current. Now, in my mind's eye, I saw the Maui steamer again. The seasick passengers covered the deck, but I didn't see Lydie anywhere.

We walked past the rock outcropping on the cane-haul road, everyone looking for ribbon—me watching Charlie Moku for a clue about my sister. Maybe he and Lydie planned all of this, the search party and Charlie pretending to look for her. Or, maybe Lydie was following a plan she kept secret from me and Charlie. That was it—it had to be. Lydie played things close. She was smart that way. She was like me.

The search party was buzzing. "Damn *buk buk*," someone said—talking about the new Filipino workers. The plantation was importing them by the boatload.

"We should call for her," a deputy said.

"Lydi-aaa," they called—her name floated out over the field.

"Ly-dieee," I called, playing along and protecting her plan, still hoping she was safe on the Maui-bound steamer. But now I wasn't sure, what with Charlie Moku following the search party—a scared shitless look on his face.

I sniffed the air like Gramps. I couldn't decide if I was smelling something rotten, or making it up. I listened to the wind for a clue, but heard only my own breathing. I looked up into the night. The yellow moon hid behind the clouds. Then, in the middle of the cane-haul road, just past the outcropping of rock, I saw a piece of red ribbon. I walked closer and saw more, the blue and red pieces tangled in the dirt. Lydie threw them away, I decided. She threw them away and good riddance to the church ladies' scraps.

Mama picked up one piece, then another, shaking the dirt off. Then Mama said, "Oh no," because there was one of Lydie's shoes lying in the middle of the cane-haul road. I picked it up and gave it to Mama, who gave me the lantern.

There was a drag mark from the shoe to the side of the cane-haul road. The sugarcane next to the road was crushed and flattened. The second shoe was lying on the crushed sugarcane, laced to a foot.

I told myself it wasn't Lydie, and followed the lantern light up the bare leg to the knee. Then I followed the trail of dried blood from the knee up the bare thigh. It's some other girl, I told myself, looking at the white blouse black with dried blood. I knew: it was a camp girl. There was one who opened her legs for a dime.

But it seemed like Lydie heard me. It seemed like she reached up, grabbed my collar and yanked me down.

It's me, Sam.

I tried to turn away, but it seemed like Lydie yanked me closer.

Look at what he did to me.

Her neck was slashed from ear to ear. One eye was swollen, and a trail of dried blood ran from her eye to her ear. Another trail of dried blood ran from her mouth, down her chin. In one hand she held a rock, in the other red Kohala dirt.

The deputies and boy scouts surrounded me, twenty-five lanterns shining on Lydie all at once. Then they stood aside for Mama.

"Jesus, Jesus help me," she said.

"Lydie—" It was Charlie Moku. That *lōlō* dropped his lantern and the kerosene spilled. Flames flew up the sugarcane leaves. Two of the boy scouts stomped out the fire, while three more tried to lift up Charlie Moku, who'd fallen into the cane.

Mama began pulling Lydie's skirt over her legs.

"Wait!"

Quick, Mama pulled back her hand.

Reverend Christian tried to change his voice. "We cannot touch anything, Julia. I'm sorry."

"We have to preserve the evidence—for the coroner's jury," Sheriff Pua said.

I looked at him: You gotta be joking.

First of all, we were stomping all over everything. And second, if we were looking at a *haole* girl, he would've let the parents carry her home.

"How long?" Gramps said.

"They'll be here in the morning," Sheriff Pua said.

"Then I'm staying," I said.

"You're going home like everyone else," Reverend Christian said, his regular voice back—like he was the king of England.

"No," I said. How could I leave her?

Sheriff Pua grabbed the back of my shirt.

"Leave him," Gramps said.

Everyone was quiet, then Sheriff Pua said, "Don't touch anything. Leave it just the way we found it."

"He won't last the hour," one of the deputies said.

I sat beside the cane-haul road, and waited for them to leave—all the lantern light going with them. I waited for my eyes to adjust to the dark, and for the moon to come out. Then I went back to Lydie. I grabbed her arms and dragged her out to the cane-haul road. I pulled her skirt over her legs, and her arms down to her side.

*"Ei ne*i," I said to her. "Only one guy I know would do this."

In my mind's eye I saw him hiding behind the wall of sugarcane—the one in the red shirt. In my mind's eye, he waited until I was gone, then began chasing her down the cane-haul road.

"Stop!" he said, but Lydie kept running until he caught up with her.

"Look at this," he said, grabbing her arm. "Someone's playing hooky from school."

Lydie stared at the dirt.

"They wouldn't like this," he said. "But I won't tell, as long as you're nice to me."

"I have to go," Lydie said.

"Where? School's back the other way."

In my mind's eye, I saw Lydie taking a step, but he blocked her way. "You ever heard of citizen's arrest?" he said, and swatted at a fly. "It means I can arrest someone if a crime's being committed. Did you know playing hooky is a crime?"

Now the fly brushed Lydie's ear. That made her shiver; her nerves fired, and her muscles loosened. Lydie yanked free her arm, pushed him out of the way and began running down the cane-haul road. He tried to chase her, but she pulled ahead, running as fast as she used to—until she ran too fast and tripped over herself. She fell onto the dusty cane-haul road, and he caught up and threw himself on top of her, pinning her down with his arms. She kicked, one shoe flying.

"I like that," he said. "Fight me."

She lifted her knee and kicked again, finding the middle of his balls.

"Fuck!" He let go and rolled to his side, his hands between his legs.

Lydie jumped to her feet, but he grabbed her skirt and yanked her down. He crawled back on top of her. "I've been nice to you! But you keep ignoring me."

Lydie struggled and managed to sit up, but he punched her in the face and she collapsed. He stood up, grabbed the back of her collar and dragged her to the wall of sugarcane, where he dropped her at his feet.

"Please," Lydie said, trying to stand. "I won't tell."

He looked up and down the cane-haul road, then kicked her in the stomach. Lydie fell back. He began unbuckling his belt.

"Please, I have a baby," Lydie said.

"I know that, you dirty Hawaiian bitch—letting that fat pig fuck you." He fell on top of her, kicking open her legs with his knees.

"Please..."

"You like it, don't you?" He pulled up her skirt. "Say what you say to that fat pig."

But Lydie was quiet now, reaching for the rock and dirt. She stopped begging and crying, and watched him rape her while memorizing every scar on his face.

And he saw. He knew what it meant, and what he had to do. So when he stood to buckle his belt, he pulled out his knife.

"No. I won't tell."

"I know you won't tell," he said, kneeling down. He grabbed her face, shoved it to the side, then slashed her neck from ear to ear.

Now, the search party gone, the sugarcane field empty except for me and Lydie—Now it was time to make sure I was right. "Tell me who," I said to her.

I looked into Lydie's eyes and found the last thing she saw before dying. There he was, his picture frozen in the middle of her black eyes.

"I thought so," I told her, then I closed her eyes forever.

"Don't worry, Lydie. I'm gonna take care of this."

1985, Honolulu
Moani

My new kayak clients sat on picnic tables at the beach park. I greeted them, but out of the ten, only two said, "Morning."

"OK." Big smile, "It's great to finally meet all of you, after talking over the phone the past few months."

They stared at me, their legs and arms crossed. "I'm Moani Kaluhi, the owner and president of Lost Paradise Kayak Adventures. Thanks for coming to the safety session today." Along with the liability waivers and medical clearance forms, attendance was mandatory before next week's launch off Moloka'i.

Then, for the one thousandth time in my kayak career, I said, "On Monday I'll be leading you on a five-day kayak run to one of the most beautiful and wild coastlines left in the world." That would be the north shore of the island of Moloka'i.

"You've all met my assistant Henry," I said. He had chauffeured the group over from their Waikīkī hotels that morning and plied them with coffee, juice and pastries while they waited for me.

"Now, before we go any further, I want to apologize for being a few minutes late."

"Mo-a-ni," my sister Pu whispered—the reason I was so late that morning.

"This morning we had an emergency." Pu had refused to leave the condo again because, she had said, she was going to throw up. We waited, but she never did.

"Moani," Pu said. "It wasn't a few minutes."

"I also want to thank you..."

"You were one hour late," Pu whispered.

"I know this morning's session is taking up your sightseeing time. But we wouldn't schedule it unless we were absolutely certain that it was necessary for your safety." We weren't trekking up Mt. Everest, but the five-day trip posed a number of safety problems. Ten-foot swells could come out of nowhere. Without protection, they could expect third degree sunburn.

"In a few minutes we'll go down to the beach where Henry's inflated the kayaks. You'll partner-up and take a spin around the inlet. I know most of you have been kayaking on the mainland, but it's important to get your feet wet in Hawaiian waters before the trip begins."

I told Pu, "Pass out the maps."

She was eating a croissant.

"By the way," I told the group, "this morning I've got an assistant, Puanani. Say hi, Pu."

"Hi," she said to me.

"Hi," the group said at once, startling her.

She looked at me.

"Go ahead," I said. "Pass out the maps."

"Maps?"

"The maps I gave you in the car. They're right in front of you, in the box."

"Oh." Pu's medical records said that she was "mentally arrested" at the age of eight—when our mother drove off a bridge with Pu and me in the back seat. Our mother drowned and Pu stayed underwater too long.

"Let's see if I remember your names," I said while Pu passed out the maps. I went from client to client, announcing each person's name, occupation and home state. The group of ten included two couples from San Francisco. The women worked together as nurses. That was good. My kayak groups tended to cast couples as the parental figures. This added a touch of family structure to camp life. Out in the wilderness, the more order the better.

There was a couple from Philadelphia on their honeymoon. They were staying at one of Uncle's hotels. There were four lawyers from New York City who had listed the same business address on their applications. One had gray hair poking out of the neck of his t-shirt, and carried a notepad and pen. Lost Paradise received hundreds of applications for our five-day trips from doctors, lawyers, shrinks and businessmen. Most were graying and thick in the middle, with clean fingernails and good teeth.

I traced our Moloka'i route on the map and pointed out our two campsites. I repeated the five-day weather report I had received early that morning. There were clouds to the northeast which would pass over the Hawaiian Islands that weekend. After that, the forecast for the following week called for clear skies and calm seas.

"It ought to be a great trip," I told them. "Now, grab your gear and let's join Henry down on the beach with the kayaks. Come on, Pu." She was eating another pastry. "How about a kayak ride today?"

"Today?"

"Now's as good a time as ever," I said. Since she moved in with me seven years ago, I had been promising her a kayak trip. But first, Pu needed to learn to swim. That meant conquering her fear of the water. We had been working on that in the condo pool.

Walking down to the kayaks I thought she was behind me. Then I heard her scream, "Moani!" I turned and found her pointing at a boy walking away from our picnic tables. He held a red fanny pack, the same that I'd seen on one of the tables where we had been sitting. I thought it belonged to the honeymooners.

"He took our things," Pu said.

I began running after the boy, who didn't realize I was chasing him until I was nearly on top of him. Then he began sprinting. He was loaded or drunk, or both, and by the looks of him, he probably hadn't eaten for days. How else could a thirty-seven-year-old female out-sprint a boy? I grabbed him by his greasy hair and yanked him down.

"Let go," he said.

"Drop it," I said, straddling his back, my knees gripping his hips.

"They're mine."

I shoved my knee into his side.

"Ow!"

Henry was right behind me, outweighing the boy three times over. He locked the boy's arms behind his back, then lifted him.

"Ow," the boy said and dropped the fanny pack.

"You've got a choice," I told the boy.

"Let go." He squirmed.

Henry tighten his grip.

The boy said, "I'm gonna sue you for assault and battery."

Henry tightened his grip.

"Let go."

"You can walk away, or wait for the police," I said. "We just called 911."

Henry let go and the boy ran off. I picked up the fanny pack then walked back to Pu.

"I can't believe you caught up with that kid," one of the lawyers said.

"I can't believe you tackled him," another said.

"Is he gonna be all right?" a nurse said. "I mean, should you have hit him?"

"I guess this fanny pack isn't yours?" I said to her.

"Oh."

I told my group, "Whoever owns these, you might want to keep a better watch on your stuff." I put the fanny pack on the table. One of the nurses' husbands walked to another table and grabbed his wallet, which he had hidden under a towel.

"Moani," Pu said, standing at the nearby pay phone. "Nine-one-one is busy."

"It's OK, Pu. You did good."

"I should try again?" Pu said.

"No, Pu. We don't need them anymore."

"No?" She looked at the phone. She wanted to play with the buttons and make another call

"See?" I said to her. "We got it back."

"He's a stealer," Pu said.

"That's right, Pu. He's a thief." I said to the group, "As you can see, even here in paradise, you can't be too careful. And you guys are prime targets. I'm good for one tackle a day, and you just saw it. So grab whatever you don't want stolen, and let's go down to the shore and talk about your kayaks." No one reached for the red fanny pack.

The honeymooners, Rick and Shari, stood nearby. Shari told Rick, "Better take it. All our vacation money's in there."

"What're the chances of something like that happening again?" Rick said, walking down to the beach without it.

"Come on, Pu," I said. "Stop talking on the phone." She held the receiver to her mouth and sang, *"I asked if she would stop and talk, stop and talk, stop and talk..."*

The yellow kayaks were lined up along the water's edge. I let the group form pairs of their own choosing. If adjustments were needed, I could make them later.

"Folks, this is your kayak, technically a tandem or double kayak because it holds two people. I've been in this business for sixteen years and these are the best kayaks available for exploring Hawaiian waters."

"Are these *baidarkas*?" one of the lawyers said. There was always someone showing off how much he knew.

"OK, that's Eskimo for tandem kayak," I said. "We'll use the word, 'kayak'. Now, let's take a minute and go over the fundamentals."

I pointed to the front. "This's the bow." I pointed to the back. "That's the stern." I stood at the front of the kayak. "The bow." I walked back to the stern. "The stern."

"These kayaks are made of"—I took a breath—"ultra-durable Nit-rylon with synthetic and natural rubbers laminated over twelve hundred denier polyester. Come next Monday, when we're paddling in the channel off Moloka'i, you'll understand why safety is my primary concern, and why I love these kayaks so much. Now, we've got the bow"—I pointed again—"and the stern"—more pointing.

The lawyer who knew Eskimo raised his hand again.

"On Monday the kayaks will not look like this."

He dropped it.

"Each deflates and folds into its own drybag, then its own backpack for storage and transport. Deflated and folded, one kayak could fit under your airplane seat."

The men smiled. They loved the technology.

"Of course, you won't have to worry about that. Transporting eight kayaks, along with all the other gear and three-hundred seventy-five pounds of food and provisions, is my problem."

The lawyer threw up his hand again.

"I just want to finish up this presentation about this beautiful piece of technology."

He nodded.

"Now, let's talk paddle." I lifted one. "This is your paddle." I held it out in front of my chest with both hands equal distance from the center of the shaft, two blades on each end.

"And this is how you should hold your paddle."

"Those of you under five-five should choose the shorter of the two lengths. If you're taller than five-five, chose the longer of the two." Both the nurses were small. So was the honeymoon-girl.

"How will we know if we've got the right length?" one of the lawyers asked.

Sixteen years in the business had taught me to repeat, repeat, repeat. "Use your height as a guide."

"Our height?" someone said.

"Just make sure the blades touch the water," I said.

They laughed like I was joking.

They chose their kayak paddles, holding them like canoe paddles, with both hands at one end. It happened every time, even though Henry stood next to the paddles holding one as a demonstration.

I walked to the pile of life vests, "These are your personal flotation devices, also known as life vests—to be worn at all times while in the kayak. No exceptions. Make sure you're buckled in. Make sure your partner's buckled in, then get seated in your kayak. Henry and I will launch you."

Once they were seated, before shoving them into the water, I said, "This is not a race. There's no hurry. Find the pace you and your partner are happy with, and that you can sustain for four hours. The group will stay with you. Henry? You want to add anything?"

"The group stays together, no matter what. You get one problem with that, then we ain't the company for you. We refund you in full, minus the donuts and coffee."

They all turned to him.

"Just joking," he said, grinning through his broken front teeth.

"By the way," I said. "Did I mention that our own Henry was on the U.S. Olympic swim team at one time? Just thought I'd pass that along."

Whenever I said this, the men would step back, the women would smile and Henry would drop his head.

We pushed them in the water and watched them flounder.

The honeymoon-guy raced to the head of the group, his life vest unbuckled.

"Let's keep an eye on what's-his-face."

"He bitched all the way over in the van," Henry said.

34

"Take me, Moani," Pu said. She lifted a paddle.

The beach park's man-made inlet was sheltered by a manmade reef. The water was calm and perfect for babies, kayak clients and my sister Pu. At the water's edge I strapped an orange life vest over Pu's bathing suit— a blousey thing our grandmother had bought to hide Pu's breasts.

"Why don't you have to wear one?" she asked, fidgeting with the life vest.

"I know how to swim."

"But you said everyone got to wear one."

"Cool it, Pu. The first rule of kayaking is never question your captain."

"But what if he's wrong?"

"Pu, did you ever think the captain could be a girl?"

She laughed. "No way."

"Pu, what do you think I am? It's my company. I'm the leader."

She laughed again. "No."

"Thanks a lot, Pu."

"Thanks-a-lot-Pu," she repeated.

"Before we get in the kayak, I want you to wade out into the water with me."

"No. I don't want to."

"It's not an option." I wanted her to get the feel of the water now, just in case the kayak tipped over.

For five years I had been giving Pu swimming lessons in our condo pool. We spent the first year just dangling her feet from the pool edge, the next year sitting on the pool steps. The next year we walked in the shallow end while holding the ledge, and the next she practiced kicking while holding the ledge. This year had been Pu's break through. The month before she had waded away from the ledge, water up to her chest, clutching both my hands.

"Come on, Pu," I said taking her hand.

She let me pull her into the inlet, until the water was chest-level.

"How do you feel, Pu?"

"Fine."

"The water's nice and warm, right?"

"Yeah."

"Suppose we got your face wet, Pu?"

"No."

"On the count of three we'll go under together. One, two, three." I tugged on her arm and went under. Pu dropped her face in the water, her eyes squeezed shut. Then she released a mouthful of air and stood up.

"Good, Pu. Now let's try—"

"No."

"Pu, you don't even know what I'm going to say."

Her teeth chattered.

"I'll let go of your hands so you can float on your own."

"No."

"Let your feet float out from under you, while letting go of my hand. I'll stay right here."

"No."

"The life vest will keep you up."

Then, without warning, she dropped her face in the water, let go of my hands and let her feet rise. Her butt bobbed to the surface.

She stayed like that for ten seconds, twenty, thirty. I grabbed her by the arm pit and lifted her.

She stood up sputtering, her new braided hair extensions hitting her face.

"You OK?" I said.

"You told me to swim."

"You're not running out of air?"

"Moani, you confusing me." She took a deep breath, dropped her face in the water again, then pushed my hand away. Her butt rose to the surface.

I counted the seconds: thirty, thirty-five, forty. When she surfaced again, I asked her, "Aren't you getting dizzy?"

"Leave me alone, Moani."

On the shore I held the kayak while Pu stepped in and sat in the bow.

"Sit in the back, Pu, so you can watch how I paddle."

"You always get to go first."

"Pu, that's not the point."

"I can do it."

"Did you see how I told them to hold the paddle?"

"Yeah."

I sat at the stern. Henry pushed us in the water. Pu gasped and dropped her paddle. I grabbed it and pushed it back to Henry, knee-deep in the water and watching us.

"Moani, we're sailing." She leaned over and looked at the water.

"Whoa, Pu. Sit upright. That's it. When you lean over, you rock the kayak."

"Moani, I'm swimming."

"Kayaking, Pu. We're kayaking."

Our grandmother had told me that when we were small, Pu was the family fish. "She would cry—cry to go to the beach," our grandmother had said. "End of the day, cry—cry when your mother said it was time to go home."

I had no memory of the first ten years of my life before the accident on the bridge, when I was ten and Pu eight. I couldn't remember the beach outings. I couldn't even remember our mother's face. I looked at old photographs and didn't recognize her. I only remembered her from behind, Pu and me sitting in the back seat of the car. My mother's long black hair fell over the seat. She used to sing along with all the songs on the radio, while sipping from a brown paper bag.

I paddled opposite my group. "You guys are doing great," I told one of the lawyer pairs.

"Think so?" one said.

"Think we're ready for the deep water, huh?" his partner said.

"We're going to have a great trip," I told them.

"I'm going on the trip," Pu said.

"Wait a second, Pu. We didn't talk about that yet. You've only just begun swimming."

"I can swim, Moani. I swim yesterday."

"Today, Pu. You were swimming just now."

"See? I told you."

"Five days is a long time to be away from home, sleeping on an air mattress," I said.

"Moani make me go faster," Pu said.

"Excuse me? The captain decides the kayak speed."

She laughed. "Where's the captain?"

1922, Kohala
Sam

I used to like to stand behind the school girls. Check all the buttons running down the backs of their blouses—sometimes they missed one or two.

But the day we buried Lydie on the hillside, I wasn't my normal self. The school girls were everywhere, but instead of checking their buttons I kept watching the way their hands shook when they brought their hankies up to their noses.

Then the gravedigger and his son wrapped straps around Lydie's coffin and began dropping her into the grave. The girls moaned.

"Girls," Sarah Christian said. "Control yourselves."

Oh come on, Sarah.

Who else we gonna cry for, but the sixteen-year-old *punahele*? Who else, but the one who was murdered, and now falling into the black hole?

Reverend Christian said his prayers. We watched the gravedigger walk to the pile of dirt and stones next to the grave, and everything got quiet. The wind stopped blowing. The birds stopped chirping. The trees stood still. We watched him lift a shovelful of dirt from the pile, then listened as the dirt and stones fell on top of Lydie's coffin.

Suddenly, the wind began whipping around us. The birds shrieked and the trees seemed to heave and shudder. Everyone started crying—even Sarah—as they watched Lydie disappear beneath the dirt. Everyone but us—me, Mama, Gramps and Bernie. We'd passed crying a long time ago, standing on the hillside next to the graves of Papa, all the babies and now Lydie.

Me? I felt like I was dead already. I wanted to tell the grave digger to stick me in a box too. Go ahead and bury me on the hillside. At least I'd be next to Lydie.

Like all the babies, after the funeral we didn't talk about Lydie. And when we didn't talk about her, it seemed like the murder didn't happen. It seemed like Lydie didn't die. And I bet you're wondering: How could you pretend she didn't die? I'll tell you how: you pretend she didn't live in the first place.

Sounds harsh, yeah?

Yeah. It was harsh. But if you saw what we saw that night—if she was your sister, her neck cut from ear to ear—you would've done the same thing we did. One thing I know is that people survive, however they can. For us that meant not talking about it. Not thinking about it. For us that meant forgetting.

After the funeral Mama told me and Bernie, "The past is past. Time to move on." That meant Bernie had to finish up at the girls' school. That meant I had to go back to the government school.

But I told Mama, enough already. "I've learned as much as they can teach me."

"Then show me," she said.

I sat with her at the table. I added and subtracted my numbers, then I multiplied and divided them. I read from the Bible. I wrote the Lord's Prayer.

"Your handwriting is sloppy," Mama said.

I wrote the Lord's Prayer again, nice and cute.

"Good enough," she said. "But if I hear you speaking pidgin, you're back in school again."

Yes Ma'am.

Reverend Christian said the same thing when he visited.

"Honest, hard work is the answer."

That was the only time he ever made sense to me. That was the only thing that helped me—work. Otherwise, I was hurting so bad, I was ready to steal Gramps's canoe, paddle out and never turn around. Instead, I took whatever jobs I could find. Sweeping, mopping, ditch digging. Shoveling horse shit from the police stables. I didn't mind what they paid me because the main thing was to keep my hands busy. Keep my head quiet.

Nothing surprised me. Not even when Sheriff Pua offered me three times my shit-shoveling pay to deliver police booze to his Kohala customers. He threw in a bonus if I rode over the mountain to his Kamuela customers. He threw in another bonus if nobody saw me.

And pretty soon I had to ask myself, why take the risk for some other guy? I built my own still and sold my booze cheaper than the police sold theirs. When Sheriff Pua found out, he threatened to break my arm.

"You touch me, I'm gonna tell," I said.

"You? A rat?" He laughed.

I laughed too, but not really. "Yeah, me. A rat. I'm gonna rat on you and all your customers. I'm gonna let everyone know who's cheap enough to drink Sheriff Pua's booze."

Then I named for him all his Kamuela customers—mainly *haoles* from oh-say-can-you-see. "They're gonna disown you," I said, "first, because you're Hawaiian. Second, because you're stupid enough to get caught."

Sheriff Pua knew: *haole* cared about *haole,* and that was about it. Look how he fucked up Lydie's murder investigation, arresting one guy, but he was the wrong guy. Then arresting another guy, but he was the wrong guy too. Finally, he said he had the right one, but Mr. Right escaped the police jail.

Listen: nobody complained or criticized. Folks couldn't have cared less.

I BREWED AND sold rot-gut. If you bought my stuff then you were desperate, and there were plenty of folks desperate in those days—not just

Hawaiians with dead babies. The island was crawling with *haoles* looking for cheap paradise. And that was just fine with me. I made more money in one day selling booze than in one month digging ditches.

Now, all four pockets stuffed with money, I knew exactly what I wanted. I went into town and bought a can of everything—sardines, corned beef, chorizo, soda crackers, cling peaches, condensed milk. For my first course, I laid sardines on the crackers. For my second course, I crushed crackers in a bowl, covered the crackers with peaches, then poured milk on the peaches. It was the best thing I ever ate in my life. I bought more and took home a box filled with cans and packages. But Gramps wouldn't touch it. He said the food was bought with "dirty money."

"Food is food, and the table's empty," I said.

Gramps slammed his fist into my face, knocking me right off the chair. Then, Mama came after me, a broomstick in her hand. She whacked it across my legs and the handle broke.

It was a good thing I'd eaten plenty that day. The sardines and cling peaches had already made me strong. I could take Gramps's fist and Mama's blows—no problem. I thought, hit me if it makes you feel better. I knew that when Gramps was finished breaking my jaw—when Mama was finished breaking my legs—I knew next week, next month, they would both sit at the table and eat their fill of my dirty money.

Next, I went after a bigger market, the plantation workers. Talk about desperate—those guys coming here because cutting sugarcane from sunrise to sunset was better than living on nothing back in Japan, Portugal, the Philippines. My first week selling in the plantation camp I made more money than Papa made in a year.

I paid all our debts and then some. I found the gravedigger who buried all the babies, then Papa, then Lydie. "This's for digging when Mama couldn't cover your bill." I tucked five twenty-dollar bills in his shirt pocket.

"Thank you, Mr. Kaluhi," he said. It was the first time anyone ever called me that.

I paid the son-of-a-bitch who had the nerve to come to our house one night, holding one of Papa's I.O.U.s. Word spread that Lipo Kaluhi's son was settling debts, and others came. None of them asked for interest, but I paid it out because I could—ten percent per annum. Now get the fuck off my porch.

It was just a matter of time before the Japani and Filipino boys began distilling their own brew. "Time to move to Honolulu," I said to Mama, "where the action is."

"What action?" Mama said.

"You know, business."

"Your business is nothing but sin."

I went to Bernie. By then she had her teaching diploma, but she wasn't teaching. "I need a bookkeeper," I told her.

"I'm not working for you," she said. "Everything you do is illegal. If you go down, I'm next."

"The only way I'm going is up," I told her.

Alone, twenty years of age, I moved to Honolulu with two thousand dollars in my pocket. I bought my first liquor store when I was twenty-five. When I was thirty-one, I won the contract with Matson Shipping. Before the passenger ships left Honolulu for San Francisco, I stocked their bars with whisky and gin, wine and champagne.

You name it, I sold it.

Then I won the contract with the Royal Hawaiian Hotel in Waikīkī, where the tourists watched the sunset sipping gin and tonic, and listening to Hawaiian trios sing about the little brown gal in the little grass shack.

Fine for them, but I wanted more. I bought a big house in the hills overlooking Honolulu. I bought dinner for a fat *haole* girl—blonde curls, painted toenails, rosebud lips—the works. I bought her a ring and a wedding dress, and the next thing I knew the first Mrs. Sam Kaluhi was lying next to me in my bed. I rolled on top of her and buried myself in her. Half an hour later, I was ready to go at it again. Half an hour later, I felt like kicking something—so I turned to her. I slapped her ass and watched it shake. I slapped her ass again and watched her run out of the bedroom. I did the same thing each night May, June and July.

In August, I sent her back to the mainland—Texas, I think it was. She didn't ask for anything, only her fare home and to make the divorce as quick as possible. The last time I saw her, she stood at the ship's railing looking for me on the pier. I was there, waiting in my car.

In those days, a brass band played at Honolulu Harbor. When the ship began pulling away from the pier, the band started playing *Aloha 'Oe*. The passengers aboard the ship threw flowers to the folks standing on the pier.

She stayed at the railing the whole time looking for me. I told myself, look at this *wahine*. Look at how loyal and faithful she is. Maybe I'm making a mistake? Maybe I should run to the pier—tell her to meet me in San Francisco? Let's try again. I'll be good.

But who was I kidding? I didn't care about her. I didn't care about anything except money. If I wasn't making money, then I wanted to hurt somebody. Even when I was making money, I still wanted to hurt somebody. If she was a fat rosebud, I wanted to slap her. If I saw a dog, I wanted to kick it. And if I heard that somebody was competing with my business, then look out. One of us was gonna lose and it wasn't gonna be me.

After wife number one left, I looked in the mirror and started puking my guts out. I stopped puking and began shitting, then couldn't stop. I felt like I was losing my insides. Just when I thought I was finished, I was running to the toilet, shitting hot, black lumps. I checked into a hospital. The doctor said it had all been in there for years—your average crap turned into poison.

"Good thing we're finding this now," he said. One more year and I would've gone home to Kohala in a box. Mama would've been forced to look up the old gravedigger—see if any space was left on the hillside next to the babies, Papa, Lydie and Gramps.

Instead, Mama and Bernie left Kohala. They lived in Honolulu with me and wife number two, plus her three brats—I don't know what the hell I was thinking with that one. I took care of them all, in the middle of expanding my business. By the time the war started, I was stocking three hotels and two passenger lines with booze, beer and wine. That was how I cared for Mama until she died. Then, after statehood, the tourists began pouring in. I shifted my business to hotels. That was how I cared for Bernie and her daughter Haunani, then Haunani and her babies, Moani and Puanani.

Now, when you talk about Moani, you're talking about a smart kid. She knew how to make money. OK, I didn't like her kayak idea. "One thing I know is tourists," I had told her back when she was starting out. "They don't come here for exercise. They want us to serve them cocktails and T-bone steaks."

But Moani saw a new market—adventure tourists. Despite what I told her, she bought more kayaks. In five years her company was booking more excursions than she could handle.

My hotel guests even asked about them.

How do you like that?

Moani was like me that way. She wasn't afraid to take her chances and see what happens. She had a good head for business, plus she was determined. When my niece Moani got hold of an idea, look out. You're in trouble.

1985, Honolulu
Moani

Pu dropped into the chair at the breakfast table wearing her pajamas and walkman earphones.

"Pu, I told you to take a shower and dress before breakfast."

"Yo soy un hombre sincero."

I carried two plates to the table.

"De donde crecen las palmas."

"After breakfast I want you in the shower, then we're driving to Uncle's."

She pulled off the earphones. "We not working today?"

"No, Pu. Remember? I called Island Cares." I needed to talk business with Uncle. Specifically, I needed a loan to get the my hotel up and running.

"We gonna see Grandma?"

Our grandmother lived with Uncle. She had been calling me for a month, ever since Uncle and his latest wife, number six, returned from their Mexican honeymoon. "Looks like we better get it over with."

Pu smeared peanut butter on her toast, then piled scrambled eggs on top.

"Pu, that's pretty disgusting."

She put the headphones back on and began humming.

"Chew and swallow first."

"Leave me alone, Moani."

"Who told you to eat your eggs like that?"

"My boyfriend."

"I thought you guys broke up."

"That was the other one," she said.

"What's the new one's name?"

She threw her hand over her mouth.

"What're you listening to?"

"Yo soy un hombre sincero, de donde crecen las palmas."

"Pu, I told you to stay out of my room."

"Y antes de morirme quiero, enchar mis versos del alma."

"Pu, you got any idea what you're talking about?"

She pulled off her headphones, "That's for me to know and you to find out."

OUR GRANDMOTHER OPENED the car door before I turned off the engine. "Been waiting how long for you," she said.

"Sorry."

Pu stepped from the car and threw her arms around our grandmother's neck.

"No, no," she said, pulling Pu's arms off. "Too hot."

"I miss you, Grandma," Pu said. She planted a wet kiss on her cheek.

"All right. All right. Me too," she said.

"So how's the new bride?" I said.

"Young. Kinda. Maybe."

She looked like she would spit, again forced to share Uncle's palace—even though she had a separate wing, with her own bedroom, bathroom, living-room and kitchenette. She had moved in with Uncle after her husband died, who wasn't our mother's real father. Our mother's real father was a big fat question mark. It was an issue never discussed. The same for my father. The same for Pu's father. And the same for our mother, who drowned at the age of twenty-eight.

Uncle stepped into the foyer wearing yellow shorts and a white polo shirt. If it weren't for the dentures and white hair, I would've sworn a man forty years younger was grabbing me by my arms. "What? We gotta beg you to drive out?"

"Uncle," Pu said and threw her arms around his neck.

"How's my Puanani?" He fingered a fake braid. "Eh, what's all this?"

"Hair ex-ten-sions," she told him, lifting a few strands and letting them fall down her back.

"Look like one colored girl's hair," he said to me.

"Cause I got colored girls' hair," Pu said.

"Nobody here get colored nothing in this family," he said.

He walked ahead of us to his sunken living room. It opened to a *lanai*, and beyond the *lanai* to a lawn that swept down to the shoreline. The lawn was studded with coconut trees, the trees skirted with fern clusters. It was exactly how I wanted the lawn at my new hotel to look. So green and cool my guests would want to roll in it.

Uncle stood beside wife number six, who sat on one of the sofas, a white poodle on her lap. It began yapping at Pu and me. She stood up. "Your uncle's told me so much about you." She held out her hand to me.

Her hair was orange, everything else pink—the belted pantssuit, frosted eyeshadow, lipstick and nail polish. I looked at the dog; its collar was pink. I looked at the dark-green awning over the *lanai* that wife number five had installed. By the end of summer it would be pink. Uncle introduced her as, "Dorothy-Lynn."

"Dixie to my friends," she said. "From Louisiana, via Texas, via Las Vegas."

"You're pretty," Pu told her, taking her hand.

"Why thank you, Sweet Pea." Dixie entwined her fingers with Pu's. "Now you're...?"

"Puanani," Uncle said.

"Pu-a-na-ni," Dixie said. "Your uncle's so proud of you, working at your own job."

It was news to me. Uncle and my grandmother were Pu's legal guardians. They never liked the idea of her working at Island Cares. "She's around retards all day?" he had said. "Just gonna make her worse."

"Puanani means pretty flower," Pu told Dixie.

"I just love you-all's names," Dixie said to me.

"Her name's Moani," Pu said. "Means breeze."

"You see?" she told Uncle. "Like a short poem."

We sat on the sofas facing each other, the square coffee table in the middle.

Dixie said to me, "Your uncle's proud to tears over you."

"Thank you," Pu said. She leaned against Dixie's arm.

"Puanani, leave her alone," our grandmother said. She sat on the sofa across from us.

"Oh I don't mind," Dixie said. "Not at all."

"I wanted to talk to you about my company," I said to Uncle.

His eyes brightened. "About time."

"I've got an opportunity, but time's of the essence." That's what the real estate agent had said.

"Listen to this girl," Uncle said to Dixie. Then he looked at me. "Anybody says you gotta do something yesterday, means they selling you one bridge in London."

"London bridges falling down..."

"Puanani," our grandmother said.

45

"Moani's gonna buy a hotel," Pu said. "I saw it."

"My goodness," Dixie said, the poodle dozing in her cleavage. "You're as ambitious as Sam."

"It's dirty," Pu said.

"It needs work," I told Uncle. "But if the engineers say what I think they'll say..."

"Getting tired of babysitting those rich tourists, looking for a thrill?" Uncle said.

Frankly, yeah.

"You think you're getting into a different business, running a hotel?" Uncle said.

"We went to the Big Is-land," Pu told Dixie. "I help Moani do in-spec-tion."

"I'll bet you help her plenty," Dixie said.

"Don't matter if you're kayaking, driving a tour bus, or running a hotel," Uncle said. "Tourists come here so they can act like college kids on spring break."

"Where on the Big Island?" our grandmother said.

"It's—it's," Pu said. "You go like this," she lifted her right hand. "Then like this." She bent her left hand. "Then you cross the bridge..."

"Kohala," I said. "There's a school and church grounds for sale."

"...then go through the forest," Pu said.

"What school?" our grandmother said, scooting to the edge of the sofa.

"It used to be a girls' school."

"The School for Hawaiian Girls?" our grandmother said.

I shrugged.

"That's *our* old school."

"When did you go there?" Uncle said.

"Yesterday. I told you I was taking Pu."

"No. You never said nothing," Uncle said.

"Since Christmas you never called," our grandmother said.

Then she said to Dixie, "She left after Christmas dinner, and we don't hear nothing for, what? Three, four months."

"They're selling the girls' school?" Uncle said.

"The owners are in Japan," I said.

"I called her," our grandmother told Dixie. "Left messages."

"I can cover the purchase price," I told Uncle.

"Guess some people think they don't gotta return calls," our grandmother said.

"But I need renovation capital, and enough to cover the first couple years' operating costs."

"Well that's something," Uncle said. "The old school's for sale."

"If Moani buys it," Pu said, "I'm gonna play the piano."

Our grandmother looked at Pu. "What're you talking about?"

"I played a song," Pu said. *"Ya, da, da, boom, de, ay."*

"Puanani," our grandmother said.

"It happened one sweet day."

"Cool it, Pu," I said.

"There was a boy next door, he got me on the floor."

"Puanani!" our grandmother said.

"My boyfriend?" Pu said.

"Damn retards," our grandmother said. "Teaching her all this stuff."

"My boyfriend?"

"Not another word," our grandmother said.

"Why that place?" Uncle said. "The buildings must be, what?" He looked at our grandmother, "A hundred years old."

"The main building's in good shape," I said. "Solid."

"Well good for you," Dixie said. She petted the poodle, black goop in the corner of its sleepy eyes.

Uncle shook his head. "Not gonna work, Moani. Who's gonna stay up there? It's gotta be one, two hours from the Kona Airport."

"The same people who book my kayak trips. They want something different. The ranch is nearby for horseback riding. There's hiking. There's the beach in Pololo valley."

"Pololū," our grandmother said.

"I've done my market research," I said—on the anecdotal side. "My kayak clients hate Waikīkī. There's a suntan oil slick on the water."

"The name of the valley is Pololū," our grandmother said.

"Pololo," I said.

"No. Po-lo-luu," she said.

"That's what I said."

"No, that's not what you said," our grandmother said.

Dixie said, "Well, more power to you."

"You gotta learn to say the name right," our grandmother said, "or don't say it at all."

"I can make this work," I told Uncle.

"Moani said I could keep this because we're buying it. But we didn't buy it yet." Pu pulled the piano key from her purse strung across her shoulder.

47

"Where did that come from?" our grandmother said. She reached across the coffee table for the piano key.

The poodle barked.

"Now you behave yourself," Dixie said to the poodle. It squinted and tried to lick her lips.

"A key from the old piano," our grandmother said.

"Do you play?" Dixie asked her. There was a grand piano in Uncle's sitting room next to the fireplace. No one knew how to play it. They never lit the fireplace.

"No," our grandmother said. "Not me. They tried to teach me, but I was all thumbs. Lydie was the one."

"Lydie could play," Uncle said.

"She could play anything she heard."

"I could play," Pu said.

"All the stuff they didn't want us to hear," Uncle said.

"Colored music," our grandmother said. "Songs from the pictures."

"I'm colored, you know," Pu said to Dixie.

"See?" Pu said, showing Dixie her hair.

"Puanani," our grandmother said.

"Who could play?" I asked our grandmother.

She and Uncle looked at me, but said nothing.

"Was she a school friend?" Dixie said.

They refused to answer.

"Oh me and my big old mouth," Dixie said. "Looks like I've walked into a ghost in the closet."

"Ghosts?" Pu asked her.

"Just a figure of speech, Sweet Pea." Dixie patted Pu's thick knee with her frosted pink nails. Pu stared at the candy-size engagement ring.

"What was her name again?" I said.

"All of this was a long time ago," Uncle snapped.

"What was a long time ago, Uncle?" Pu said.

"Your friend?" Dixie said.

"Our sister," our grandmother said.

"Oh, that's right," Dixie said. "What were you telling me, Sam?"

"Had the twins, Henry, Uncle"—our grandmother pointed at Uncle with her chin—"the triplets, Baby Anne. Now I'm forgetting them."

"What happened to them?"

"All dead before their first birthdays," our grandmother said.

"Simon before his fifth."

"I can't imagine what it must have been like—to lose so many babies," Dixie said.

"What was the order again?" I asked our grandmother.

"It must have broken your poor mama's heart," Dixie said.

Our grandmother listed the order of her siblings.

Uncle's jaw clenched and unclenched.

"Oh now I remember," Dixie said. "Is this the one you told me about, Sam? The one that was murdered?"

"She was *murdered*?" I said.

"Who?" Pu said.

"What was her name?" Dixie said to Uncle. "Oh, I'm terrible."

"Lydie," our grandmother said. "That's what we called her."

"Lydia," Dixie said, sitting back. "That's right. What a terrible story."

"She was murdered?" I said to Uncle.

"That poor thing," Dixie said.

"Enough," Uncle ordered.

The poodle sat up.

"What's Lydie got to do with anything?" he said.

"But, what happened?" I said.

"Business. That's what you came here to talk about," he said. "Either you buying the property, or not. Either you making money, or you losing money."

"I know, but—"

He sat up, resting his elbows on his knees. "Moani, *pau kēlā*."

"You understand?" our grandmother told me. "This is finished. Over. A long time ago."

"I don't want you asking any more questions about this," Uncle said.

"About what, Uncle?" Pu asked.

He grabbed the poodle. It whimpered as he carried it out to the *lanai*.

We said nothing. Even number six kept her mouth shut. I could tell Dixie was already on guard against Uncle. Just the way he liked it.

1985, Honolulu
Bernie

Damn that girl—asking about Lydie when Sam told her to leave it alone. Digging up our private business in front of an outsider. Moani was just like her mother, always doing something to embarrass me. Never taking no for an answer.

I blame Sam for spoiling Moani. When he told me he was sending Moani to Trinity Girls School, age eleven, I told him he was asking for trouble. She didn't belong with all those *haole* girls. Sure enough, within the year Moani was walking into stores thinking she could have whatever she wanted. Then, her senior year, she applied to mainland colleges when we had a perfectly good one right here.

You watch, I told Sam. She'll come back thinking she's better than us. But my brother said that we should give Moani the opportunities we never had. So we drove her to the airport that morning to say goodbye. Oh, there was plenty of crying. *Leis* up to her nose. Then Sam gave her five hundred dollars—cash. Imagine that. A seventeen-year-old girl walking around with five hundred dollars.

Even with all that cash, at the end of her first week up there she called us. Now she needed more money for books. I told her, why're you buying books? Isn't that what the library is for? At the end of the month she called again. This time she needed winter clothes. I told her, you wouldn't need those expensive things if you had stayed here where you belong. At the end of her first semester she called, yet again. Now she wanted to share an apartment with some girls. What was wrong with the dormitory? I said. It's too noisy, she said. I can't study. Sam said the apartment would help her education, but who was he kidding? An apartment full of girls?

After college Moani came home, acting like she knew everything, and asking why, why, why all the time. She turned up her nose at the food I cooked because, she said, she was now a vegetarian. Fine, I made an omelette, but she wouldn't eat that either. She told me the eggs could have been chickens. Can you beat that? The chickens were more important than her grandmother's feelings.

And what did Sam do? He bought her a car!

For one year Moani did nothing but drive to the beach with a beat-up canoe strapped on top of the new car. Then she decided to start her own business. What kind of business? I asked her. When she told me, I didn't even know what she was talking about. What's that, I said, a kayak? She pointed to the canoe on top of her car.

I couldn't get over it. My brother Sam sent Moani to the best girls school in Hawai'i, and after that a mainland college. He was ready to put her in charge of an entire hotel. But Moani threw it away. She wanted to paddle around in a kayak with tourists, her skin turning black. Her arms starting to look like a weight lifter's.

Then she wanted to move out of our house, convincing Sam to buy her an apartment. I told him, can't you see what she's doing? She's using you. But Sam said it was good for Moani to live on her own and learn to be "independent."

I laughed. Independent? Driving around in a car her uncle bought her? Living in an apartment he gave her? Running around in a bathing suit all day? From what I could see, Moani was turning into a beach-bum—doing exactly as she pleased. She was worse than her mother. She was worse than my sister Lydie, who did just as she pleased and look what happened there.

FROM THE BEGINNING I knew Lydie was in trouble. What else did she expect, crawling out our bedroom window to meet Charlie Moku every night? After Lydie left, I would lock the window and lay on our bed. One night I pulled my nightgown up to my neck, then lay the pillow over my chest and stomach wondering if I was feeling what Lydie was feeling that night.

Six hours later, when the crickets petered out and the mynah birds began yakking, Lydie woke me up, tapping on our bedroom window from outside. I went to the window and stood there—Lydie and Charlie Moku standing outside in the shadows.

She pointed: The window. Open it.

I unlatched the window; that was it. Let Lydie pry it open. That was what she got for sneaking around in the dark. Her shoes scraped against the outside wall as he lifted her. She stepped through the window, then lay next to me on the bed, hands across her stomach and smelling like the reef at low tide. She turned her head away from me, and in a minute I heard her deep steady breathing and felt the heat of her body. Half of me wanted to ask: What's it like when his skin is against your skin? And when he kisses you—is it true what the girls say? Do they really do that?

The other half of me hated her, listening to her fall asleep. She left me behind with the other girls—all of us pretending with our pillows, dreaming about things we didn't know. Lydie didn't dream. Lydie was the dream. Oh I wanted to slap her.

Then, one morning while making the bed, I heard something fall on the floor. I looked up and saw Lydie holding on to the bureau, her hair brush on the floor. She turned toward the bed, grabbing at the air like she was blind. Then she fell on the bed the way Papa used to fall on Mama's bed.

51

"Eh you," I said. "Get off."

She lay on her side across the bed, and wouldn't answer me.

"Suit yourself. You finish making the bed."

In the kitchen Sam and I ate last night's rice with tea, then a pile of toast.

"What's she doing in there?" Mama said to me. Then she called into the room after Lydie.

"I'm not hungry," we heard Lydie say.

"Miss Picky-Picky," I said.

When it was time to go, I walked into our bedroom. Lydie lay across our bed on her stomach, her face to the side and staring straight ahead. The back of her white blouse was soaked with sweat.

"If you're sick, better get under the covers," I said. "If not, let's go."

"I'm not sick," Lydie said, sitting up on the bed.

"You look sick."

Lydie stood, felt along the bed to the bureau, then from the bureau to the door. She lifted her schoolbag off the hook on the wall and walked out of our room—didn't even finish making the bed. That was just like Lydie, thinking she was the Queen of Sheba, leaving me to tuck in the bedspread she had rumpled and straighten the pillows she had smashed.

Each morning we walked through the sugarcane field, across Government Road, then up through the forest to Girls' School Road. But that morning Lydie couldn't keep up with me on the path beside the irrigation ditch. I crossed Government Road and waited beside the edge of the forest. "Where are you?" I called across the road into the field.

"I'm coming," she said from somewhere behind the wall of sugarcane.

"I'm not waiting anymore." But I waited. Then I yelled back, "I'm going," and began climbing the forest path. I walked into the clearing where girls were smoking.

"Where's Lydie?" one said.

"Taking her own sweet time," I said.

On Girls' School Road I waited again. The smokers walked out of the forest without Lydie. "Didn't you see her?" I said.

"She didn't come through yet," one said.

"Better hurry, Bernie," another said. "Else you'll ruin your goody-two-shoes record."

"Better wash out your mouth," I said to her. "I can smell your smoke-breath from here."

I walked back to the clearing, the smoke hanging in the damp air. I looked down the forest path for Lydie, but saw nothing. "Lydie!"

The school bell began tolling. Each ring made me madder than the last. Lydie was making me late. She was getting me in trouble. Instead of climbing the path to the Girls' School, I walked down through the forest looking for her. Close to Government Road I saw Lydie hanging onto the trunk of a thin tree.

"Lydie." I walked up to her, about to let her have it. Then I saw a clear puddle at her feet, a string of spit hanging from her lip. A dry heave knocked her forward and she spit up water. She grabbed the tree trunk to keep from falling and she lifted herself—one hand crawling over the other up the tree trunk. Full height, she turned to me, her face drained, her lips gray. "Think I might be in trouble, Bernie."

"What did you expect?"

The school bell rang again. Now it was 8:30.

"You can go," Lydie said.

"I know I can go."

Then she spit up more water.

"Come on," I said. "We'll walk slow." I lifted her schoolbag on one shoulder, mine on the other. We climbed the forest path to Girls' School Road, followed the road to the gate and walked across the schoolyard to the classroom building. There I gave Lydie her bag.

"Do I smell, Bernie?"

"Yeah," I said, as I leaned close and sniffed. "But not that much."

I walked to the dining hall where I had kitchen duty that morning. Before going in, I looked back at the classroom building. Lydie just stood beside the porch, holding her schoolbag to her chest.

Four hours later she sat in the dining hall with her noisy gang—the smart-alecs and smokers. That day Lydie was quiet. I watched her eat, slowly chewing and swallowing each mouthful. Then she waited before taking another bite. She ate the same way I would eat eight years later while carrying my daughter Haunani and trying to keep down my meals.

PRETENDING. THAT'S WHAT we did in our family. Me? I was the star pretender. I pretended I wasn't relieved the morning Sheriff Pua told Mama that he had found Papa's body in the middle of Government Road, no bruises. No broken bones. He fell in a puddle of water and couldn't get up.

I felt like skipping all the way to the manse when Mama told me to tell Reverend Christian the news: It's not a baby this time. Today we're burying Papa. That afternoon, standing beside his open grave, the birds sang while the gravedigger shoveled dirt on his coffin. I dropped my head like I was supposed to, but inside I felt like I could finally breathe. I felt like I could finally look up and not be afraid of what I might see.

There was more pretending when Mama found out that Lydie was pregnant. Mama made plans to get rid of her during the last three months, but she didn't tell Sam and me until the day Lydie was to leave.

"Arrangements," Mama called them, as we ate breakfast and Lydie packed her things. There was someone named Gladys.

"A Maui relation on your father's side," Mama said.

I pretended it was an average morning, but after breakfast I asked Sam, "Who do we know on Maui?"

"Maui?"

"Where is Mama sending Lydie?" I said.

"Mama's sending her somewhere?"

"Didn't you hear her?"

He gave me that stupid look.

"Stop pretending you don't see what's happening."

More stupid, all over his face.

In our bedroom I watched Lydie pack her things into two cardboard boxes Gramps had doubled to make a suitcase. Mama brought in a towel and blanket for her, then went through the clothes Lydie had packed. She pulled out two skirts. "I don't know why you're taking these," Mama said. "They don't fit you any more." She pulled two of my dresses off the hook on the wall. "Just until she comes back," Mama said to me, then gave them to Lydie.

What could I say? My clothes were the only clothes that fit swollen Lydie. I was like Papa and Sam, short and stocky. Lydie was like Mama, with the height of the Puna District in her bones.

When Mama left the bedroom Gramps put the skirts back in the suitcase. *"Bum bye* your skirt gonna fit," he said to Lydie. "You take them."

Mama asked Gramps to take Lydie through the sugarcane field to Keawa'eli Bay. From there, they would go by canoe to Māhukona Harbor, where Lydie was supposed to catch the Maui-bound steamer.

On the porch Lydie turned to me and waved her hand. "Bye, Bernie." Then she skipped down the steps like she was eight years old again.

If you ask me, she couldn't wait to get out of there. It didn't matter that she was going to live with a stranger. Anything was better than living in Mama's jail. Once Lydie began showing, Mama had refused to let her out of the house, or let anyone visit. She threw dirty looks at Lydie every morning, noon and night. She threw the same dirty looks at me eight years later when I gave birth to my daughter Haunani—Haunani's father who-knew-where.

"At least Papa isn't here to see this," Mama said, watching Lydie leave with Gramps through the backyard.

"If Papa was alive, he'd be sleeping it off inside." I braced myself for a slap, but I didn't care. "He wouldn't have noticed a thing."

"He would have noticed," Mama said. "She was his favorite." Her eyes followed Lydie down the lane beside the wall of sugarcane—Lydie and her long bones and high forehead. I couldn't help it. The tears began falling. It didn't matter how much I tried. Lydie would always be the one they loved the most.

Four months later she returned the way she had left, walking beside Gramps through the sugarcane and into the dusty backyard. She wore the same faded dress she had left in. Only now her stomach was flat, her thin arms hanging at her side. Little Girl came out from under the house, sniffing. When she realized it was Lydie, she wagged her tail and dropped her head. Gramps held the cardboard suitcase on his head. As they climbed the porch steps, I saw him wiping tears from his eyes, like it was a happy occasion. Like Lydie was a young bride coming home to visit her country family.

When Lydie walked into the kitchen, I saw the true story. The fear I had seen in the forest that day when Lydie puked up her empty stomach had hardened into loss. Lydie was sixteen years old going on forty-six. Dark shadows circled her eyes. Her cheeks were hollow, her lips thin and cracked. She was a grown woman now, and filled with sorrow.

Lying beside Lydie her first night back, I watched the rise and fall of her chest as she slept. "Lydie," I whispered.

She didn't answer.

"I want to ask you something."

But she turned on her side.

I kept my question to myself. It took me a lifetime to say those simple words: Where is your baby? When I was finally ready to give them life, it was too late. We had long ago buried the answer on the Kohala hillside.

1985, Honolulu
Moani

My lawyer kept telling me I needed to consider the possibility of "predeceasing" Pu. He called this a "contingency" and urged me to appoint a guardian. But I didn't have the authority, I would tell him, because I wasn't Pu's legal guardian. Uncle and my grandmother were.

He would get cocky: "Do you think, Moani, it might be time to do something about that? Once and for all?"

But even if I was Pu's guardian, who could I appoint as my stand-in? Let's face it, nobody wanted to take care of a thirty-five-year-old retard. Our own grandmother couldn't even handle the job.

And the question of taking care of Pu led me to another question: what about me? Pretend Pu was dead and I was alone. Who would take care of me one day? Even worse, pretend Pu was dead and pretend I was dead too.

Who would remember us?

Even though I was on the verge of a major career change, from kayak-girl to resort developer, all I could think about was the fact that I had no babies. I would have no grandchildren. No descendants. When I died, we were finished. Our family, our blood. Gone.

This made me second-guess decisions made when I was twenty. I remembered the boyfriend in Michigan and the afternoon he drove me to the hospital for an abortion. The winter sky was low and gray, the field outside the hospital covered with new snow. I second-guessed decisions made when I was twenty-five and living in Honolulu again. I got married and could've had my babies then. Everyone kept telling me that there was never a right time. Everyone said to just have the babies, and figure it out as you go along.

Fine for them, but I had plans. I wanted to build my business first and establish financial security. I realized that wasn't going to happen with the husband. He was a California transplant who, it turned out, was afraid to work. Scotty complained that it made his stomach hurt. I sent him back to California with a check for six hundred dollars. I bought a fleet of tandem kayaks, and a car mechanic's garage that I remodeled into my new company offices. Never looked back.

Now, sixteen years later, it was time to plan again. In the short-run, we launched the Moloka'i run next Monday, and I had to decide whether Pu was ready for a five-day kayak trip. Since I wanted to sell the business by the summer's end, either she went on a kayak trip soon, or she wouldn't have the chance again. In the long-run, I wanted to sell Lost Paradise to buy the Kohala property. Then I needed to find financing to renovate the property. But I didn't like what I had heard from Uncle on Tuesday. "Not gonna work..." "You can't..." "It won't..." "You shouldn't..."

That left my bank, which had wooed me for my Lost Paradise business accounts. It was Friday, and I had made an appointment with the bank's business loan officer. "Sorry, Moani," he said. "Your condo won't begin to provide the collateral needed to cover the amount you want to borrow. Why not go with something smaller?"

"Smaller leaves me with only half the job done. How about shares in the company I incorporate to run the hotel?"

Blink, blink.

"Just thinking out loud," I said.

"A hotel?"

"I didn't say? The reason why I want the loan?"

"I thought it was for more kayaks," he said. "You're planning on building a hotel?"

"I found the perfect site."

He shook his head. "Save the hotels for your uncle." He was one of Uncle's golf partners.

"I grew up in the business, remember?" While my high school classmates were vacationing in Spain, I used to cover the front desks at Uncle's hotels. I knew reservations, promotion, bookkeeping and concierge services. I knew housekeeping. I could strip and make a bed in two minutes. Wipe down the bathroom in three. Vacuum, dust, fluff in another four.

"You're making a mistake," he said, pushing his chair back from the desk. "Most guys would give their pinkies to have your company."

"How long do you think I can keep up this schedule?" I said.

There. That stopped him. "All right, Moani. See if you can find a contributing creditor to match the collateral on your condo. Then come back and we'll see what we can do."

"You want me to go to my uncle," I said.

"It's an obvious choice."

"Then you'll give me the loan?"

"We'll talk about it."

"Let's put this in writing," I said.

"You know I can't do that," he said.

I left the bank, realizing a follow-up visit with Uncle was inevitable. A groveling session, likely. I decided to see him on the Monday after we returned from Moloka'i. Or Tuesday. By the end of the week at the latest.

EVERY YEAR I attended the Trinity Girls School alumni weekend. Friday night was the dinner, when alumni showed each other updated family pictures. Saturday was Family Day, when alumni picnicked, showing each other the actual family, or in my case, Pu.

My fault, my grandmother would say when the issue of men and my failure to find another husband and produce children came up. Pu scared away the men. "Who wants to marry you," she would say, "when they find out they getting a retard too?"

Without pictures to display at the dinner, I slipped on a knit black dress I had bought. It wasn't a fair exchange—my classmate's family pictures for my black dress. One day they would have grandchildren; one day I would just have an old black dress. All the more so, then. In the short run, I knew I had to make the best of the flat stomach kayak paddling gave me.

Pu sat on my bed watching me adjust the straps over my shoulders. "It's too small," she said.

"It's supposed to look this way." I stepped into the dress-sandals.

"You gonna fall."

"No I won't." I teetered across the carpet to the dresser, looking for earrings.

"You look stupid."

"Pu, didn't I tell you to get in the tub before Gina comes?" Gina was our babysitter.

"You said I could go."

"Tomorrow, Pu."

"When I marry my boyfriend, you can't tell me what to do."

"I thought you guys broke up?"

"We broke up. But now? Now we made up."

"When you finish your bath there's chocolate-chip ice-cream," I said. "Come on. We'll use the new soap."

In the bathroom I squirted blue bubble bath into the tub.

Pu stomped in, pulling her t-shirt out of her shorts.

"I'll be back in ten minutes, Pu."

"I-be-back-in-ten-minutes."

"Quickly, I want you bathed before I leave."

"I-want-you-bath-before-I-leave."

I was alumni president and supposed to give a speech after dinner. In my bedroom I sat at the desk, a pen and stack of blank index cards in front of me.

Fifteen minutes later I cracked open the bathroom door. "Are you wrinkled enough?"

She didn't answer.

I walked to the tub. Pu sat in the suds staring at the faucet.

"Time to rinse and dry," I said.

Pu didn't move.

I knelt down, reached in and felt for the plug. Pu slapped at the water, splashing me.

"Stop it."

She laughed, her round shoulders heaving. Then she threw an armful of suds out of the tub. It hit me in my chest and face.

"You little shit." I found the plug and pulled.

Pu blocked the drain with her foot. "No."

I knocked her leg from the drain.

She kicked the water, suds flying into my hair.

I stood and grabbed a towel. "I'm not kidding, Pu. I want you out of that tub, now."

She began crying, her small breasts dripping.

I threw a towel over her shoulders. "Dry off. Now."

"I hate you." She threw the towel on the floor.

"Fine. Gina will be here soon. Want her to see you like this?"

"You always lie to me."

"I said you could go tomorrow—Family Day."

"You a liar."

The front of my dress was soaked. I began walking out, but slipped on the wet tile and fell on my ass. Pu leaned over the bathtub and started laughing.

I pulled off the dress sandals, turning my right ankle, then the left. I crawled to the counter and hauled myself up. Then the doorbell rang. I limped through the living room.

"Whoa," Gina said when I opened the door. "You look like shit, and the party never even started."

59

WEARING *MU'UMU'US* SCRATCHING our necks and falling to our ankles, we stood in circles during cocktail hour. My classmates displayed pictures of their buck-toothed kids and black-eyed husbands. I thought of Pu, by then watching *The Sound of Music* for the two hundredth time, chocolate-chip ice-cream turning into a soupy swirl she liked to drink from the bowl. I didn't carry a picture of her.

"How about you, Moani. Any children yet?" It was Charlotte. When we had boarded together, Charlotte would go home each Friday and return on Sunday evenings carrying a box stuffed with treats. In February her mother made heart-shaped sugar cookies. In March they were clovers.

"Oh that's right," Charlotte said. "You take care of your sister. How is she?" Even the pleated *mu'umu'u* couldn't hide her dimpled ass.

"She's fine." I thought of my black dress drying on a hanger in the bathroom.

"Oh I envy you, single and free," she said. "I can't remember what it was like, what with Mitchell and the boys."

"Do you date a lot, Moani?" another classmate asked. Four from our senior-year dormitory huddled around me. We were sixteen years old again, and they wanted the juicy details.

I shrugged, "Off and on."

"And—so—what do you do?"

A year ago I had sex with my second-in-command, John. I knew it was a mistake, but it was close to my birthday and I felt entitled. We bumped teeth and knees. Then he snored so loud it woke up Pu.

I told my classmates, "We go to dinner, movies, you know."

They closed in. I smelled the white wine on their breath. "Is there anyone special? Or do you see a bunch?"

They wanted the fantasy. The lover who carried me through doorways, then kissed my naked, throbbing body. "We'll see." I was ready to drop the subject.

"Who?"

A lie fell from my mouth, "One of my clients I met a couple years ago."

"Moani. Shame, shame—dating your clients."

"So there's hope for you yet," Charlotte said, smiling too hard. The lines crisscrossed at the corners of her eyes.

"One day I might be as lucky as you," I told her.

Charlotte's smile held, but her cheek flickered.

Then I looked across the banquet room and realized I had no close friends. I had spent sixteen years building Lost Paradise, defining my client base and devising marketing campaigns. Consulting with lawyers over company disclaimers and client waivers. The rest of the time I spent worrying about Pu catching the bus alone, and wondering whether Island Cares was properly staffed. What if there was a fire? What if someone choked? And who was the retard teaching her to eat scrambled eggs and peanut butter?

After cocktails we sat for dinner. After dinner the waiters served coffee and dessert, a withered pear sitting in a swirl of red goop. Just the kind of thing Pu loved.

At this point in the evening I was supposed to deliver my welcoming remarks at the podium, and introduce our guest of honor. She sat shriveled in a wheelchair at the next table, between Trinity's current headmistress and one of the trustees. A girl sat next to the woman. She had tucked a napkin around the woman's collar before dinner began. Now she held a cup with a straw to the woman's lips.

I checked our program. The woman's name was Sarah Christian Gooding. "Teacher and headmistress at Trinity Girls School from 1933 to 1968; born in the District of North Kohala, August 4, 1894."

"She's ninety-two years old?" I said to our treasurer, Marleen.

"So they say."

"No wonder the chin-wiper. Am I really supposed to introduce her? How will she get to the podium?"

"You have to give her the award." Marleen reached under the table for a shopping bag. Inside there was a wood plaque.

"Does she even know where she is?" I said. "It looks like she's asleep."

I had forgotten my speech notes at home and blamed it on Pu. I walked to the podium with the plaque, hoping something clever would come to mind. At one point I heard myself saying, "We're not getting older, we're getting better."

Worse yet, my classmates laughed.

Then I introduced Sarah Christian Gooding, reading from the program. And that was when I saw it, '...Teacher and Headmistress, School for Hawaiian Girls, Kohala, 1916 to 1933.' If that was true, then she knew the school I wanted to buy. And she must've known my grandmother and her sister—the one they would not speak about. The one they called Lydia.

I read from the plaque, "...and with abiding gratitude..." while the girl pushed Sarah to the podium, Sarah's ginger-root fingers gripping the wheelchair's armrests. Cameras flashed as I tried to hand her the plaque. She wouldn't take it, but seemed to read it. I couldn't really tell. Her eyes were puffy, red-rimmed slits. Then she turned toward the banquet room, blinking her lash-less eyes. The girl lifted the plaque from my hands. "She can't hold it."

Now my classmates stood, applauding the old woman we had never heard of until that night. Sarah raised her arms like a baby, waiting to be lifted. The room hushed. I looked at the girl, who reached beneath one of Sarah's arms. "Take the other one," she said. We helped Sarah to the podium where she gripped the edges and pulled herself to the microphone.

"Be seated," she said, with a strength I didn't expect.

In one gesture, my classmates smoothed the backs of their *mu'u-mu'us* and sat down, ankles crossed, hands in their laps.

"It's all nonsense," Sarah said, her chin trembling. Bet she hadn't spoken all year.

"You Trinity girls. You waste your lives thinking you're good for only one thing. Well, that's up to you. It's too bad we haven't seen better. I know where you come from. I know the privileges you've enjoyed. Well, let me tell you, at the School for Hawaiian Girls many of my students didn't have money for a pair of shoes. Not even a pair of shoes. But they were strong and smart and..." Her voice wavered.

"Do what you must," Sarah continued. "But do something with yourselves—for Godsake." She loosened her grip, fell back from the microphone and into the girl's arms.

The room responded as only Trinity girls would after someone takes a dump on us: we stood and applauded. For me it was worse, because I had to help the old bitch back to her wheelchair.

The girl pushed Sarah back to their table while I addressed the room again. "Thank you Sarah Christian Gooding, for reminding us of the true meaning of Trinity, and the duties and responsibilities we share as graduates."

There was more applause and Sarah broke into a smile, actually waving at the room.

The next morning I called Sarah's nursing home. The operator told me the doctor made rounds Saturday morning. "You should come by this afternoon."

I told Pu there would be an emergency stop before going to the beach. "It'll be short," I said.

We sat at the breakfast table. "You always say that," Pu said. "You lie because you a liar."

I had arranged for Gina to stay the night and into Saturday for the picnic. I wanted her to watch Pu while I spoke with my classmates' husbands. At least one of them would know about venture capital sources for my hotel. Otherwise, they always wanted to talk about kayaking with Lost Paradise. Like most of our clients, they sat in air-conditioned offices all day dreaming of adventure—and so did their friends. Altogether, my Trinity-related bookings represented fifteen percent of my business.

Then, on our way out the door, the phone rang. Pu and Gina were already at the elevator.

"Good mooor-ning." Uncle never identified himself. "What you up to today?"

"We're just leaving."

"I got Dixie here. She wants to talk to you," Uncle said.

"No... no. You..." I heard her whisper to Uncle.

"Moani, you there?" Uncle said. "Dixie wants to go on your kayak trip."

Was he kidding?

"You got room? On your upcoming trip?"

"She can't go on a kayak trip."

"Leaves this Monday, yeah?"

"Wait a minute. This isn't a dinner cruise off Waikīkī."F

"Course we're gonna pay."

Whoa. "Can she even swim? Has she ever sat in a kayak before?"

"Yes. No. And we bought sun screen and a big hat."

There was more whispering from Dixie: "Leave her alone... She doesn't..."

Uncle again: "We're gonna go on a test ride."

Pu and Gina returned. "We had to let the elevator go," Gina said.

I said, "Uncle, people like Dixie shouldn't be in the sun, period."

"Hi, Uncle!" Pu said.

"Puanani!" Uncle yelled. I had to pull the phone from my ear.

"We're leaving right now for the beach," I said.

"We're gonna meet you folks there," Uncle said. "Which beach?"

"No," I said. "This's a school event. You can't meet us."

"Meet us!" Pu said. "Kailua."

"Kailua? That's where you're going?" Uncle said. "We'll see you there."

"Wait—"

He hung up.

"What's happened?" Gina said.

"Remember the redhead I told you about?"

"You said it was more like tangerine," Gina said.

"Dixie!" Pu said.

"Pu, don't yell."

"Wife number five?" Gina said.

"Six."

"Not," Gina said. "Six already?"

"She's pretty," Pu told Gina.

"Uncle wants me to take her on the Moloka'i run."

"Yeah!" Pu threw up her hands.

"Pu, I said don't yell."

"We all go together," Pu said.

"Slow down, Pu. I didn't say you could go."

"But I was swimming."

"You rode in a kayak, once."

"Liar. I was swimming by myself at the beach. I was."

1922, Kohala
Bernie

The night we found Lydie, I couldn't let her lay there like that, her dress around her waist and everyone looking. But when I tried to pull her dress down, Reverend Christian stopped me. He said we had to preserve the evidence.

So now Lydie was 'evidence.'

And Mama began cry-crying.

"Julia," Reverend Christian said. "As soon as the coroner's jury inspects the site tomorrow, we'll bring her home."

Now Lydie was a 'site.' And I had no idea what a coroner's jury was.

"I'll stay with her," I said.

"You'll do no such thing," Sarah Christian said.

"My dear," Reverend said, "there is nothing you can do for her now."

"I can keep her company," I said.

His eyes flickered. Oh I knew what he was thinking: the old ways were taking hold. Soon, I would begin wailing over Lydie's body like the old-timers once did. The next morning you'd see me with teeth knocked out, missing an eye.

What did Reverend Christian know about us? Since when had anyone heard the chants for the dead in Kohala District? I didn't know them. Gramps didn't know them. I didn't even speak Hawaiian, not to Mama, not to Gramps. I used to try with Papa, but he would scold me. *Ōlelo ho'ohewa,"* he had said. *"You want to speak our language? Then do it right."*

But what was the right way?

Mama knew. "Learn to speak good English," she had said. It wasn't that hard, what with the Girls' School drilling us every day: I am; you are; he/she/it is. And no one spoke Hawaiian anymore. Speaking English just became easier.

"It's a long wait until morning," Sheriff Pua said.

"I know."

Gramps put his jacket over my shoulders and gave me his lantern. The search party walked away. I sat in the small circle of light from the lantern, watching the black sky grow wide and deep. A wind blew across the plain. It made the sugarcane leaves hiss. Then the wind calmed. The smell of red Kohala dirt mixed with Lydie's blood. The scent settled over the cane-haul road, filling my nose and creeping down the back of my throat. I walked to the crushed wall of cane and Lydie's body. One of her arms reached overhead, the other stretched out to the side. She held the sharp sugarcane leaves in each fist—her head fallen back and her eyes wide open.

I asked myself: If I was the one lying here in the sugarcane field, what would Lydie do for me? My answer came fast. I put the lantern beside the road, returned to the crushed wall of sugarcane and dragged Lydie out by the ankles. On her right foot she wore Sam's old brown shoe. But on her left foot the shoe was missing, her stocking bunched at the ankle. I held up the lantern looking for the lost shoe. But the sugarcane was thick-thick. The night black-black.

I pulled her skirt over her legs. The white blouse was brown with dried blood. I tucked Gramps's jacket around her shoulders. I smoothed her hair and the stocking at her ankle. Then I closed her eyes. And with them closed and the slash across her neck covered, Lydie looked as if she was only sleeping. An ant crawled over her hand. I flicked it off, but there was another crawling across her forehead.

I sat beside Lydie on the cane-haul road. Crickets chirped in the sugarcane. An owl swooped overhead. Somewhere across the field a dog barked. Then a rooster crowed, but dawn was far away. The lantern glowed and dulled. The wick hissed and smoked. The clouds broke apart and the yellow moon appeared. The stars followed, glittering across the black dome as if it was an ordinary night. As if girls fell asleep in the sugarcane field every night.

Dawn arrived, flat and gray from the blanket of clouds that covered the District that morning. And look who finally came to help. My brother Sam led a horse by the reins. He walked right past Lydie without looking, then sat beside me. He handed me a jar of tea and milk, and a half loaf of bread.

I shook my head.

"Suit yourself." He tore pieces off the loaf, stuffed them in his mouth and washed the bread down with tea. He lit a cigarette, squinting with each drag, then he let the blue smoke curl out from his mouth. Mr. Tough-Guy. He smoked the cigarette, then lay back on a small patch of grass between the wall of sugarcane and the road. "Let me know when they get here," he said and pulled Papa's old cap over his face. Well, that did it for me. I stood up and kicked his bare foot.

He sat up.

"How can you sleep next to Lydie?"

"You think I'm sleeping?" he said.

"You got your nerve."

"Kick me again, you asking for it."

"You couldn't even look at Lydie."

"I don't need to look. Now shut the fuck up."

"I'm telling Mama," I said.

"Make sure and tell her every fucking word."

"Think you're so tough."

It was 6:30. I picked up pieces of red and blue ribbon lying in the cane-haul road. From 8:00 to 9:00 I flicked ants out of Lydie's hair. At 9:00 we tried to lift her onto the horse, but we couldn't.

The clouds broke. The sun warmed the field. Now I wished I had the tea and bread. "Sam, what's a coroner's jury?"

"Bunch of *haole*s, gonna say Lydie's dead."

66

"Why're they taking so long?"

"Gotta grab the wife's ass first. Eat their bacon and eggs."

The sun was high and hot, a swarm of flies hovering over Lydie, when we saw a dust cloud rolling in from Government Road. We heard a car engine and horses' hooves beating against the ground.

"Sam, I moved her. We found her back there," I pointed to the sugarcane. "They told me not to upset the evidence."

"Oh yeah?" Sam stood, watching the dust cloud above the sugarcane field. He crossed his arms over his chest and said, "Fuck 'um."

It turned out that the coroner's jury was five men. Four had been there the night before—Sheriff Pua, his two deputies and Reverend Christian. The only new person was the mill manager. He arrived on horseback, like Sheriff Pua and the deputies. Reverend Christian drove up in his new car.

When Sheriff Pua saw Lydie lying beside the cane-haul road he told Sam, "You weren't supposed to move her."

"So what's the difference?" Sam told him.

"You've destroyed the evidence," the mill manager said. The buttons strained across his belly. He had moved to Kohala at the beginning of the year.

"What evidence?" Sam said.

"You little fool. You've upset the clues," the mill manager said. I could tell he hated Hawaiians, especially ones like my brother—with nothing to lose.

"There's your clue." Sam pointed at Lydie. "Look for the guy who's got blood on his hands." Then he looked at the mill manager. "Let's see your hands."

The mill manager dismounted, his belly shaking. He followed Reverend Christian and Sheriff Pua to the crushed wall of sugarcane, trampling the spot where we had found Lydie the night before. Sheriff Pua returned to the cane-haul road with Lydie's missing shoe.

Sam grabbed it. "That's mine."

"Now look here," the mill manager said. His blue eyes were bloodshot. I had heard stories.

"Never mind the shoe," Reverend Christian told the mill manager. "Let the boy have it. What harm will it do?"

The group walked to Lydie. Reverend Christian lifted the jacket. The mill manager aimed his riding stick at Lydie's face.

"No, stop," I said.

But he jabbed Lydie's nose. Her head fell to the side, and the slash in her neck split wide open.

"Son-of-a-bitch." Sam grabbed the mill manager's riding stick, jumped on the man's back and pulled the stick across his throat.

"Samuel!" Reverend Christian said.

Sheriff Pua and the deputies watched, then pulled Sam off. The mill manager fell on all fours, coughing. Each deputy held Sam by an arm.

"I kill you," Sam said, "you touch her again."

The mill manager tried to stand, holding his throat. But he fell on his knees and coughed.

"She's not a dog," Sam said, breaking free. He shoved the mill manager onto his back, then grabbed the riding stick and flung it into the field.

"You'll pay for that," the mill manager said, hoarse. Reverend Christian helped him to his feet. Now that he was standing, I saw that the mill manager's pants were soaked, the red dirt sticking to the wet spot between his legs. I began laughing and couldn't stop.

"Bernice," Reverend Christian said.

I threw my hand over my mouth.

"I'll be pressing charges against you," the mill manager told Sam.

Sam pretended to lunge for him and he jumped back. Then Sam stopped, pointed at his wet pants and began laughing.

"Samuel!" Reverend Christian said.

The mill manager slapped his pants, but the dust clung to the wet spot.

Now the deputies started laughing.

"That is quite enough," Reverend Christian said.

The deputies walked to Lydie, lifted her by the ankles and arms, then carried her to the horse Sam had brought. Sam helped them heave Lydie over the horse's back. Then he caught my eye and we both burst into laughter. That got the deputies going again.

"Come on now," Sheriff Pua told us. "No horsing around."

We exploded.

"Abraham, I am surprised," Reverend Christian told Sheriff Pua, who bowed his head. Then he told me, "Bernice, let your mother know I'm ready when she is."

The mill manager trotted off on his horse and good riddance. Reverend Christian followed him, leaving us in a cloud of dust from his car.

I looked at the wet spot in the dirt that the mill manager had made. I looked at the pile of horse shit, and at Lydie's arms and legs, dangling over the side of the horse. On one foot she wore a shoe, on the other only the stocking—the stocking toe hanging past the horse's belly. It looked so stupid.

I thought about the night I was leaving behind, sitting in the dark next to Lydie just so the mill manager could poke her in the nose. I thought about the afternoon ahead, burying Lydie on the hillside. Nearby there were ten graves—all our family. I began laughing so hard that I fell against the horse.

There was a hand beneath my arm. Sam pulled me up.

"I got an idea, Sam," I told him. "Let's all play dead." I threw back my head and closed my eyes. "How do I look, Sam?"

Now Mr. Tough Guy was getting all weepy.

"Better take her home," Sheriff Pua told Sam.

"Come on, Bernie," Sam said. "Mama's waiting."

That was all I needed. The thought of Mama waiting to bury another kid made me laugh so hard my stomach hurt. We had to be the most ridiculous family in the District. Maybe the entire Territory of Hawai'i.

AFTER BURYING EACH baby, we had circled their graves on the hillside with rocks. But the rain loosened the rocks. Some rolled down into the stream bed. Saplings grew into trees, their roots creeping over the hillside, dislodging other rocks and markers. We didn't know who was where anymore. Or what was what. I looked at the tree and thought I heard Baby Henry. He died after coughing one week straight.

When Papa died, Mama wanted more than a mound of dirt and rocks for his grave, but he left no money for even a headstone. So she asked the gravedigger to bury him at the base of the *hala* tree, toward the edge of the hillside where she could always find him.

The day we buried Lydie, she asked the gravedigger to look for a spot near Papa. But the gravedigger showed her his map. It turned out everybody else had the same idea. The *hala* tree was full.

He showed Mama a spot next to a two-foot pillar marking the grave of some Japani who couldn't get in his own cemetery and was forced to rot with the Hawaiians on the hillside. "At least you'll know where she is," the gravedigger said.

When he was done digging, we stood beside the hole next to the Japani pillar listening to Reverend Christian read the same passage he read for all the babies and Papa: "Though I walk through the valley of the shadow of death, For Thou art with me; Thy rod and Thy staff, they comfort me."

It was a good prayer—about as good as they came. But I had heard it too many times by then, and didn't know what it meant anymore. Thy rod? Thy staff? I never saw those things before. How would they bring comfort? When?

As they lowered her into the ground Reverend Christian read: "Surely goodness and mercy Will follow me, All the days of my life."

But I saw no goodness in our lives. And if God was merciful, then why keep taking our babies? Then why go after Lydie?

Reverend Christian nodded to the gravedigger, who began shoveling dirt over Lydie. Her classmates had sniffled through the service, but now they began cry-crying, watching that dark hole gobble up Lydie. What a terrible place to put a girl.

Reverend Christian prayed: "Hear O Lord, When I cry with my voice: Have mercy also upon me and answer me."

Reverend Christian's voice and the classmates' crying faded. I listened hard for the answer, knowing it was creeping toward me. About to slip off the tip of a leaf. Mix with the sting of an ant. I had heard the whispering since the church service. Yes, there it was. The voice that was blowing across Kohala that day. Now it grew closer and louder, until it punched me in my stomach. The last thing I remember was Sam and Gramps grabbing my arms to keep me from falling. The voice said: A Hawaiian girl. Probably asking for it.

SHERIFF PUA BEGAN visiting every day, reporting about the investigation. They had found a bloody shirt and arrested a mill worker. The next day he sat at our kitchen table and told us that they had arrested the wrong person. "But don't worry, Julia," he told Mama. "We're gonna find the one who took Lydia from you."

When he said Lydie's name, I remembered the slash across her neck.

"He's gonna hang for what he did to Lydia," Sheriff Pua said.

This time, I saw Lydie's eyes staring at the hidden moon. The third time he said her name, I remembered the sound the flies made hovering over her body while we waited for the coroner's jury.

The next day Sheriff Pua reported that the rumors of a confession by the suspect were just that. "Don't pay attention to rumors. You should only believe official reports from my office about Lydia's case."

This time when he spoke Lydie's name, a strange thing happened. The spoon beside his tea cup seemed to melt into the tablecloth. His tea cup seemed to dissolve in his mouth when he took a sip.

Sheriff Pua stood up from the table. "If it's the last thing I do, Julia, I'm gonna avenge Lydia's death."

The kitchen began melting. The cupboards, sink and table spilled their forms over the floor. Then Sheriff Pua himself began fading into the thick gray mix.

I looked at Mama. Her eyes were darting from Sheriff Pua, to the table, to the floor. She saw the same things I saw. Our world was melting away.

The next day Sheriff Pua knocked on the front door, but I stayed in the bedroom, and Mama wouldn't answer the door either. By that evening, I could make out red and green again. By the end of the week the knife's edge was clear and sharp against the table cloth. The white pillow cases fluttered against the blue sky.

I knew we should've followed the investigation and Sheriff Pua's reports. I should've been praying for Lydie's soul. All girls should be remembered. So I told myself that just for that day I would not say Lydie's name. But the next day, I told myself the same thing. And again the next day. I knew Mama told herself the same thing, because she didn't say Lydie's name either. None of us did.

A month later the plantation burned the sugarcane field. I watched the cane blaze, wither and evaporate. I watched the cranes rattle into the fields, then scoop up the remaining cane stalks. They hauled them down to Kohala Mill in trucks, leaving the field empty and clean.

At first, it felt like a new start. But the promise of fire and the new planting season fell apart at the end of the year. I walked into Olson's Store and saw sacks of sugar stacked in a pyramid, the bags printed with the Kohala Mill label. I knew I was looking at sugar from the cane field fed by Lydie's blood. The next day in the school dining hall, I watched girls spoon Lydie into their tea. In the school kitchen, I folded my sister into the cake batter.

THERE. THAT WAS the story my granddaughter Moani wanted to hear. A story about murder and death. And it seemed to keep getting worse. After Lydie died, there was only Sam and me. When we die there'll only be Moani and Puanani, and how can Puanani count—becoming retarded and all of that? That left Moani, already thirty-seven, no man in sight. No hope of children or grandchildren. It was her own fault, working all the time and acting like she knew everything. Who wants to marry a girl like that?

When Moani dies, we're finished. It's the end of our line. The end of our race. All those babies Mama labored to deliver amounted to nothing. Two generations later, we're about to dissolve into the Pacific Ocean. Forget everything you've heard about happy-go-lucky Hawaiians living in an island paradise. It's an island, and we're Hawaiian. But that's about it.

1985, Honolulu
Moani

At the white, wrought-iron gates to Sarah Christian's nursing home, the security guard rang her bungalow. Then he gave me a laminated map of the grounds. We drove past clusters of bungalows and the hotel-looking hospital to the visitors' parking lot. From there we walked up a wide concrete path lined with benches and railings, white and yellow ginger hedges, hibiscus and fern.

"Why don't we live here?" Pu said.

"Not until you turn into one old fut," Gina told her.

"*Oh my darling, oh my darling...*"

"Cool it, Pu."

"*...oh my daaar-ling Mrs. Fut.*"

Gina stomped her foot and laughed.

Sarah lived in No. 34. The girl from the night before met us at the front door. She was younger in daylight—maybe under twenty. "Granny might not be up," the girl said. "She's been sleeping all morning."

We entered Sarah's bungalow—a living room, dining area and kitchenette. The living room opened to a *lanai* surrounded by a thin strip of grass and white ginger hedges. A bamboo wind chime hung beneath the awning. The wind blew, but the sound of the bamboo was drowned by the blasting TV: chariots raced around the Roman Colosseum. Whips cracked, horses screamed. The Romans cheered.

From the front door, we faced the back of a sofa. The girl walked around the sofa to the front, which faced the TV.

"Granny?" she said.

I stepped closer. It was Sarah, lying beneath a blue blanket. Tufts of white hair peeked out from one end.

"Granny? It's the lady from last night at the party."

"Guess this's a bad time," I said. "Looks like she's sleeping."

"Is this the old fut?" Pu said. *"Howzit going, Old Fut?"*

Gina ran out the front door and burst into laughter.

I fished for a business card in my wallet, then handed it to the girl. "Maybe when she's up, you could call me."

"Oh my darling..."

"Pu, stop."

"Oh my darling..."

"Enough, Pu."

"Oh my da-a-rling-"

"Shut up, Pu."

Pu's fingers flew to her mouth, then her chin fell to her chest. I stepped outside and told Gina to take Pu back to the car.

Back in the bungalow Sarah's eyes were open now, darting back and forth across the TV screen: at the Colosseum the Roman emperor stood up and held out his hand, poised to decide the fate of a fallen gladiator.

"I think Sarah knows some of my relatives," I told the girl. "My grandmother went to the school she talked about last night. Sarah was probably her teacher."

The girl looked at my business card. "I heard about this company."

"You can reach me at any of those numbers."

"This's really you? Your company?"

"Or leave a message," I said. I wrote our home phone number on the back.

"And you're trying to find your family?"

"No. My grandmother's sister was—" I couldn't say 'murdered.' "She was killed. I wanted to find out more about her."

Sarah coughed.

"I want to buy the school Sarah spoke about last night. It's for sale." The girl nodded.

"Is Sarah your grandmother?" I asked.

"I'm her"—the girl counted the links of kinship on her fingers—"step-grand-niece. My mother married her brother's son," she said. "He would've been my"—more finger counting—"step-grandfather. But he died a long time ago I heard."

From the other side of the couch, Sarah said, "You're Lydia's child."

"Excuse me?"

Sarah stared at the TV: a Roman soldier stripped a slave to his waist. The Colosseum roared. A lion paced. I walked to the front of the couch and knelt beside Sarah.

"I'm not Lydia's child. Lydia didn't have children."

"She most certainly did," Sarah said.

"I never heard—"

"Of course not," Sarah said. "No one knew about Lydia's baby." Then Sarah made another sound in the back of her throat. Gas escaped. It hit me in the face and I had to lean back. Sarah hacked, then gasped for breath. The girl lifted and bent Sarah at the waist, then slapped her back.

"Maybe I should come back another time," I said.

"Spit Granny," the girl said. She lifted a blue plastic bowl off the floor.

"Do you need help?" I said.

"Oh no. We're fine," the girl said.

"Is there a better time to visit?"

The girl looked up while slapping Sarah's back, "Usually Saturday afternoon's good. Only last night we didn't come home till late. She goes to bed pretty early."

"Can I call?" I asked.

Sarah spit.

"You can call," the girl said.

Sarah looked up at me, tears in her eyes. "You..."

"Easy Granny."

"You're cruel to your sister," Sarah said, tears ran down a wrinkled trough in her cheek.

In the parking lot Gina struck a tough-girl pose, leaning against the car and smoking. Pu sat in the back seat, the doors open to catch a breeze. She sang, *"Oh my darling Clementine..."*

"When did it happen?" Gina said, getting in the car. "What you were talking about?"

"Thou art lost and gone forever..."

I started the car. "I don't know. No one wants to talk about it."

"Dreadful sorry, Clementine."

AT THE BEACH we walked past the table where Charlotte stood, a ketchup bottle poised over a hamburger. She shook the bottle, the back of her heavy white arms swinging left and right.

"Hello," I said.

She turned, ketchup pouring over the table.

"Mom!" one of her three sunburned boys cried. "Look what you did."

I walked to the food tables. Pu and Gina followed, carrying the grocery bags filled with snacks Pu chose at the store, chips and dip, peanut-butter chocolate-chip cookies. We tucked them wherever there was room. Then I asked Pu, "Should we eat first, or take a dip first?" The water was calm, the winds gentle.

"Swim first," she said, surprising me. I thought she would want to eat, given the spread of food in front of us. It covered three picnic tables—one table with just desserts. A gang stood at the nearby grill, tongs in hand, burgers, hotdogs and chicken sizzling.

"You want to swim first?" I said. "Good idea, Pu."

"Good-idea-Pu."

"Pu, I told you not to repeat what I say."

She thought about this, "No you didn't."

"Then I'm telling you now. OK?"

Down in the water, I held her hand as we waded in until it reached her chest. "Pu, am I ever mean to you?"

"Yeah."

"When?"

"All the time."

"Come on, Pu. Tell me when, exactly."

"Exactly morning, noon and night."

"What do I do that's so mean?"

"Everything you do is mean, cause you a big, fat meany."

She dropped her face into the water and let go of my hand. I slid under the water and watched her from below. Her eyes were squeezed shut. She lifted her legs off the sandy bottom and her butt rose to the surface. I reached for her hand, but she swatted it away and stood up.

"Pu. What a good job."

She wiped her face. "I'm swimming."

"Suppose you open your eyes underwater, like at the pool the other day?"

"I didn't open my eyes at the pool."

"Well, how about trying that now? The thing is, if—"

She dropped into the water.

I followed. Her eyes were open. I waved under water and called out, "Hi, Pu."

She gasped. A silver air bubble escaped from her mouth.

She surfaced and cried, "Mo-a-ni."

"What?"

"No fair. You made me laugh."

We returned to the food tables. "After lunch, I want to take you into the water again."

"I'm swimming, Moani."

We found Gina and the paper plates, then began at the end of the table where they'd placed the salads. On the opposite end lay a mound of hamburgers and hotdogs.

"How're you doing this morning?" It was Charlotte. She wore a t-shirt down to her knees that said 'Trinity' on the front.

"It's not the morning anymore," Pu said, checking her watch.

"You remember my sister Puanani?" I said. "And our friend Gina?"

"I see someone's been in the water," Charlotte said to Pu.

"I'm swimming because we gonna kayak."

"My goodness," Charlotte said to me. "You take *her* on a kayak?"

"Come on, Pu," Gina said. "Let's make your plate."

"Puanani!"

It was Uncle. He strutted toward us holding Dixie's hand. He wore swimming shorts and an unbuttoned Hawaiian shirt. Dixie wore a red bathing suit with the cleavage cut down to her waist and a sarong tied at her hips.

Pu threw her arms around Uncle's neck. "Moani made us late."

"So mean, yeah?" Uncle said to Pu.

"We had to see Mrs. Old Fut," Pu told him.

Gina laughed again. I didn't think it was that funny.

"The lady who knows Grandma," Pu said.

"Who knows Bernie?" Uncle asked me.

"I remember you," Charlotte said to Uncle. "You're Moani's grandfather, right?" Her husband and son stood beside her.

"This is my *uncle*, Sam Kaluhi," I said.

"Of the Hideaway?" Charlotte's husband said.

"All eight of them," Uncle said. "Look for our new rental car company by the end of the year."

It was the first I'd heard of it.

"Guess the business instinct runs in the family?" the husband said, looking from Uncle to me. I had spoken to Charlotte's husband at other Trinity picnics. He always told me he wanted to go on a kayak trip.

"One of us got a business instinct," Uncle said. "I don't know about this one. She doesn't know a good thing when she's got it. Owns the premier kayak company in the state, but now she tells me she's getting out. Says she's gonna give me competition in the hotel business."

"Is that right?" the husband said.

"She's planning on building her own hotel," Dixie said.

Charlotte wrapped her arm around her son's shoulder, but he squirmed away.

"I've got my eye on an opportunity," I said. "Think I can make it work."

"With a little help from you-know-who," Uncle winked at Charlotte.

"So you can't do it on your own," Charlotte said.

"Of course she can do it on her own," Dixie said.

"No. I can't," I said. I didn't like Dixie cheerleading on my behalf. "I've always needed help."

"There you go," her husband said. "No man's an island."

"When you understand that one," Uncle said. "You're on your way."

Pu returned to us with a loaded plate.

"Pu, I said to eat lightly. We're going back in the water later."

"No you di-dn't," Pu said to me.

"Oh my," Dixie said. "There goes my diet."

"How come we gotta eat lightly?" Uncle said.

Then Charlotte said, "I guess we can open the picnic to a few more guests."

Uncle and Dixie were about to grab paper plates but stopped.

"This's family day," I said.

"It's meant for our regular families," Charlotte said.

"This *is* my regular family."

"You know what I mean," Charlotte said.

"Let's get back to the boys," her husband said.

"If we let alumni bring everyone under the sun..." Charlotte said.

"My family has a right to be here, like anyone else's."

"She didn't mean anything," the husband said.

"Yes she did," I said. "She made my family feel unwelcome, and she acted like my sister's an idiot."

Charlotte walked away. I followed, then stepped in front of her. "For the rest of the day, my family is off-limits to you."

"You can't tell me—"

"And don't test me."

UNCLE WAS NOT a big man. I was an inch taller. But he was strong, still at age seventy-seven. He stood in the water with Dixie, his shoulders packed and solid, his chest barreled. His skin was tough and burnt, especially next to Dixie, who was as white as paper wherever there weren't freckles. Uncle's idea of training Dixie for a five-day kayak trip consisted of floating her in an inflatable dinghy off the beach.

He held it steady as Dixie slid in butt first, then swung her legs over the side and into the dinghy. He handed her a canoe paddle, pushed the dinghy forward, then turned to me and smiled, making two thumbs up.

Dixie pursed her pink lips as she tried to paddle. Within a few strokes she ran aground. Uncle pushed her back in the water. A small wave rolled toward her, one foot in height. It met the dinghy on its starboard side, providing a gentle lift, but it was too much for Dixie. She panicked, dropped the paddle, leaned to the right, then the left. Then she shrieked and capsized in three feet of water. Kids nearby stopped playing and watched.

I waded to her.

"Did you see that wave?" she said, finding her footing. Water fell in sheets from her lacquered hair.

"Looks like you've been baptized." Uncle smiled.

"Was that something or what?" she said, wiping her eyes so as not to smudge the goop.

"Ready for anything now," Uncle said.

"I don't know about that," I said.

"Dixie." Pu ran into the water. "Dixie, you swim too."

"Pu, you're in the water alone," I said.

"I can swim."

"Of course you can," Dixie said.

"See," Pu said, then she plunged face-first into the water.

She stood up again, "And I open my eyes under water."

"Now I have never been able to do that," Dixie said.

"The kayak trip involves five days of paddling on the open ocean," I told her. "This time of year the seas will be calm—"

"There you go," Uncle said.

"But we've seen swells seven, eight times the size of what just knocked you over."

They stared at me.

"You ever had to say, you know, *'aloha 'oe'*, to anyone?" Uncle said.

"Oh, Sam," Dixie said.

Pu sang, *"Aloha 'oe."*

"If Moani thinks it could be risky—" Dixie said.

"Aloha 'oe."

"It's her company after all."

"E ke onaona noho i ka lipo."

"Now listen to this one," Dixie said, turning to Pu.

"One fond embrace."

"I could just squeeze you."

"Well boss," Uncle said, "how's about it?"

"A ho'i a'e au."

Dixie wrapped her arm around Pu's shoulder.

"You still have to fill out all the paper work," I said. "It's extensive."

"Until we meet again."

1985, Honolulu
Sarah

Why did I go to that dinner? I missed my television programs and couldn't sleep for days. It wasn't worth it: I have no use for a two hundred dollar plaque. Those Trinity girls were always so wasteful, giving me a wall decoration because they realized I was not yet dead.

I told my girl Silvie to keep it, and find some use for it. A hot pad for the table. I wanted nothing. At the age of eighty, I began throwing out the mountain of things that once held meaning—furniture, clothes, books, pictures. They were nothing but wood, plastic, cloth. I could not understand why I clung to each object for so long.

Awards. Nowadays they give them to anyone for anything. Silvie told me her five-year-old received an award for graduating from kindergarten. I could see how proud she was, and said nothing. But it was all nonsense. It sent the wrong message—that the child had accomplished something. Well, reward the child for doing nothing now and she will never do anything later—which is the point, isn't it? To encourage. To teach the student to reach beyond herself.

I taught my entire life and knew when a child was thriving or languishing. And if she was languishing, then she was in trouble. There was an art to teaching, which involved the ability to empathize and communicate. It could not be learned. Either one had it, or one didn't. Over my career I interviewed hundreds of young women with teaching degrees from the best schools, even graduate degrees. Of course they were intelligent. But could they put themselves in the student's place? Communicate at the student's level? Most could not. A few tried. Good teachers were either born with this talent, or developed it at an early age: the ability to read people.

I learned to read Father. I learned to read my brother Daniel, and my husband Everett Gooding. And I learned to read my Kohala school girls. Their polite responses to my questions opened the doors to their homes. When I listened closely, they told me of births and deaths, love and loss, all with the drop of their eyes. A pause between words. A shift of their brows. At the end of my life I cannot remember what I ate for breakfast. I rely on Silvie, who tells me it is time for lunch, time for my program, time for bed. I trust her to tell me that night has fallen. I do not need to see for myself the lengthening twilight. I know that these are my final days. I know that they do not matter in themselves. Their purpose is to remember, and wait. I am not sad. But I am bored. The Trinity girl's visit helps. It gives me an occupation: to collect my Kohala memories. To sort through them for my student, Lydia Kaluhi. A relation of the Trinity girl—or so she said. The girl seems to believe that Lydia will provide some clue to her own life. Silly, spoiled girl, like all those Trinity girls. Making a claim on my memory as if she were entitled.

I will decide that issue later. For now, I remember my Kohala days quite well, and the green valley called Light in the Darkness. In fact, I remember my Kohala days perfectly. Watch. I close my eyes and when I open them, I am there again. North Kohala, 1922.

THERE WERE SOME things I would not tolerate, like the Hawaiian boys stalking the church grounds after Sunday services. They had not attended services—although no other class of boy in the District needed it more. And I did not appreciate their staring and laughing at those of us who did.

We gathered on the veranda to the church meeting house, where my students served refreshments after the service. The boys smoked and loitered in the parking lot, smirking and God-only-knew.

I kept an eye on them. There were five, kicking at the dust with their huge, bare feet. They petted the horses, then ran their filthy hands over the cars. I doubted they owned a suitable pair of pants to enter the church, let alone a pair of shoes. They were from a class of Hawaiian I still see today—the class that is resistant to improvement and in the news for murder and drugs. They drop out of school, cannot hold a job and fill the prison and welfare rolls. They are destined to lead dull, impoverished lives outside the influence of good government and Christian morals. They were exactly the class of boy I was determined to steer my girls away from.

Then Sam Kaluhi walked out and spoke with them. I was hardly surprised. Although he was only fourteen years old, he had already established himself as one of the District's worst delinquents. The smell of tobacco hung on him. I had seen him sitting on the Hāwī street corner in the middle of the day, when he should have been sitting behind a desk in the government school or working. I watched him buy five dollars worth of treats for himself in Olson's Store. Now where did a boy like Sam, son of the destitute Lipo Kaluhi, find five dollars? Where did any Hawaiian boy earn that kind of money? It was a wonder his mother persuaded him to go to church that Sunday. The boys laughed with Sam, leaning against the fence separating the horses and cars from the lawn leading to the veranda. Then my husband Everett began walking across the lawn toward them.

"Everett," I called, hoping to stop him.

He spoke with the boys until, just as I feared, he gestured toward the veranda, inviting them to join us. After more than six years in Kohala, Everett still insisted on ignoring convention. One simply did not mingle with such boys, this rule being as much for the boys' comfort as our own.

But from the beginning, Everett had followed his own counsel. We had arrived in 1916, after my graduation from Mount Holyoke and Everett's from the Theological Seminary in New Haven. Everett had written to Father, asking for permission to marry me. In the ensuing exchange, Father learned of Everett's training and wish to minister and teach. Father offered him an assistant ministership for five years and, assuming all went well, full ministership—at which point Father would retire. Everett accepted, notifying me of his decision after the fact.

"How could you make such a decision without consulting me?" I said.

"I was certain you'd be thrilled to return to your home. You talk about it all the time."

"No I don't talk about it all the time," I said. Two or three times at the most. "I never said I wanted to return." Not on a permanent basis. "Even if I had, isn't it only fair to discuss the matter with those whose lives will be affected first, before making the decision?"

"I can't believe you're accusing me of unfairness. I did this for you."

"No. You did not do it for me."

"It's the chance of a lifetime," he said. "What I've always wanted. A congregation of my own—with native people who need help."

This was the first I'd heard.

"And your father... It sounds like he needs help too."

He had a point of course.

I was young and stupid, notwithstanding Mount Holyoke. In other words, I did what was expected of me and accepted Everett Gooding's proposal of marriage. This meant that I accepted the terms of our married life together which Everett had unilaterally chosen: to minister and live in Kohala.

Father did not attend our small wedding in New Haven after Everett's graduation. The travel would be too difficult, he had written. Since Father could not attend, somehow this meant that Everett's mother and sister would not attend. I met them two days later in Philadelphia, where we stayed in Everett's childhood home for a week, then traveled by train to Chicago, then to San Francisco where we stayed for two weeks. We traveled by passenger liner to Honolulu, where we treated ourselves to a week at the new hotel on Waikīkī beach. Everett couldn't get enough of the water, burning himself from the sun the first day out.

From Honolulu we boarded the inter-island steamer, and a day later stepped on the dock at Māhukona. We had been traveling for two months. I had been gone five years—four at Mount Holyoke in Massachusetts, then another year waiting for Everett to graduate.

Father stood on the dock waiting for us. He had aged more than five years. Completely gray, he could have been 80 years old instead of 62. And he seemed to have shrunken at least three inches.

"Oh, Sarah," he said. "Finally you're home."

I could not remember him ever holding me. He draped *maile leis* around our necks and embraced me, crushing the sweet leaves. For that, Father's embrace and sweet *maile*, I wiped away all doubt over returning to Kohala. I decided that Everett was wiser than I, and had chosen well. I thanked God for him, and Father, and for giving me the grace of faith.

An hour later, even the condition of the manse did not dampen my spirits, although it startled me. In the parlor the windows were shut, the curtains drawn. Mildew hung in the air and had spotted the walls. Hills of old newspapers covered the carpet. With each step a dust cloud rose and the mildew odor worsened.

I could not understand. Father had always hired a girl from the plantation camp for cleaning, another for laundry. I said nothing, snuffing out the questions that made the most sense—including my question about my brother Daniel's whereabouts. I expected to see him waiting with Father at Māhukona. Then I expected to find him waiting at the manse. But it was empty, save the dust. When I asked after him, Father muttered something about Kamuela on the other side of Kohala Mountain. But what could be more important in Kamuela than our arrival?

I did not ask. Within an hour of returning to Kohala, I was a child again. The rules of Father's house remained in force: never ask. Never speak unless spoken to.

Without information, I did what I had always done. I dreamed of a perfect world. I decided Daniel was giving needed assistance in Kamuela. Yes, the minister's son was every man's mate. Why not? Father had embraced me at the dock. Mother could be right around the corner.

Young women, such courage and foolery. Father's warm disposition and my trust in Everett strengthened my resolve. This would be my house. My home. These were my men, and I would care for them.

Everett and I undressed and lay on the new bed and mattress Father had bought as our wedding gift. "Goodnight, Everett," I said. But when I turned to him, he was already sleeping.

The next morning I lay beside him listening to doves cooing outside the window. The dawn sky turned the white walls in the bedroom pink. It was my old bedroom, where I had slept since childhood. I could not remember the white walls pink at dawn, nor the doves cooing. I could not remember feeling a bed cradle my body like ours did that morning, Everett's warm back slowly expanding and contracting. He had promised me on the boat between San Francisco and Honolulu that if, within the year, I was not happy, we would leave Kohala.

I fit my body around his back, my faith complete in dawn's pink light. Such comfort. Had it been here all along? I never believed it possible in the manse. At best, I had found safety as a child, never comfort, by tucking myself behind the skirts and shirts in the closet, then falling asleep in the quiet darkness.

I was not disheartened walking through the parlor, the dust appearing thicker than the night before. The foliage outside the manse had covered the parlor windows, preventing light from entering. I could hear the centipedes crawling in the corners, and the sound enlivened me. After breakfast I would circle the manse outside to see what needed to be cut back. I would open the windows and begin airing the parlor and dining room. No wonder Father looked ill, breathing the putrid air.

In the kitchen, he sat at the table with the stack of Honolulu newspapers he had received with our arrival. I startled him when I walked in, then his eyes softened. He rose from his chair and walked to me, his arms open. Then he stopped, dropped them and turned to the stove. "Coffee," he said. "I made a big pot this morning."

He poured me a cup and asked, "How is he?" He placed my cup on the table across from him.

"He should sleep," I said, sipping. I had forgotten the taste of Father's strong, bitter coffee.

I looked over the kitchen. The stove was caked with grease, the walls and floor splattered, the curtains above the sink hung in tatters. The sink was filled with dry, dirty dishes. Father had yet to buy an ice box, and still used a screen-covered kitchen safe. There was a single bowl on one of the three shelves, but I could not tell the contents.

"The place," he said, staring at the newspaper. "I haven't had the time. The plantations keep growing. Now they want their own services, and they need a bigger school." He looked at me, then at the week-old Honolulu newspaper. "You'll find help to hire in no time. We'll take a ride later. Did you see the new car?"

"We rode home in it from the dock yesterday."

"Oh?" He looked up at me. "Oh yes."

His beard had grown out, the white ragged ends touching the top of his chest. His face had thinned and the crease between the eyebrows had deepened into a cleft that rose and splintered across his forehead. "You two rest today," he said.

"I don't feel tired."

"Maybe you don't, but he needs the rest—not used to the humidity and heat. Once he's ready there's much to do. We've started building a meeting house. You'll come by later and see."

"Will Daniel be back today?"

Father turned the page. "Hard to say."

I heard Everett's footsteps in the hallway. He walked into the kitchen wearing pants and a clean shirt, the shirt tail out. His face was gray.

I did not expect a morning kiss, what with Father sitting there. But I had become accustomed to Everett's attention in the morning. At the hotel in Chicago, I had left Everett to sleep one morning, while I drank my coffee and read the papers downstairs. Everett followed me to the restaurant, then tiptoed up behind me and kissed the back of my neck. I jumped. "Don't worry," he whispered into my ear. "We're married now." He sat down and drained his glass of juice. "Why, Sarah," he had said. "You're blushing."

Father did not hear Everett walk into the kitchen and continued reading his paper. I reached for Everett's hand, but he pulled it away. I poured him a cup of the bitter coffee and told myself that it was all for the better. Those public displays of affection never sat well with me in the first place.

Everett pulled out a chair at the table.

Now Father looked up, "Well." He folded the newspaper and told Everett, "Slow and steady these first days. Rest is important. What a journey. I couldn't do it myself anymore."

Everett sat at the table and lifted the coffee cup, then stopped.

Father continued, "It isn't so much the length of the journey, but the dramatic change from cool temperatures to this heat—and from the dryness to tropical humidity. When Sarah's mother first arrived—when was it?"

My God.

Father continued, "I came in '74, she came in '76. When her mother first arrived, oh how she suffered."

Father had never mentioned Mother before.

Everett closed his eyes, felt for the saucer and slowly replaced the cup—coffee spilling on the table.

"Now that's it," Father said, rising from his chair and throwing his paper on the table.

No. Say more about Mother.

"You're back in bed until noon," Father told Everett.

Everett opened his eyes. "No, I'm fine." But when he pushed the coffee away his hand shook, rattling the cup and saucer.

"One day this will be your house," Father told him. "But for now it's mine. I want you in bed through the morning. Sarah will bring you some tea and toast."

You must say more about Mother.

"Like Sarah's mother, you will come around."

Yes, more.

"We're getting up slowly," Father said, standing behind Everett, hands beneath Everett's arms.

Please, Father.

Everett smiled, "I'm really fine." But standing full height, he swooned.

"I've got you," Father said. "Plenty of rest." He wrapped his arm around Everett's lean middle. He looked at me. "And plenty of bread and butter with his tea."

Father could be so cruel. I had almost forgotten.

"There's half a loaf in the bread box, butter in the safe," Father said to me; then he led Everett out of the kitchen, down the hallway, chattering all the way. "This afternoon I'll be back. We'll put you on the porch. Oh, the evenings are mild and fine here. The breeze from the mountain is God's breath."

I found the loaf, a pot of orange marmalade and a jar of tea. I brewed a mild pot, which I served with the toast. I could not find the butter.

I left the tray on the night table next to Everett, then I drove to the Japanese Camp where I hired two girls. They came to the manse every day for a month. We began in the kitchen. They removed everything from the cupboards and washed the plates, glasses and flatware. They scrubbed the pots and wiped clean the cupboards of the droppings from mice, roaches and lizards. They sneezed and sneezed, but continued. They hitched their skirts to a sash around their hips, revealing their short muscled legs, then scrubbed down the floors and walls. One carried an infant on her back the entire month. The child never cried, just as she had promised.

I hired one of the girl's husbands to do yard work. He cut back the overgrowth. I hired a carpenter from the Portuguese camp, who pried open the windows and replaced the screens. In Hāwī I went to the new general store owned by the Danish immigrant, Dag Olson. Unlike the mill store, Olson imported goods the camps' Japanese and Korean workers relished—dried seaweeds, peppers and plums. And there were crates of dried fish which stank, but that my cleaning girls savored at lunch with rice.

I bought ammonia, nails and plywood. Olson quietly made up the bill; then he stammered out the English, "You brother, he should deliver to you?"

"My brother?"

"He is my help."

"Where is he?" I looked around the store.

"Soon he gonna come. He bring you order?"

"Yes," I said, still looking. "Is he here?"

"Soon."

"You must tell him to come immediately," I said. "With or without the order. It doesn't matter."

"Sure."

"Has he been with you long?"

"Oh sure. He is good worker."

"Yes, but do you know where he is? Why hasn't he been home?"

"I can bring myself, if you need today."

"No, no," I said. "It's Daniel I want. Send Daniel."

EVERYONE WATCHED EVERETT lead those boys beneath the veranda. Charles Moku was easily the largest of the gang. He was so brown he almost looked black. He wore a smugness I found laughable: that overgrown, barefoot ragamuffin assumed the countenance of an accomplished man. In fact, his family lived in the dank shadows of Hālawa gulch. It was said of the ten siblings that no two shared the same father. No one knew how they survived.

As the boys stepped onto the veranda, everyone took a step backwards, then turned their backs and continued their conversations. I saw Everett's glare, but did he actually expect us to hold a conversation with them? About what? I was not sure they even spoke English—or what I considered proper English.

The boys followed Everett to the refreshment table. I believe that was the first time the boy Charles saw Lydia, who was serving cake with her sister Bernice and two other students. I believe it was the first time because the boy's mouth dropped open when he saw her. He dropped his eyes as if he was afraid to look up at her.

I didn't like it. At the Girls' School we did our utmost to steer our students away from such boys and toward wholesome activities. It was important to wipe away the Hawaiian girls' inclination to cavort and carouse. In addition to their education, one of our purposes was to influence the most important decision the girls would make, for marrying well was essential to their lifelong health and happiness.

While a busybody from the Kamuela Women's Auxiliary yapped on and on to me, I watched Lydia hand Charles a plate stacked with cheese sandwiches, a slice of cake and a bun.

"Tea or coffee?" Bernice said to him.

Charles stared at Lydia.

"You'll choke without something to wash that down," Bernice said.

A lopsided grin spread across the boy's face, displaying the biggest set of teeth I had ever seen, white as bleached coral.

"Or you could pump water from the well," Bernice said.

Lydia elbowed her, then placed in his hand a cup and saucer, the cup filled with tea and milk. It rattled and spilled as he took it from her. The boys found a place near the step to the lawn with their loaded plates. They fell to their haunches, placed the plates in the middle of their circle and began stuffing their mouths with their fingers. They lifted the tea cups around the rim, gulped and wiped their mouths with the backs of their hands. It was hard to watch.

Now, that Sunday old Lipo Kaluhi Sr. accompanied Julia and the children to services, it being his custom to attend once or twice a year. Lipo Sr. lived with his son, Lipo Jr., his daughter-in-law Julia and the children. Or rather, I should say that their home appeared to be his base. It was reported that he camped for weeks along the coastline, casting his nets and searching through the rocks. He wandered the valleys singing in the old native way—that quivering, tuneless nonsense.

Given the old man's usual attire—a tattered pair of pants cut off mid-thigh, a tattered shirt he often tied about his head—his church appearance was always startling. That Sunday he wore a brown suit, the jacket lapel pressed to a shine, a white starched shirt buttoned up his rough neck, wrapped with a black tie. His oversize leather boots caused him to shuffle when he walked down the church aisle to sit with the family that morning. Later he would shuffle two miles into Hāwī. There he would sit by the roadside with other native men waiting for the cars to pass, at which point they would lift their hats and canes in the air.

Lipo Sr. shuffled out to the boys while holding Julia's arm. Very good, I thought. It was about time someone rebuked them for disrupting our coffee hour, then send them on their way. When the boys saw Lipo Sr. approaching they stood. Lipo Sr. touched each boy's shoulder with his weathered hand. Then he turned toward us—Father, myself and the Kamuela chatterbox, still speaking without pause.

Lipo Sr. held Charles's arm and shuffled back beneath the veranda, the other boys following with Julia. He stood beside us waiting for an entrée, but the chatterbox wouldn't stop. Finally, Father threw up his hand in front of her.

Her gloved fingers flew to her mouth. She turned to find the gang of barefoot Hawaiian boys behind her and jumped. Lipo Sr. stepped too close to her and she gasped, then backed away—thank goodness. But now we had to deal with the old man and the boys.

"'O 'oe,'" Lipo Sr. said to Father. "Here are the grandsons of the men who dig your church." He pointed with his chin toward the sea three miles away. "Bring sand from below. Cut stone. Build walls. Here is the foundation of your church."

Charles was the tallest of the group, at six-four or six-five. He towered over Father. "Charles Moku," Lipo Sr. said to Father. "Grandson of Nōweo."

Father's eyes brightened.

"Yes, Nōweo. Take you around the District. Show you where everyone lives. Take your wife to Kona when she is sick."

Father reached for the boy's hand, whose defiant eyes had shifted into quiet black pools surrounded by a dense crop of lash. Lipo Sr. held another boy's hand. "Edward Kauka," Lipo Sr. said. "Grandson of 'Iehu."

Father's eyes softened.

"Yes, the one feed Miss Christian."

The silly boy attempted a bow of sorts. But Father lifted him by the shoulders, insisting on a handshake.

"My regards to your mother," father told the boy.

And I had heard pieces of this story. When I was an infant, Mother had caught a fever. Father had taken her to Honolulu, leaving me with a Hawaiian family for a year.

Well, shared history was pleasant to learn about on a Sunday afternoon, and it seemed to lessen the boys' threat, but it hardly excused their rude behavior. I could guess there was plenty more where it came from.

Sure enough, a week later I was not at all surprised to see the same boys walking out of the forest onto Girls' School Road at 3:30 when we dismissed the day students. Cigarettes dangled from their mouths and they wore the same tatters from the Sunday past.

Then I saw Lydia and Charles. They stood apart from the students who were walking down the road. He gazed upon Lydia and she up at him. It was clear they were having a private conversation, and I did not like that one bit. There was no doubt in my mind the two were involved. I didn't know when it had begun—at church the Sunday past, or perhaps they had been seeing each other for some time already. Regardless, it had to stop immediately. If the situation festered then, sure enough, it was bound to happen. We would lose Lydia to maternity.

For some of my girls this was inevitable. I could tell by looking at the girl's family, no two siblings from the same father. Oh there were broods of bastards throughout the District. The girls from these families wore the same dress day after day. They reappeared at school after weeks of absence without an acceptable excuse. And worse, after contacting such a girl's family, it became clear the mother herself was not concerned—so why should the girl be?

This was not Lydia's mother's way. I knew Julia Kaluhi would not have approved of her daughter cavorting with a boy like Charles. I doubted he could write his own name.

The next day I called Lydia out of class to my office. She sat in front of my desk, her hands in her lap. "You must promise me," I said, "that you'll have nothing more to do with that fellow I've seen you with."

"Yes, Miss Christian." My students never used my married name, Gooding. Of course, I could have insisted.

"I'm telling you this for your own good. You do not need a boy like that in your life. He'll take your attention away from your work here, and nothing should interfere with that. Possessing your own career, learning self-reliance, is the most important thing we can give you."

"Yes, Miss Christian."

You see, I believed in persuading the child, rather than issuing orders supported with threats of punishment. I believed my words carried more power than the gaze between Lydia and Charles that had held them beside the forest noticing no one else but each other.

"Promise me that you'll not see that boy again," I said.

Lydia looked at me. "I promise, Miss Christian."

But the next day I saw him sitting at the corner of Girls' School Road and Government Road.

Of course he would have noticed Lydia. Everyone did. The photographer I had hired for the graduating class picture remarked on her "classical" features and asked to photograph her. I knew his work, scenery and portraits. It was all quite flattering. Nothing immodest. I told him I would deliver his proposal to Lydia's mother.

But Julia objected, I learned from members of the Hawaiian Club. "She said she didn't want a *haole*"—the woman caught her breath—"an outsider taking pictures of Lydia."

"Then he offered her ten dollars," another said.

I could not blame Julia, wife of the perpetually unemployed Lipo Jr. It was up to her to feed her children.

The photographs of Lydia were a success. The photographer loosened her hair, which fell over her shoulders. He crowned her head with a wreath of silk flowers and asked her to wear a grass skirt we had used in Tribes of Israel—there was always some production going on. He posed her seated upon a grass mat with a *'ukulele* in her hands. I suppose it added a nice touch: native maid plucking a sweet tune. But he could not coax her to smile, not the way she had smiled for the boy Charles. She looked past the camera lens, wanting to be in another's company.

No it did not surprise me that Lydia captured Charles's eye or the photographer's imagination. I had even seen women stop, turn and stare after her—visitors from the Coast or Honolulu who traveled up to Kohala for our pleasant valleys and fresh air. For the view of Pololū and Hāmākua at the end of Government Road.

And when she began seeing the boy Charles, Lydia's features transformed. Once they had been a refreshing mountain stream. But now the stream had been let loose over a cliff, and tumbled into mist and light. That was how I knew she continued to see him, despite my warning. The light in her face and the mist in her eyes told me so.

And what could I have done? Warn her mother Julia of course, but beyond that, how could I have prevented her from making a terrible mistake? I could have ordered, threatened, but all for naught since Lydia Kaluhi had a mind of her own. Of course she sat for the photographer, but refused to smile. Of course she promised not to see the boy again, but saw him nonetheless. She was, in the end, a Hawaiian girl with a mind of her own and destined for trouble.

1985, Honolulu
Bernie

When Moani first went to Trinity, she said she needed extra money for P.E. clothes.

What's that, I asked. P.E?

Sports, she said.

I went to Sam. We're paying all this tuition so she can play?

He told me it was different nowadays. Girls were supposed to run around. Get strong.

After we bought the P.E. clothes, Moani joined the volleyball team and wanted that uniform. The next thing I knew, she joined the basketball team and wanted that uniform. Then there was softball, and they had their own uniform too. She joined the swim team and would you believe that little bathing suit cost more than the softball uniform? There were fees for traveling, and victory parties at restaurants. Would you believe they had parties at restaurants for the losers? And another thing: I didn't like her being involved with so much sports. After all, she was a young lady. What about that time of the month? I said to her.

She laughed. She told me I was old fashioned. She told me that she could do anything she wanted to do, then showed me the box of tampons with the girl riding horseback.

That's supposed to prove something?

Yes, she said. She showed me a book called Sex Education, filled with pictures of naked boys and girls. Plus close-ups of you-know-what. Plus pictures of sponges she was supposed to stick up there. I took it straight to Sam: Did you know they're teaching her this? A thirteen-year-old girl?

He looked me in the eye and said it's about time.

So he wanted to get personal? Fine. I told Sam that if he ever said anything about me having Haunani out of wedlock again... If he ever said anything about Haunani having Moani and Puanani... I'd yank Moani out of Trinity and he would never see either of us again. I was the grandmother. I could do that.

MOANI HAD IT easy. At the School for Hawaiian Girls there was no such thing as tampons and girls riding horseback. No one said anything about what was happening to our bodies. My first time it ruined my nightgown and the bed sheets. I thought I was dying, but Mama just handed me a stack of folded rags and told me to use extra bleach in the wash water.

And once I started bleeding I had to show Sarah Christian a bloody rag each month. That was the policy and how they thought they could weed out the pregnant girls. That's how they thought they could make us think twice before letting the boy's finger slide down there. The morning of my first inspection I left a used rag on the bureau. I should have wrapped it in the newspaper right away, stuffed it in the corner of the my schoolbag. Mama saw it and gave me hell. "So dirty of you," she said.

I felt bad-bad. I tried to pretend that it was like any other morning, wrapping the stiff rag no one was supposed to see except Sarah Christian. I tried to pretend because that was the only way I could get myself dressed, then up through the forest to school—Lydie trailing behind me as usual. The only thing that made me feel better was knowing that soon she would have to go through the same thing.

We began our school day with a prayer and a hymn. I couldn't sing, knowing what would happen after the hymn. Sarah sat at her desk in the front of the classroom. "Let's finish our inspection quickly. There's much to do today. Girls for inspection, line up beside my desk."

Chairs scraped across the wood floor.

"Lift your chairs, please," Sarah said.

I walked to the end of the line beside Sarah's desk.

"Oh, very good, Bernice," Sarah said. "Now you're a woman."

Like it was an accomplishment. But it felt like I was being punished. Each girl stepped up to Sarah's desk and opened the folded newspaper, then dropped the rag in the waste can and returned to her desk.

When my turn came, I watched Sarah Christian write my name at the bottom of the inspection list. Then I handed her my bundle of shame.

"You don't *give* it to me," she said.

The other girls laughed.

"I just need to *see* it."

"Oh." I began unwrapping the paper.

She threw up her hand. "That's enough, just to see if it's there." She made a check next to my name, the red ink glistening.

There was more laughing. I walked back to my desk.

"Really, Bernice," Sara said. "Don't *keep* it. Why would you want to keep such a thing?"

I dropped the rag in the waste can. Now Mama would give me hell for throwing out a perfectly good rag.

I had kitchen duty that day. We cooked a pot roast and served it with mashed potatoes. The kitchen matron assigned me to serve the teacher's table. I prepared their plates in the kitchen and put them on the serving tray. But before carrying the tray into the dining room I licked my finger and ran it through the mashed potatoes on Sarah's plate.

"Thank you, Bernice," she said when I put the plate in front of her. "This looks very nice. I'd like a cup of tea with my lunch, please."

As I walked to the tea and coffee service, she leaned across the table and whispered something to the other teachers. They all laughed.

Back in the kitchen I watched Sarah through the pass-through, my lunch getting cold on the counter. I didn't care. I needed to see her eat the potatoes. The next day we made beef stew from the leftover pot roast. I made sure I got the job of serving the teacher's table again.

A month later I came home from school and Sam was in the yard petting a chicken like it was a puppy. "Where did you get that chicken?" I said.

"Ask me no questions, I tell you no lies."

He thought he was so smart, when he was just plain hungry all the time. Mama was feeding him more than she fed me and Lydie, but it was never enough. At dinner, Sam would finish his plate in a minute, then look for more in the empty pot. He began stealing chickens and fish. Raiding vegetable gardens and fruit trees. Robbing grocery stores. The week before, he had carried a twenty-pound sack of rice into the kitchen, proud. But Mama had ordered him to carry it right back out.

"Stay there," I told Sam, petting the chicken. I ran into the house and our bedroom. I grabbed a handful of clean rags from the back of the bureau drawer. In the kitchen I found the carving knife, then ran back to Sam in the yard. "Now kill it," I said, holding out the knife to him.

Sam looked at my rags. He knew what they were for. I had seen him snooping in our bureau. "What're you doing with those?" he said. The chicken pecked at the air.

"You afraid to kill that chicken?"

Sam grabbed the chicken's head and gave it a twist. The head fell to the side—its eyes closed and the beak parted.

"Lōlō. Why do you think I'm standing here with this knife?"

Sam took the knife, held the limp chicken in front of him and whack—the chicken's head flew off. It landed in the dirt beside the house. From beneath the porch Little Girl crawled out. She sniffed and licked the chicken head.

"Hold it up," I said.

"What?"

"I'm gonna kick you, you don't do what I'm telling you."

He held up the chicken by the neck.

"Not like that." I grabbed the chicken and turned it upside down, then held one of the rags under the bleeding neck.

"What're you doing, Bernie?" Sam said.

"Ask me no questions, I'll tell you no lies."

My chicken-rags didn't last long. The best thing I found for monthly inspection was all around us: red Kohala dirt and water. It turned the color of dried blood nicely and fooled Sarah Christian, who wrinkled her long nose each month when she looked at my dirty rag. Inside, I was laughing at her: she couldn't tell the difference between blood and dirt. But on the outside, I was laughing with everyone else at the girls who didn't have dirty rags to show yet.

That was the way it went. At first, we were ashamed to show. But once we did, we went after the girls who didn't show. It meant they were still kids. In each class there was one: a girl with a flat chest and nothing down below. In our class it was a girl named Grace who was as tall as a boy and looked like one too—a shadow over her mouth. Each month it was the same. Sarah Christian would say to her: "Still nothing for you?"

Grace would shake her head.

"Hmmm," Sarah would say. "All right, let's see what happens next time."

Then, the year my class matriculated, another pregnant girl made it close to her delivery time before the Girls' School found out. A rumor circulated: we would have to show Sarah Christian our bloody privates. All the girls acted so shocked. But after six years at the Girls' School nothing surprised me.

No matter which way I turned, it seemed like being a girl was bad news. Everybody kept telling me what to do. Don't run. Don't talk. Sit quietly. Bleed for the next forty years, but pretend I don't bleed. Pretend I don't bleed, but prove that I bled. Make babies, but pretend I didn't do it. Do it, but pretend I didn't like it. Push a baby's head out of my privates, but pretend a stork dropped her on the porch.

Sarah Christian called assembly. "As you know, girls, the inspection program is for your own good. I cannot think of another way to proceed, so we shall proceed as we always have with our monthly inspections. Let me remind each of you that here at the Girls' School we operate on the honor system."

That was the first time I ever heard that, the honor system. Now it was an honor to show her my bloody rags.

"That means that we—I—trust each of you to do justice, love mercy..." she paused and we completed the prayer with her, "and walk humbly with thy God."

1985, Honolulu
Moani

We were supposed to leave Honolulu for Moloka'i early Monday morning, with the kayak launch no later than 1:00 so we could make camp before sunset. But there was a downpour that morning. Then the winds at the airport reached sixty miles per hour and the airline canceled our 7:00 a.m. flight. I stood at the airline ticket counter with my third-in-command Henry, and Pu.

The ticket agent said, "The earliest flight to Moloka'i won't be until"—she checked her screen—"until 10:00 this morning. Did you want to reschedule for that flight?"

"No. Book us for early tomorrow morning," I said. "Same time. Same flight."

I turned to Pu. "Sorry, but today's trip is a wash."

Henry yawned and stretched.

"If we don't get to Moloka'i until 10:30 or 11:00, then we won't be launching until 2:00 or 3:00," I told her. "Not good."

"No?"

"Means we'll be paddling to camp in the dark."

Her teeth chattered. "I thought Dixie was coming." I had told Dixie to meet us at the airport at 6:00 A.m. sharp.

"Wherever she is, we can't wait for her."

"But... So we're going?" Pu said.

"No, we have to wait until tomorrow."

"We wait for Dixie?"

"No, Pu. We're waiting for better weather."

"But maybe if we wait then Dixie can come?"

"Hopefully she'll sleep in again tomorrow morning."

"Why?"

"Nothing, Pu." We walked to my ten kayakers standing in the interisland airline terminal—the four lawyers, the two nurses and their husbands, and the honeymooners. They stopped talking as we approached, their arms wrapped around their chests. They saw the weather. They knew the news was bad.

I squatted in front of them and laid the Moloka'i map across two of their backpacks. "I know you've been planning on this trip for a year, maybe more, but safety is my first concern in anything."

Honeymoon-guy acted surprised and stomped his foot.

"Given the weather we're seeing this morning," I said, "the airline tells me that they've rescheduled our flight for 10:00, at the earliest. So, it could depart even later."

I pointed to Moloka'i. The lawyers squatted next to me to study the map. "By the time we arrive, collect the kayaks and gear, and transport everything from the airport here"—I pointed—"to our launch site here"—more pointing—"eat lunch, inflate the kayaks, get everyone in the water, it'll be 3:00 or 4:00 in the afternoon."

"You said 2:00 or 3:00," Pu said.

"Now, here's our campsite," I pointed again. "There's no other campsite in between. The first day out, people paddle slowly. I've never made this campsite in under four hours. That means we'll be paddling in the dark, beaching and setting up camp in the dark." I looked up at the nurses, who were nodding. Women get the safety thing quicker than men.

"And that won't happen," I said. "Not in my company."

One of the lawyers said, "Supposed we're stuck here tomorrow?"

Another said, "We'll just have to come back."

"But come you back..."

I squeezed Pu's hand.

"...when summer's in the me-a-dow."

"If we're stuck here tomorrow," I said, "then we're stuck here tomorrow."

"Or when the valley's hushed and white with snow."

I pulled on Pu's hand. "We go through the same exercise until the weather permits a safe launch."

"Tis there I'll be in sunshine or in sha-a-dow."

"That's my bottom line: a safe launch. A safe trip." Honeymoon-guy looked at the map. The rest of the group stared at Pu.

"Oh Danny boy, oh Danny boy, I love you so."

"In the meantime," I said, "you've packed all your gear, checked out of your hotels and now you have to check-in again. Unpack again. Repack tomorrow morning."

The nurses continued to gaze at Pu.

"Circumstances like this arise from time to time."

My contract specified that the launch date was contingent on favorable weather, and, if necessary, would be adjourned until safe launching was available.

"Even though I've made you aware of this, I know it's a big disappointment. We have an arrangement with one of Waikīkī's premier hotels. They'll house you at a seventy-five percent discount on their room rates." It was one of Uncle's Hideaways, where the honeymooners had been staying. Once called quaint and charming by the travel guides, now the City wanted to provide it with historic landmark status.

"Of course I'm picking up your fare back to the hotel," I said. "Plus your lunch, dinner and breakfast tabs through tomorrow at the hotel's restaurant. Nothing fancy, burgers and chops, pie and coffee."

Their eyes softened. People love free food.

"Or, if you're game, I'll meet you tonight at the Canoe Beach Lū'au. Dinner's on me."

There were smiles all around.

"Waikīkī at its best—or worst. And the food's not bad."

"All you can eat," Henry said, his hand on his stomach.

"Sorry about this," I said. "But there's no way I'm letting you paddle out there in the dark. I'm committed to making this trip one of the best memories of your lifetime, but that only happens if you're safe."

"Just can't be helped," a lawyer said.

Another stood and stretched his arms overhead. "Nope."

"So what if we're a day late getting started?" a nurse said.

"Better safe than sorry."

"I always wanted to go to an authentic luu-ow," the other nurse said. They laughed.

"I'll see you guys tonight," I said.

"Does that mean we get to see you in a muu-muu?" a lawyer asked.

"I don't wear *mu'umu'u*s," I said.

"Yes you do," Pu said. "You wore one the other night."

AFTER CANCELING THE kayak departure and driving Pu to work at Island Cares, I drove to Uncle's office to discuss a loan on the Kohala property. He sat in the wingback leather chair behind his desk, a rose-colored marble slab that rested on four marble columns. He bought it with wife number five in Italy.

"We could fly over next week," I said. "You should see the property for yourself." I pushed the photographs of the old school across the marble.

"I thought you were supposed to be watching Dixie on Moloka'i today?"

"You were supposed to get her to the airport by 6:00 this morning. She never showed."

"Why're you in such a hurry to buy this property?" He wouldn't look at the pictures.

"I don't want to lose the deal."

"I told you already, anything worth doing today, still worth doing tomorrow. Has your seller got any other bidders?"

"None that I know of, but I want to move on this place. The price could change."

"The price's not gonna change any time soon, you listen to those *lōlōs* up the street"—he pointed with his chin toward the state capital, five blocks away from his office—"don't got one ounce of business sense.

"Can't you see? They're dumping this property. It's probably got major problems. The only change in price's gonna be downward—you play your cards right."

It sounded like he was in. Maybe.

"I won't sign the sales contract unless I know there's capital for the renovations and at least two years' operating costs."

"You're not listening to me, Moani. You don't need to sign nothing."

"I know I don't have to sign, but I want to. I want to get started. I want to open for business on January 1." It was late May. "I'm sick of kayaking. This's my last season."

"Then good thing you're taking Dixie now."

"She's got no business in a kayak."

"She needs to get out."

"So take her shopping," I said. "She doesn't know how to paddle."

"That's a good one. Like your clients know anything about paddling and swimming with sharks."

"She'll fry out there," I said. "She'll get sunstroke."

"We went to the drug store. I bought enough sunblock for your whole crew."

"This is an open ocean trip. We're paddling in deep blue water for four hours straight. She's sleeping on a thin air mattress."

"She's tougher than you think," he said.

"Her baggage can't weigh more than eighteen pounds."

"Not a problem."

"Her makeup bag probably weighs that much."

"Hey. Be nice."

"She has to be at the airport tomorrow morning no later than 6:00."

He pushed the pictures back across the desk toward me. "You think you can make this place into a hotel?"

"It's the perfect place. I know I can."

"Got my doubts about the 'place' part. I still haven't heard a good reason why anyone would drive all the way up there, when they got all the hotels in Kona."

"The place is beautiful. People will go there for the same reason they go to the hotels in North Kona."

"North Kona's not Kohala."

Speaking of Kohala... "I ran into someone who knows you—a lady at alumni weekend. Her name is Sarah Christian."

At first he didn't answer, then, "Never heard of her."

"She knows Bernie."

He reached for the pictures and straightened the stack.

"She said Lydia—"

"Now what did I tell you about that?"

"She said Lydia had a baby."

He sat back in his chair, the red leather framing his white hair and mahogany face.

"Is it true?" I said. "Did she have a baby?"

"How much did I spend on all those fancy schools? And you believe anything a stranger tells you."

"She's the only person willing to talk about Lydia."

He held up his finger. "Listen to me. You better stop poking your nose in all of that—happened so long ago. It's got nothing to do with you."

I said nothing, watching Uncle reach for the checkbook, then take the pen in hand. I told myself I was making a mistake by taking his money. Simultaneously, I coached myself: Why not? Uncle had offered help for sixteen years. Besides, I had called around. No one else was willing to invest in a dilapidated property, or a kayak guide who thought she could develop a hotel and take care of her retarded sister at the same time.

INSTEAD OF DEPOSITING Uncle's check at the bank first, I drove to the Department of Health and requested a copy of Lydia's death certificate.

"Wait till your number's called," the clerk behind the intake window said. "Next?"

There were five chairs for thirty people. All of us stood along the walls waiting for news of births, deaths, marriages and divorces—the official word on the unofficial soup that makes a family. The clerk called my number. At the intake window I reached for the pink copy, but she snatched it away. "Five dollars."

I paid her and began reading.

She tapped on the glass and pointed to a sign that read: Step To Side.

I turned away and read the death certificate for Lydia Kaluhi, born April 29, 1906, North Kohala, Territory of Hawai'i. Died April 24, 1922. Cause of death: Unnatural. Number of births: 1. Number of living children at death: 1.

Sarah Christian was right. Lydia had a baby. Suddenly, I remembered a girl from college in Michigan, a pre-med student named Mary. She had worn the same green corduroy pants through the long winter. One afternoon she described her gross anatomy class to me while we walked across the snow-covered campus. "Want to see my cadaver?" she said.

"Sure," I said. "Maybe next week."

"Come on."

"I'm supposed to be somewhere."

"It'll be fun," she said.

We walked to the Medical School, then down the hall to the air-conditioned examination room. The cadaver was covered with a white cloth; its arm hung off the table. Mary lifted it by the hand. "See?" she said, holding it up. They had pulled back the skin revealing the bone and sinew connecting the fingers and forearm. She showed me a finger nail, painted bright red. "Makes her seem real, right? Whoa Moani..." She kicked the stool on wheels toward me. "Take a seat. Deep breaths."

"It smells in here."

"You get used to it," she said, pushing her thick-lens glasses up on her nose. There were twenty tables in the room, cadavers covered with white cloths on top of each.

Outside the snow fell. Inside, Mary pulled back the cloth, laying bare the woman's excavated organs. She pointed with her pen to the small slit in the cadaver's cervix, a dimple on the surface of a plum. "It means she gave birth at least once."

I stepped back to the intake window, "Excuse me?"

"You cannot cut line," the clerk said. "You gotta go back to the end and wait your turn. Next?"

I walked back to the forms desk and the stacks of requests for birth certificates, marriage licenses and death certificates. I filled in a birth certificate request for Lydia's baby, first name unknown, last name Kaluhi—

maybe. Mother's name: Lydia Kaluhi. Mother's place of birth: Kohala. Father's name: unknown. For date of birth I wrote, "1921-22?" For place of birth I wrote, "Kohala, Hawai'i?"

"This's all you got?" the clerk said when she saw the request. "You don't got dates, names." The end of one false eyelash sprang off her eyelid. "How I'm supposed to find a match?"

"Try anyway."

I waited against the crowded wall, Uncle's check in my wallet. A shirtless, barefoot boy ran by. The woman next to me grabbed his arm. "I told you to stop running." He pulled away. The clerk called my number. "Only thing we found was this," she said and showed me another pink copy. "But it's the wrong island."

"Let's see," I said.

"Five dollars."

I paid, then studied the birth certificate. It told me that Lydia Kaluhi gave birth to a baby girl on September 2, 1921, Island of Maui. The infant's name: Lydia Moku. Mother's name: Lydia Kaluhi. Father's name: Charles Moku.

I found her!

I looked around, wanting to tell someone. The shirtless boy ran past me again, grunting and warm.

At the forms desk I prepared requests for a death certificate and marriage license for Lydia Moku—date of death, unknown. Date of marriage, unknown. Then I prepared another request for a birth certificate for any child Lydia Moku might have had. Infant's first name unknown, last name Moku. Maybe. Birth date, unknown. Birth place, Maui. Maybe.

"You're kidding, right?" the clerk said.

"Do I look like I'm kidding?" I said.

She showed her supervisor, "She got no dates, no names. She got nothing."

The supervisor studied my requests, then told me, "This isn't much to go on."

"Sorry."

"Why not ask someone in the family?" the supervisor said. "The more you can give us, the better we can help."

There was a loud splat. The barefoot boy began howling. "Good for you," his mother said. "Didn't I tell you to cut it out?"

"Unfortunately, they can't help," I said.

The supervisor handed my requests to the clerk, "See what we've got on these." Then she told me, "Don't expect miracles."

The clerk returned with a copy of a death certificate for one Angelina Moku.

"Angelina?" I said. "Her name was Lydia."

"That's all there was," the clerk said.

I'd lost Lydia's baby the same hour I'd found her. The copy said: Death due to multiple injuries suffered from motor vehicle accident, July 17, 1973. Number of births, 1; number of living children at death, 1.

"But is she the same person?" I asked.

The clerk stared at me.

"I mean, is Angelina also Lydia?"

"All I know is that's what I found," the clerk said.

I turned back to the crowded waiting room. The barefoot boy had collapsed at his mother's feet.

I looked back at the clerk. She carried a paper plate wrapped with brown paper to the supervisor's desk. "Only had chicken cutlet," she told the supervisor.

"Makes no difference to me," the supervisor said.

I used the pay phone in the lobby and called my grandmother. "I need to ask you something."

"What's this about Dixie going kayaking?" she said. "She's got no business out there."

"Did Lydia have a baby?"

I could hear her breathing.

"I need to know."

"Moani—How—?"

"Tell me what happened."

I imagined her slumping across the kitchen counter where she kept her phone.

"Moani, you heard what Uncle said."

"What did she name the baby?"

"He doesn't want you asking questions," she said.

"You could tell me."

"I don't even know what happened," she said.

"But, how could you not know?"

"That's how it was in those days," she said.

"But, your own sister?"

"And besides, all that was finished a long time ago," she said.

"Who's Angelina Moku?"

"I've got no idea," she said.

"Is she the same person as Lydia Moku?"

"We told you already, Lydie's got nothing to do with you. I'm hanging up."

"Don't hang up."

"You've got some nerve."

"I'll find out no matter what."

She hung up.

I walked to the State Library. In the microfiche room, the librarian showed me the cabinets containing reels for newspapers from 1960 on. I asked for the reel dated July 1973—when Angelina died. The librarian showed me how to scroll, focus, copy, then left me alone in the dark room with the other researchers scrolling back and forth in time.

It didn't take long. Suddenly I sat face to face with my future, the obituary notice for Lydia's baby. Angelina Moku, a.k.a. Lydia Moku, survived by one son, Charles Moku of Maui. "I found her," I said and looked for the librarian. But she had returned to her office. I looked at the other researchers. They sat behind the cubicles, lost in their own stories. I dropped a quarter in the slot to copy the article, then remembered the premed student Mary probing the cadaver's cervix, her eyes filled with hope.

AT LOST PARADISE headquarters I had built along the wall in the main room a counter and sink, installed a large refrigerator, stove and microwave. There was a conference table and desks for my second- and third-in-command, John and Henry. But those two liked to do their business while sitting on the conference table with their feet on a chair. Off one side of the main room there was a garage where I parked the company's vans, and stored the kayaks and gear. Off the other side there was my office. It was nothing fancy, just my desk, a sofa and a mini-fridge that Henry was prohibited from opening. It was an ideal space for a kayak business, so it didn't surprise me when the real estate agent told me that within a week of listing the premises for sale, she had received a half-dozen inquiries. I figured they were all my competitors.

When I arrived, the real estate agent was waiting in my office with a prospective buyer—an upstart from New Zealand who thought he could run his own kayak operation. It looked like he was only sixteen years old.

"Suppose you guys walk around the place?" I told the agent and the kid. I needed to make a call first.

The real estate agent's cheek twitched. I was already late.

"Hey, no problem," the kid said.

"There's juices and soda in the fridge," I said. "Help yourself."

"Cool," the kid said.

There was a stack of telephone messages on my desk, one from my accountant about scheduling a meeting to value my company. It said: 'Urgent.'

I put it aside and called telephone information for the Maui number for one Charles Moku. Then Pu walked in from Island Cares. I checked my watch, not realizing that it was 4:30 already. She flopped on the couch next to my desk. I opened the mini-fridge, found an orange and began peeling it for her. Then information gave me a number.

"Moani?" Pu said.

I held up my hand while writing the number.

"Mo-a-ni."

"Pu, would you please? I'm trying to do something here." I dialed the number, but there was no answer and no answering machine.

"Are there more cookies?"

I hung up the phone. "Here," I said, tearing the orange sections apart.

"I had oranges for lunch," Pu said.

"Another won't hurt," I said. "If you're still hungry after the orange, then I'll give you a cookie." I ate one of the orange sections.

"Hey, those're mine," Pu said, snatching the rest of the orange. She sniffed a piece.

"Pu, what are you doing?"

"Pu-what-you-doing?"

"Guess what I found out today?" I said.

"Guess-what-I-found-today."

"Pu, this's a big deal. I think we have a cousin."

She shook her head. "We don't. We don't have cou-sins, because Grandma, because, because our mother didn't have a sister or brother."

"This cousin comes from Uncle and Grandma's sister. She had a baby."

"She's our cousin?" Pu said.

"No, she would've been, let's see..." I worked through the kinship relations in my head.

The real estate agent stuck her head in my office and pointed at her watch.

"Be right with you," I told her. Then I told Pu, "See, Grandma and Uncle's sister had a baby."

"The baby's our cousin?"

"She would've been our mother's cousin."

Pu's teeth chattered.

"That baby..."

"Our mother's cousin."

"That's right. She grew up and had her own baby."

"I don't want this." Pu pushed away the orange. "It's too cold. Are there cookies?"

"I'm thinking he must be about our age."

"Who?" She opened the fridge.

"The cousin."

"See?" Pu said. "There's chocolate chip."

"It means there're more of us than we thought," I said. "And that our family's bigger than we thought."

"I knew that."

"Pu—How'd you know that?"

"Because I'm gonna have a baby."

1914, Kohala
Sam

All my years in business, you figure I must've met some sons-of-bitches. And you'd be right. But I never met anyone like Reverend Christian. He was worse than any of those guys he preached about from the old testament—those slaves-turned-kings who betrayed their own brother and killed their own kids in the name of Jehovah. At least our guy, Kamehameha, murdered honestly—in his own name. He prayed to the war god, then made war, because that was his business. He wanted the whole show for himself, and he never pretended he was doing it for anyone else.

Listen, Reverend Christian even drowned his own kid. I saw it with my own two eyes, when I was five or six—on the day Papa took me upstream looking for shrimp. Instead of shrimp we found Reverend Christian pulling his son Daniel up the trail that ran along side the stream. Papa put down the shrimp basket and lifted me on his back.

We followed Reverend Christian and Daniel upstream to the pool under the waterfall—twice the size of my own swimming pool. Even at that age, I knew who belonged where, and that boy didn't belong up at the pool. He was eleven or twelve, but Reverend Christian wouldn't let him go anywhere. We never saw him down at the beach or upstream at the pool. The Christians didn't mingle, and they did everything backwards. They taught their kids to walk first, and swim later.

At the pool Reverend Christian pulled off the boy's shirt. Daniel's body was so white I could see the blue veins crawling over his ribs. Reverend Christian tied a rope around Daniel, who tried to pull it off. Reverend Christian smacked him, then ordered the boy into the pool. I couldn't hear everything because the waterfall was so loud. He told Daniel, "Kick ... arm," and threw him in the pool.

"Look, Papa," I said.

Papa held his finger to his lips.

We watched Daniel's yellow hair fly above his head. He hit the water and his mouth opened like he was screaming. Over the roar of the waterfall I heard Reverend Christian yell, "Swim!"

Daniel stuck out his arms, then went under. He came up and went back under the water three times, each time his mouth filling with water when he tried to suck in air. The fourth time he stayed under, his blond hair floating up to the surface of the water.

Reverend Christian pulled him to the side of the pool. He stood over the boy, looking down. "... tell you ... kick ... keep ..."

I looked at Papa.

But Papa just shook his head: this ain't our business.

"Tell you ..." Reverend said.

Daniel grabbed Reverend Christian's leg. He sounded like a pig getting a spit stuck up his ass.

Again I looked at Papa.

Again he shook his head: we're not supposed to be seeing this.

Reverend pulled Daniel off his leg. So Daniel grabbed Reverend's jacket and ripped the sleeve.

"Now ... done," Reverend Christian said.

Daniel let go.

"... godsake," Reverend said, then he threw Daniel in the pool.

This time Daniel just closed his eyes like he was falling asleep, arms and legs out to the side.

"Swim," Reverend Christian said.

But the water around Daniel was calm, except for bubbles.

"... last time," Reverend said, pulling the rope. Then he fell back. The rope broke.

"Daniel!" Reverend Christian yelled.

I looked up at Papa. The vein in his neck was going in and out, in and out.

Reverend Christian grabbed a stick, ran across the slippery rocks, then fell. I heard his chin hit the rock. Up again, he ran to the side of the pool. "Daniel!" He held a stick out to the boy. But now Daniel was floating into the middle of the pool, underneath the waterfall.

"... God," Reverend Christian said.

Everyone called Papa *luhe*, droopy, because that's what he was—a drunk. But Papa could be fast too—like that day, running to the pool to save Daniel Christian.

"Lipo," Reverend Christian said when he saw Papa.

Papa jumped in the pool, swam to Daniel and pulled him out of the water. On the rocks, he turned Daniel on his stomach and began slapping the boy's back.

"Daniel," Reverend yelled.

If I was Daniel and heard Reverend Christian calling me, I would think twice about coming back. But no, Daniel did what his father said. He began coughing and spitting up water.

Meantime, Papa was rubbing his back, drawing out the water.

"All right Lipo, that's fine," Reverend Christian said.

All Papa had to do was look at him, and Reverend Christian shut his mouth. You didn't mess with Hawaiians like Papa, who never apologized for being pissed off all the time. Papa couldn't have cared less about Sunday mornings and Jesus. "Just one more stupid *haole*," Papa had once told me, "who couldn't keep his mouth shut." He had a point. The Roman soldiers were everywhere, nailing folks to the cross. If you can't keep your mouth shut in the face of that, then you're a hopeless cause.

Papa turned Daniel over, laid him on his back, then began massaging his feet. When he finished with the feet, Papa worked the legs. Just like Gramps did the time he pulled the Japani boy out of the water down at the shore. First, you drain the chest. Then you work the feet, the legs, the stomach, the arms—making sure all the life comes back.

Listen, if only half the life comes back you've got problems. Take my niece, Puanani. She drowned at age eight and never found her way back home—not all the way. I thought the same thing would happen to Moani.

She didn't talk for two months after the accident, but eventually she came around and thank goodness. It was bad enough having one retard in the family, let alone two.

Papa watched Daniel's lips turn from blue to red, and his cheeks from white to pink. I watched too. I could tell Daniel would look like his father one day, with the face of a scrawny chicken and a beak for a nose.

"That's quite enough, Lipo," Reverend Christian said.

Papa lifted Daniel into his lap.

"I'm grateful, but I think he's fine now."

"'*A'ole,*" Papa said—refusing to speak English. "*The child is not yet born,*" he said—just the way the old-timers used to talk, everything in a riddle.

Reverend Christian stepped back. He had lived in the district for more than forty years. He knew what Papa meant: Daniel was between death and life.

"*Take my boy home,*" Papa told Reverend Christian. "*When you return, I will give you your boy. All your boy, not half a boy.*"

Me? I started cry-crying. *Bum-bye* Reverend Christian would drown me too.

But Papa didn't notice me. He told the boy Daniel, "Like this," then took deep breaths.

Daniel cried.

"*Maika'i,*" Papa said. "*Cry plenty. Crying is good.*" The year before he tried to make the newborn twins cry, but I had only heard Mama crying.

Reverend Christian took me as far as Government Road. "You know the way home, now don't you, Samuel?"

"You gonna kill me?"

"Don't be silly, boy."

"Like Mrs. Christian."

"Listen to me, boy." He grabbed my shoulder, then loosened his grip—trying to act nice. "Mrs. Christian had to go home—back to her own people."

I tried to pull away, but he wrapped his fingers around my arm. "She just couldn't—" he tightened his grip. "No one needs to know about what happened today, right boy?"

I yanked loose my arm, ran across the road and into the sugarcane field.

When I walked into the house Mama said, "Where's Papa? Where's the shrimp?" Then she sat at the table with her chin in her hand, and stared out the window: Papa had blown it again.

There was nothing to cook for dinner.

But Papa came home with the shrimp basket full.

During dinner Mama said to me, "What's happened to you? You didn't eat all day."

"I'm not hungry," I said, watching Papa suck on the shrimp. He ate half the basket.

Papa never talked about that day. He never talked about the boy Daniel, who he gave birth to. Papa taught me how to keep my mouth shut. Listen, once you learn how to do that, you're on your way.

Unfortunately, my niece Moani never learned this basic lesson. She refused to keep her mouth shut about Lydie, even though I gave her a direct order to back off. Even though she saw that her questions were hurting me and Bernie. You see? Moani had a mean streak. Moani did what she wanted, when she wanted, and fuck anyone who got in her way. How come I knew this about her? Because she was just like me.

Moani was trying to make me talk about Lydie. That meant I had to talk about the night I found her in the sugarcane field, and the afternoon when we buried her on the hillside. Moani was making me remember the days I worked hard to forget—and not because I wanted to. Listen, I didn't have a choice. The only way I survived was by forgetting the past, and looking to the future. But Moani was making me go back to the hillside—beautiful Lydie lying at my feet. Moani was breaking my heart.

1922, Kohala
Sarah

Weren't we all like the Apostle Thomas? Doubting His presence, though it be revealed again and again? In the sunrise each dawn; in the moonrise each dusk.

That was the subject of Everett's first sermon at Light in the Darkness, which he delivered during our sixth month in Kohala. I thought it was a great success. I told Everett so that evening, but he pointed out all the things he had forgotten to say. Still, his relaxed shoulders and easy smile through dinner told me he was pleased.

After dinner we sipped coffee on the porch, Father, Everett and I, the mosquitoes kept at bay by the cool evening. Everett popped shortbread squares in his mouth. I watched him as the dusk sky shifted to midnight blue, all the while holding my secret inside. My monthly was three weeks late. Now, with each day that passed, my elation grew. I believed a future lay ahead in Kohala. A future as rich and pleasant as the evening on the porch.

Then, there was a rush of heavy footsteps across the wood floor inside the manse. The screen door flew open. Everett jumped from the wicker chair, sending it flying against the porch railing behind him.

"Sarah."

Daniel.

I ran to him and he grabbed me. I pulled back, embarrassed by our contact, aware that Everett and Father were watching. Not even a handshake had passed between us when Father sent me to Mount Holyoke six years before. I pulled back and saw a different person from the little brother I had left behind. A dozen scars covered his face. Beard stubble covered his chin. His nose tore to the left at the bridge. His eyes were afire, veins shooting from the red rims to the once-clear blue pools. He was only eighteen years old.

"When did you get here?" he said. The stench from whisky and his filthy clothes made me dizzy.

"It's been six months. Where have you been? Why didn't you come?"

"I thought something was different," he said, looking through the window into the parlor.

I caught my breath and pulled back.

Daniel tightened his grip around my arms, then smiled through his broken, grimy teeth.

Again I tried to pull away.

Now Daniel's fingers dug into my upper arm, his thumbs in the bone.

"You're hurting me," I said.

Daniel lifted me off the floor, and swung me around. "You're back," he said. Then he saw Everett standing behind me, and dropped me to my feet. He offered his hand to Everett, who stood against the porch railing with shortbread crumbs clinging to the corner of his mouth.

"We've looked forward to meeting you," Everett said.

"Been tied up recently," Daniel said with a wink.

"Oh sure."

"Would've gotten here sooner—if I'd known," Daniel said.

"You didn't know?" I asked Daniel, looking at Father.

He sat slumped in his chair, the cup and saucer in his lap. He stared at the porch floor.

After asking for Daniel my first few weeks home and receiving no answer, I had put my questions to rest. I had become accustomed to Daniel's absence. I had become accustomed, once again, to ignorance.

"Beautiful place you have here," Everett said to Daniel.

"Think so?"

"Oh, it goes without saying. Yesterday I walked up into the valley where the waterfall collects at a pool. Nothing like that in Philadelphia where I was raised. It was breathtaking."

"Some would say," Daniel said. He turned back to me. "You've been cleaning up the place?"

"What do you think?"

"You painted everything?"

"So far the kitchen, bathroom and part of the parlor."

"My bedroom?"

"I wouldn't go in your room unless I checked with you first."

"What's this here?" Daniel said, reaching for the shortbread tin.

"Have some coffee with us," I said.

"Yes, I'll make another pot," Everett said.

Daniel threw two squares in his mouth and washed down the crumbs with the coffee in my cup. "Not this time."

"But you just got here," I said.

"I'll be back tomorrow. I promise."

He did not return the following night, or the next one. He did not come again until two months later. Just after we had gone to bed, I heard the kitchen door open, then slam shut. Daniel marched down the hall, past our bedroom to his bedroom. I could smell the liquor evaporating off his clothes through the wall. I heard him rummaging in his bureau and desk drawers. He kicked open the bedroom door, stomped down the hall and let the kitchen door slam shut again. I heard him whistle and curse at his horse. The next morning I found a pile of manure beneath the laundry lines.

EACH SUNDAY MORNING we ate our breakfast early, then Everett and Father would walk up to church. There, Everett would review his sermon notes while Father arranged the flowers and checked the hymnals and prayer books. We had been following the same routine for more than five years.

That Sunday, one month before Lydia died, I had dressed early, then used Everett's old shirt and an apron to cover my church clothes. After they left, I cut and breaded a chicken for our dinner after services. I rolled a pie crust, filled it with fruit and put it in the oven. My back to the door, I stood over the stove, tending the chicken browning in the skillet.

"Think there'll be enough room for me today?" I dropped the chicken thigh I was turning. Hot grease splattered on my hand. I turned and saw the silhouette of a man in the screen door. He pushed it open and stepped into the threshold.

"Daniel."

He lifted his hat from his head and held it to his chest, soap and vetiver filling the kitchen. "Thought I'd visit today," he said. "Were you going up soon?"

Now I felt the grease burning my hand and dashed to the sink where I held it under the running water. I turned to Daniel again, the morning sun exploding from behind him. "Look what the cat's dragged in," I said.

"Nothing too bad, I hope."

"I hope." I dried my hands.

"Damn, Sarah. What smells so good?" He walked to the stove and checked the chicken. "Golden brown, just how the old bastard likes it."

"Daniel."

"What else you got going in here?" He opened the oven door and saw my mango pie. "How much's he paying you? I'll double it." Daniel stood up from the oven, his faced flushed. "It's not fair that he's got you all to himself."

"I'm not here alone. There's Everett."

"Who-vrett?"

"If you visited now once and awhile you two would be friends."

"He doesn't want to know me, now does he, Sarah?"

"Of course he wants to know you. You're the closest thing he has to a brother."

"In that case I pity him."

"You..." I took the pie out of the oven. "Have you eaten? There's eggs and potatoes from breakfast."

He pointed to the pie.

"It's too hot."

I sipped coffee while Daniel ate the leftover eggs, then I fried two more. "What are you up to, coming here out of the blue?"

"Thought it was time to pay my respects." He wiped the plate clean with toast.

"*You're* going to church this morning?"

"Don't act so surprised, Sarah. A man's gotta greet his maker now and then."

"Well, I'm glad to hear you say that." I studied his clothes, suitable for riding.

"Spit it out, Sarah. You got something on your mind."

"I heard there's a woman," I said.

"Oh, Sarah."

"A Hawaiian woman—and children. For godsake, Daniel."

"Come on, now. Why listen to gossip like that?" He held up his cup. "Is there more?"

"How can you live like this?" I asked. At the stove I poured the last of the pot, thick with coffee grounds.

"You believe everything those old biddies tell you?"

"Sometimes, yes," I said, walking down the hall to our bedroom for my hat.

Daniel called after me. "You're still as mean as ever."

Back in the kitchen, I expected to see him slicing into the pie. Daniel had cleared the table and was wiping it with a wet rag. When he saw me, he put down the rag and adjusted my hat, tilting the straw brim to one side. The movement kissed my forehead. He smiled at the effect, his blue eyes glistening.

"Come back after service," I said. "Let's have dinner together."

"I might just do that."

We crossed Government Road and walked into the valley and up Girls' School Road. "Heard your boy Everett isn't doing a bad job," Daniel said.

"What would you know about Everett's work?"

"Looks like he's willing to put up with Father. I don't know if I should congratulate him, or throw him in a looney-bin."

"If you behave yourself, this could be a pleasant morning between you and Father. A family reunion."

"As long as we keep a mile's distance between us."

"Then why visit?"

"Listen, Sarah," he said. "Hear that?"

"You waited until Father was gone this morning before coming to the house."

He grabbed my hand, forcing me to stop. "The best birds on the island live right here. Listen."

It was nothing more than the usual forest chatter, as the sun burned off the dew and the valley heated. I pulled away.

"Remember when we used to walk up this road together?" he said.

"I'm sure Father wants to see you."

"And the day you taught me to whistle?" Daniel said.

"There's no reason why the two of you should keep ignoring each other."

"We used to make bird calls and listen for their answer."

I walked ahead.

"Remember the cardinal? He used to fly all the way to church with us each Sunday."

It was a pair actually, which we had named Rosie and Robert.

The church was empty, with Father and Everett working in the back office behind the vestibule. Daniel and I sat together in the front row, where we had once sat as children on either side of Mother. I waited for Father to appear with vases of flowers and a pitcher of water. I was anxious to see his reaction to Daniel. I hoped for the best, a chilly reception. But I braced myself for the worst, Father's demand that Daniel leave.

The church members arrived, filling the pews behind us. I looked at Daniel, who had closed his eyes, revealing the blue veins etched across his pale lids. I reflected on that Sunday's gospel and lesson: The Kingdom of God Lay Within. Everett had written his sermon and practiced its delivery the week before. Father had coached him to touch his chest at each mention of the word "within." Everett laid both hands upon his chest the night before at the dinner table. Father had corrected him. "Just a hint of emphasis is all that's needed."

Paradise lay within. I understood the lesson's truth and felt a glimmer of peace. I needed it so. Now, more than five years after our return, Kohala's humid valleys were suffocating me. So did the arid lands of Kawaihae and the high, cold plains of Waimea, the two—the dry and the cold—hemming in the District. Each time I shopped in Kapa'au and Hāwī my spirits fell, believing there would never be anything grander than this. These were the same small towns I had known as a girl, filled with the same petty people.

And my dream of a family eluded me. At first I had prayed for three children, but after awhile prayed for two. Two would have been fine. A boy and a girl, or two boys, or two girls—it didn't matter. Then I pleaded for at least one. But there was never more than the three of us living in the manse, which was, once again, tidy and trim.

How much I wanted to leave that place of disappointment. I decided it was time to tell Everett. I had given Kohala my best, but it had returned nothing.

I heard a baby cry, followed by footsteps leaving the church. Daniel leaned against me and whispered, "I need to find the little boys' room."

He won't come back, I thought, but decided his brief appearance was good enough. If this was all the religion Daniel practiced for the rest of the year, so be it. I never believed in pushing people into religion—especially the fallen. Daniel was only twenty-three, so he had plenty of time to find salvation, and today was his first step. For that I added thanks in my prayers, then found myself tearful. Daniel would be saved. The Lord was merciful. Have faith, I told myself. Trust that Everett will honor his promise to me: if I was not happy in Kohala we would leave, and make a new life for ourselves somewhere else.

Midway through the service, I walked back to the church entrance for the collection baskets. From the open door, I saw Daniel outside near the cars and horses, smoking. As we sang the offertory hymn, I began passing the baskets down the pews from the back of the church. Then I heard his footsteps climbing the church steps, and glanced back. He stood in the doorway studying the congregation, as if he were looking for someone. He stopped at Lydia, who sat with her mother, sister Bernice and brother Sam. Daniel strutted up the aisle to the row behind the one where Lydia sat.

We sang, *"...Thou my best thought in the day and the night..."*

Father too. He sat in his chair near the lectern. When he saw Daniel, he stopped singing mid-verse. He closed the hymnal and watched.

Daniel forced himself into the crowded pew behind Lydia. He pawed his way over a family singing, then brushed Lydia's hat as he sat directly behind her.

Lydia grabbed it before it fell. Then, with her mother and Bernice, she turned to see the cause of the commotion. Daniel gave Lydia a quick wink down his nose. She slowly turned around and did not sing again.

Lydia's brother Sam turned around. Even then, fifteen years old, Sam's face was aged and rough, his eyes arrogant. He looked Daniel over from head to toe. Then Sam turned to the front again, his brown fists pressed against his thighs, the calloused knuckles turning yellow.

116

The collection basket's heft grew. I passed it down the row where Daniel sat. The family next to him gave their child a nickel. The young boy hesitated, looking at his mother. She nodded: let it go.

He dropped it in and peered up at her again. She smiled at the boy and handed the basket to Daniel.

My brother passed it along without so much as looking at it. He stared at the nape of Lydia's neck, and her long black hair tied in a blue ribbon. Then Lydia stood up.

And Daniel, that fool... Daniel stood up too, then trampled over the family next to him to reach the end of the pew. But when he saw Lydia walk to the piano in the front of the church he sat back down—forcing a space for himself at the end of the pew. Lydia waited for Father's cue, then began playing the second offertory hymn.

Now I understood the story my students had told me earlier that week. I had sent Lydia and two others to Olson's Store for cloth and trim. The errand should have taken no more than two hours, but the girls did not return until after 4:00. They reported that the store clerk, who they did not know was my brother, had refused to help them. Then he left the store, forcing them to wait. When he finally returned he was red-faced and red-eyed, and insisted that my order had not arrived. Olson appeared, checked the storeroom and found the cloth.

"Why didn't you speak up to begin with?" I told them. "Find Mr. Olson earlier?"

But my students practiced what I had taught them, that patience was a virtue. They did not know the value of their time. And I could not teach them because I did not value my own time. I taught my girls to wait for men and children and store clerks. For the day to end, and for the night to end. For rain, and for the rain to end. They waited as girls will wait, girls with names like Patience and Grace. They waited as I waited, age twenty-eight, for miracles.

AFTER SERVICES, DANIEL stayed for coffee, while Father returned to the manse. Daniel's teacher from the government school was the first to approach. "Daniel Christian, is that you?" she asked. Her mouth was filled with cake. "How long has it been? Seven, eight years?"

I gave her failing marks for discretion and tack. I would not have hired her at the Girls' School to sweep the floors.

"Where's your father?" another fool asked him. "He must be thrilled to see you at the Light in the Darkness again."

I could not believe their naïveté: Did it look at all like my brother was a sheep in the fold, living on the word of the Lord?

"I thought I was seeing things," the mill timekeeper said, a smirk on his face. He had approached Daniel with a group of men. They all wore bleached and starched collars beneath their pressed jackets.

"Keeping busy I hear?" one said. They dropped their voices to speak, then broke into laughter.

I saw that Daniel was again staring at Lydia. She was serving coffee and tea with her sister Bernice and another student. The girls chatted about some silliness, except for Lydia, who, under Daniel's gaze, was quiet.

"What're you doing?" Bernice asked her. Lydia had placed teaspoons beside the cake slices instead of forks. "See what happens when you stay out so late?"

Daniel smiled at the mistake, his thin lips red and wet.

Lydia kept her eyes on the task at hand, slicing the yellow pound cake, sliding the pieces off the serving knife and onto the plates.

After the coffee hour she told Bernice, "I don't feel well. Maybe I'd better leave early."

"Maybe you better do your share and sweep the hall first," Bernice said.

During the Sundays past, Lydia had worked slowly, lingering in the meeting hall kitchen. I knew what she was up to. Despite my warning that she stay away from Charles Moku—Despite the rumors that she had given birth on Maui the summer before—Despite all the trouble those two had caused, they still met. I had seen him at the end of Girls' School Road on Sundays, where he sat on his haunches waiting for Lydia. There was always something dangling from his mouth.

Lydia knew that delaying their meeting until the District was seated at their Sunday dinner tables reduced the risk of being discovered. God only knew where the two ran off to. But this Sunday Lydia quickly finished sweeping. She saw Bernice leaving, and ran to her. "I'll walk down the road with you."

"I'm walking up to school," Bernice said.

"We're walking down, Lydia," I told her. "Reverend Gooding and I will walk with you."

"Oh, very good," Everett said when he saw that Lydia would accompany us. "We'll have a chance to talk and get to know each other better."

"Yes, Reverend Gooding," she said.

"You know, Lydia, I've been worried about you," Everett said. He had heard the rumors of Lydia's pregnancy too. He told her, "If you ever need to speak to someone—"

I stopped him, "On Sunday we need not worry about anything."

"Oh, I don't mean worried as in troubled," he told me, then he addressed Lydia. "I just want the best for each of our students."

"Thank you, Reverend Gooding."

The night before he had been on his high horse again. "You actually demand that each girl show you her bloody underwear?"

We sat on the porch after dinner. Father sat inside the parlor, reading the week-old Honolulu newspaper.

"It's the most demeaning practice I've ever heard of," Everett said. "Do they do this together? In public?"

"The parents agree to the policy," I pointed out.

"And if they don't agree they can send their daughters to the Government School, where they'll sit in class with children from the camps who can barely speak English?"

"You don't understand these people like I do. I was raised here."

"Were they your friends? Do you really know them?"

"You're being silly. These girls don't have the same modesty we do. You've seen the women at the shore picking through the rocks, their skirts hitched above the knee."

Father stepped out onto the porch. "You have to understand that the Hawaiian is only three generations removed from human sacrifice," he told Everett. "We're talking about a culture where brother married sister. Even now, with a good one hundred years of Christian teaching under their belts, you'll still find illegitimate, unbaptized children under every rock in the District."

"I'm not talking about illegitimate children," Everett said. "I'm talking about human decency."

"Decency is it?" Father said. "The way they joyride about? Cavort at all hours? The decent thing to do is lock them up until they're twenty."

"Oh, you can't mean that."

"I most certainly do. There's no sense of shame. No sense of sin. Do you see? Their families don't condemn the behavior. The illegitimate infant is welcomed into the fold, given to another relation—*hānai*, they call it. There. They even have a name for it. We've got to take a firm stand against sin, otherwise it's rewarded."

"It doesn't sound like a bad system at all."

119

"Everett—" I felt my face flushing.

"Otherwise, what would you suggest?" Everett said. "Abandoning the child? Throwing the poor thing in an orphanage in Honolulu? What good does it do to condemn the girl for the rest of her life over a mistake made when she herself was still a child?"

"You have to look at this from the rational point of view," I said. "Unless a clear message is given—that this sort of conduct is unacceptable, period—you lose control."

"Here, here," Father said. He returned to the parlor and his chair, snapping the newspaper back into place.

THE THREE OF us walked down Girls' School Road. Everett said to Lydia, "I see you're quite the musician."

"Thank you, Reverend Gooding."

"Have you thought of further schooling?"

"No, Reverend Gooding."

"For example, earning a teaching certificate?"

"Yes, Reverend Gooding."

"Musical training is something all girls, well, boys too—it's something everyone needs."

"Yes, Reverend Gooding."

"And there's always a need for good teachers."

"Yes, Reverend Gooding."

"Think of your career as something you possess," Everett said, "an investment. Something that will grow in value the more you study it."

"Yes, Reverend Gooding."

Then Daniel stepped out of the forest, snuffed a cigarette with his boot and walked toward us. "Well, Daniel," Everett said.

"You're back," I said. "You shouldn't be sneaking—" I stopped myself. I couldn't reprimand him there, in front of Everett and Lydia. "Will you be joining us for dinner then?" I said.

"Yes, time to catch up," Everett said.

Daniel stared at Lydia, who herself stared at the road. I could think of nothing else but to provide a quick introduction. "Daniel, this is one of our day students, Miss—"

Daniel held out his hand.

"We've met already." Lydia looked straight ahead, refusing his hand.

"When a gentleman offers his hand," I said, "polite ladies permit a greeting."

"When I meet a gentleman I will remember."

Daniel's eyes brightened.

"Now just a minute—" I began.

But Everett interrupted. "You won't meet gentlemen with remarks like that."

"Then it's a good thing I'm learning a career," Lydia said.

"I think an apology is in order," I said.

"Absolutely," Everett said.

Lydia stepped in front of Daniel and curtsied low, her hem fanning out over the dust and gravel.

Daniel's nostrils flared.

"Is this right, Miss Christian?"

"Now that's quite enough," Everett said. "I don't think your mother would approve of your behavior."

She stood. "Yes, Reverend Gooding." Then she turned and walked ahead of us.

"I had no idea she was like that," Everett said. "She's not at all like the other one. What's her name?"

Daniel watched Lydia walk away, his steps slowing to kicks.

"What on earth gets into these girls?" Everett said. He turned to Daniel, his voice lighthearted once again. "Come join us for dinner."

Daniel did not answer, glaring at Lydia's back, her waist twisting with each step, her hem fluttering as she ran around the bend in the road. We heard Lydia and Charles meeting, their voices wafting up the road to us. Oh, she would hear from me come Monday morning.

Daniel's dusty shuffle slowed to a stop in the middle of Girls' School Road.

"Daniel? There's pie for dessert," I reminded him.

He muttered something I could not understand, then broke away from us into the forest on our left, onto one of the many trails leading to Kapa'au.

Everett and I continued walking until we heard the sound of branches cracking. The birds screamed, then fell silent.

1922, Kohala
Bernie

Charlie Moku just couldn't leave things alone. It was bad enough he caused all the trouble in the first place, making Lydie *hāpai*. Then, three weeks after the funeral, he had to remind us of everything—when we were trying so hard to forget.

I was pouring hot water over the dinner dishes when I heard shuffling out on the front porch. I found him standing on the other side of the screen door.

"Please, Bernie," he said. "Help me."

I looked for Mama. She was in her bedroom.

"You crazy coming here?" I said, walking across the parlor. "You better get going."

When I got close, I couldn't believe it. The last time I had seen him, he was waiting in the forest for Lydie. She was one of the tallest girls at school, but when she arrived I saw that Charlie towered over her. He put his hands, as big as dinner plates, on her shoulders. They walked right past me down through the forest, the trees throwing long shadows. The wind from Kohala Mountain blew. The underside of the leaves flickered, making Lydie and Charlie sparkle in the yellow and white light. I looked again, and they were gone.

But now Charlie Moku was bent and thin. Dried pus surrounded his swollen eyes. And there was Mrs. Moku, standing in the shadow. Now I knew we were in trouble.

"I want my baby," he said. "Help me find her."

Mrs. Moku stepped into the light. "Let us care for the child." It looked like she had two black eyes.

"I don't know what happened to the baby," I said.

Charlie Moku choked.

"You didn't ask?" Mrs. Moku said.

I dropped my eyes. I only knew that Lydie stayed with someone on Maui. Then I told Mrs. Moku what Mama said: "What's done is done."

"You really believe that?" Mrs. Moku said. "That a wrong cannot be made right?" She opened the screen door. "I cannot believe you think that way. Don't you want to know your sister's baby? See that she's safe?"

No. I didn't. I just wanted everything to go back to the way it was.

Then we heard Mama's quick footsteps. "What's this? Who's there?" She stood in the middle of the parlor looking at Mrs. Moku standing in our threshold.

"Julia—" Mrs. Moku said.

"I don't know you." Mama stayed put.

"Tell me where my son's baby is."

"I don't know what you're talking about." Mama crossed her arms over her chest.

"We'll never talk about it again," Mrs. Moku said. "Don't separate my son from his child. The child from her family."

"No idea what you mean," Mama said.

Then Mrs. Moku put her foot inside our parlor. She raised her forefinger. "The child belongs to us too."

"I don't know anything about a child."

"Lydia..." Mrs. Moku said.

Mama's face fell. We hadn't heard Lydie's name in the house for two weeks, since Sheriff Pua's last visit.

"Lydia wanted father and child together," Mrs. Moku said.

"You get out of here," Mama said, walking to the door.

Mrs. Moku stepped back out on the porch. "This isn't right. How can you live like this?"

"I'll ask you to leave only once," Mama said.

I never heard a boy sob like Charlie Moku was sobbing.

"Don't do this, Julia," Mrs. Moku said. "It's a terrible thing. Forcing us apart. Dividing a family—a father from his own."

She paused, then told Mama, "You think you're protecting yourself but everyone knows what happened. You don't want the child, but we do. Tell me where she is. I'll never say another word about this."

Mama slammed shut the big door we never closed. I looked out the parlor window. A sliver of moonlight lit the night. Gramps climbed the porch steps. With Mrs. Moku, he helped Charlie walk out of the yard and into the lane. Little Girl followed them, her ears and tail dropped. Mrs. Moku turned and looked at our house. I was standing in the window. She pointed to me and mouthed: talk to her.

At the kitchen table, Mama sat with her sewing basket and a pile of mending. She made a stitch in the blouse, then put the needle and thread down. She held her hands up to the light, curling and stretching her fingers.

"Why won't you say?" I said.

Mama jumped in the chair, her hand flying to her chest. "Don't come up behind me like that."

"What happened to the baby?"

Mama pointed her finger at me. "Don't ask me questions. You know better than that."

WORD TRAVELED FAST in those days. We didn't need a telephone. I heard Charlie Moku went fishing that Thursday, but didn't come home. Sheriff Pua and a search party began at Keawa'eli Bay. They covered the windward shore past Pololū. There was no sign of Charlie, his canoe or fishing nets.

That's it, everyone said, and too bad. Charlie Moku decided to paddle out until the sharks found him or the sun cooked him.

It wasn't the first time I heard of suicide by canoe.

But the next week Sheriff Pua and a deputy found him near Waimanu. According to the deputy, Sheriff Pua gave Charlie hell for wandering off and worrying his mother. Then he ordered Charlie to return with them, but Charlie refused. He told Sheriff Pua, "Tell my mother I'm sorry, and not to be sad. We forgive everyone."

You see? Everyone wants to be remembered well. That was my granddaughter Moani's problem. She thought we had forgotten Lydie. And if the world forgot Lydie, eventually the world would forget Moani.

But she didn't have to worry. Everyone remembered her. Just look at the bulletin board at her office. There had to be one hundred pictures from her clients, their kids, even their dogs. And at Christmas... At first she saved all the cards. Then, a couple of years back, she began throwing them out soon as they arrived. That's when I knew something was up. Moani was getting tired of the business. It didn't surprise me when she told us she wanted to sell everything.

At some point in your middle years—it's different for everyone—but at some point you realize you won't live forever. Moani had a long way to go before it was time to worry about death, and whether anyone would care about her when she was gone. Those questions about the by-and-by, and whether we're going to heaven or just rotting in the ground—Those questions were the concern of an old-timer, like me. Well, listen to this: I couldn't give a damn.

When I'm gone, who cares? Unless I'm Abraham Lincoln, eventually nobody will remember me, whether or not I leave behind a tribe of descendants, or nobody—like Moani. Even Abraham Lincoln won't last forever. How many times did you say his name last week?

And if we're forgetting about presidents, then why was Moani insisting that I remember Lydie? If I didn't want to talk about Lydie, then what gave Moani the right to talk about her? Lydie was mine first. It was my right to remember her. My right to forget her.

I didn't have to explain Lydie to anybody. The same way I didn't have to talk about my daughter Haunani. I was the one who lived with the loss. Nobody else felt her death like I did. I decided not to talk about it. I decided to forget. No matter what, my girl was never coming back. Every morning I woke up and remembered that she was gone. My beautiful girl who hurt me so much.

1985, Honolulu
Moani

In the doctor's examination room Pu sat on the exam table, her legs dangling over the side.

The nurse whispered to me, "When was her last pelvic exam?"

"You can talk to her," I said. "She's not deaf."

Clipboard in hand, the nurse asked Pu, "When was your last period?"

"What are those for, Moani?" Pu asked, looking at the stirrups at the end of the exam table.

"Didn't they examine you at St. Teresa's, Pu?"

"We had to stick out our tongue and go, ahhhhh."

I told the nurse, "Her last period was about six weeks ago."

"You never had her examined before?" the nurse said.

I guess not.

"When was *your* last exam?"

"Let's see..."

"We'll deal with your sister first," the nurse said. "She's a little late?"

Pu said, "It looks like the things for horses."

"Yeah. She's late," I said.

"What are those things called?" Pu said.

"And the date of conception?" the nurse asked me.

"Pu, we talked about this. When did it happen?"

"I told you."

"No Pu, you wouldn't tell me. Now you need to answer the question."

For weeks she had been telling me about a boyfriend at Island Cares, but I ignored her. Yesterday, after she told me she was pregnant, we had driven back to Island Cares. I wanted her to point out the son-of-a-bitch. But the building was empty and the director was locking up for the night.

I told the director Pu's story. I asked Pu to tell us who did it and where. Pu pointed to the lunch room, usually lit with rows of flourescent ceiling lights. A window overlooked the work area.

"Tell me his name, Pu."

But she wouldn't say.

The director insisted that nothing could have happened in the lunchroom or work areas. "Just look at all these lights," she said as she flipped on the switches. "People are walking around all day long. The center opens at 7:30 and closes at 4:00. No one stays after hours."

"Then how did my sister get pregnant?"

"First of all, is Puanani really pregnant?" the director said, turning off the lights.

"Yes I am," said Pu.

"And you're assuming that if she's pregnant, it happened here," the director had said. "But your sister's only with us from 8:00 to 3:30. Otherwise, her welfare is up to you."

I TOLD THE nurse, "We're not sure about the conception date, or the pregnancy."

"Yes we are," Pu said.

"That's why we're here."

"We are sure. We are."

"Cool it, Pu."

"She needs to strip from the waist down," the nurse said, handing me the blue paper gown.

When she left the room I told Pu, "You heard the lady."

"I don't want to."

"We need to find out, Pu. The doctor needs to check you." I realized I could've bought a home-pregnancy kit.

"I know I'm having a baby."

"For the hundredth time, Pu, what makes you sure?"

"Just know."

"Well, I'm not sure. So we're taking the exam. Let's get out of your shoes first, Pu."

I knelt and loosened the sneaker laces while Pu unzipped her pants. "This gonna hurt?" Pu said.

I decided I would go to the police if the exam was positive. How could Pu consent to sex? It sounded statutory to me.

Pu began sliding the pants over her hips. Then the door flew open. Cool air rushed in the small room. Pu gasped. "We're not ready yet," I said.

"Sorry," the doctor said, but walked in anyway.

I stood up and faced him. "A few more minutes," I said. I didn't like the beard or the fat pink fingers he would be sticking up Pu's pussy. "And do me a favor. Next time knock first, then wait for my answer."

I went back to Pu's sneaker laces. There was a knot on the left one. I heard the door close behind us. The knot in her sneaker lace loosened.

"Let's step out of the shoes and get the pants off."

But Pu held up her pants, staring at the door. "I don't want to."

"Come on, Pu. You said you're pregnant, so you have to get tested. I want the pants and panties off. I want to be out of here in half an hour." I had adjourned the Moloka'i launch another day for the pregnancy exam.

"No."

"Pu, I'm getting mad."

She leaned against the exam table. "What do they do with that?" The stirrups.

"You have to put your feet in them."

"How?"

"If I show you, will you take off the pants and let the doctor examine you?"

She nodded.

I lay on the table and lifted each foot into a stirrup.

"Why you sitting like that?"

"Because the doctor's down there," I said. "That's how he examines me—to see if I'm pregnant."

"You having a baby?"

"He's down there to examine you."

She looked under the table, "Why's he there?"

I pointed between my legs. "There. Down there."

"What's he doing there?"

"He's there to examine you."

"Where?"

I grabbed my crotch.

Shock spread across Pu's face.

"I told you about this, Pu."

"No you didn't." Tears filled her eyes.

"See, Pu? You'll have this gown over you." I draped it over my knees. "He won't see you. You won't see him."

"No." She began crying.

I lifted my right foot out of the stirrup, then the left. "It's over really fast. And I'll be right here."

"You had to do it?"

"Yeah, Pu. I had to do it too."

"You had a baby?"

"Pu, gees." I took a breath. "You know I don't have a baby."

"Why?"

"Pu, could we please get on with this?"

"How come you don't have a baby?"

"I just don't, OK, Pu?"

"Then I could have a baby brother," Pu said.

"No, my baby would be your niece or nephew."

"Your baby?"

"Pu, I'm really getting tired of this."

She looked at the stirrups. "The boy didn't make me do that."

"Who? Tell me his name, Pu."

"It wasn't like this." Tears streamed down her face.

"Yeah—but—Come on, Pu. If you're pregnant, then somebody was in your crotch."

"No."

"That's the only way you end up with a baby."

"No."

There was another knock at the door. "Come in," I said.

The doctor's eyes darted from me to Pu, then dropped to her hands still holding up her pants. "Want to reschedule?" he said.

"We're having a slight problem here," I said. "It's my sister's first pelvic."

"Her first? But she's"—he looked at the file—"thirty-five years old."

I looked at the floor, the exam table.

"Well, I could bring in some help," the doctor said. "Patients like this."

"Excuse me?"

"And there's sedation," he said.

"Step into your shoes, Pu."

"Just a suggestion," he said. "I'm trying to help."

"How about checking her through her clothes. You guys do that too, right? Tell me what you're feeling?"

"Really a bad idea," he said. "Eventually I've got to do the pelvic."

"Just for now," I said.

He didn't protest.

"OK, Pu. You get to keep on your pants. But I want you to lie down on the table. The doctor will feel your stomach." Pu walked toward the exam table, but as she did, so did the doctor, who put his hand on her shoulder.

She jerked away. "No," she said to me. Then to the doctor, "You're nasty."

MY SECOND—AND third-in-command were waiting for me at headquarters.

"You're late," John said when Pu and I walked in at 10:30 in the morning.

"Goodies," I said, holding up a pink bakery box. I placed it on the table next to them. "Did you guys have breakfast?"

"We've been here since 4:00 in the morning," John said.

"We should be on Moloka'i right now, driving to the launch site."

Henry handed me a stack of phone messages. I still hadn't returned my accountant's call. Pu walked back to my office, sat in my desk chair and opened her chocolate milk.

I told them, "The weather report said there was rain and rough seas in the northeast."

"In the northeast," John said. "That won't affect us. We've launched with the exact same forecast."

"The report said tomorrow through the weekend will be fair," I said.

"And I didn't like doing your dirty work this morning at the hotel," John said. He ate one of the rolls in two bites. "If you delay the launch again," he grabbed another roll, "you tell them." He'd gotten cocky since our knock-teeth, knock-knee sex last year—which I tried to forget about.

I looked through the phone messages.

"One of those's marked ASAP," Henry said.

"Which?"

"The first." It was the kid from New Zealand, anxious to make an offer on my company headquarters. "He keeps asking me what the company's worth," Henry said.

"What'd you tell him?"

"Told him to talk to you."

"If she's ever around," John muttered.

A man appeared at the entrance. "Hello?"

I didn't recognize him.

"You wanted to talk about inspecting some buildings on the Big Island?"

"Right," I said. The engineers. I couldn't remember scheduling a meeting today when we were supposed to be launching on Moloka'i. I took him back to my office and offered him a seat on the sofa beside my desk. Pu wore her walkman earphones. "This's my sister Puanani," I told the engineer. "Pu? Pu?"

She waved me away.

"I'll be with you in just a sec," I said to him, then walked back to the conference table and returned with the box of rolls, "Pu, how about eating something?" She had skipped breakfast again.

She took a bear claw.

I held the box out to the engineer. "Fresh from the bakery."

"No thanks."

I took the box back out to John and Henry. "When I'm done with this meeting, why don't we go to lunch?"

"I'm outta here," John said. "Tomorrow's the last time I'm loading the kayaks and gear at four in the morning, driving to the airport, then coming back here."

"What's that supposed to mean?" I said.

"They're getting restless," Henry said.

"Is that a threat?" I asked John.

"You should've seen their faces this morning," Henry said.

"Look, we're launching tomorrow. For sure. As long as the weather holds."

"Excuse me?" The engineer called from my office. "She doesn't look too good."

"Moani—" Pu's face had lost its color.

I ran into my office still holding the pink bakery box, and shoved it beneath Pu's mouth. She vomited the bear claw and chocolate milk.

The engineer grimaced. "Maybe this isn't a good time."

"Oh we're fine," I said.

Pu, looked up, nodding. "I feel better now."

"Feel like you could eat lunch?" I asked her.

Pu nodded.

"How about lunch?" I said to the engineer.

"I'm having a baby," Pu said to him. "And Moani can't."

THAT AFTERNOON I called Charlie Moku again. An answering machine picked up my call. The outgoing message was delivered by a child, who repeated the words whispered to him by an adult. "We not here—(so please)—please leave a message—(when you hear)—when you hear the beep."

I was about to greet my only cousin for the first time. I heard the beep, momentarily lost my voice, then found it again. I told him my name. I told him that Sam Kaluhi was my uncle and Bernie was my grandmother—the only surviving sister of Lydia Kaluhi who was Angelina's mother. I left my office and home numbers. "I just wanted to say hello and that it would be nice to meet one day—" But the machine cut me off.

UNCLE SUGGESTED DIXIE sleep over that night. We would all go to the airport together the next morning and Dixie wouldn't miss the flight. Pu and Dixie ordered pizza and I called the babysitter Gina, who arrived with a six-pack of beer.

"Isn't this fun?" Dixie said, carrying the pizza boxes to the coffee table in the living room. "A slumber party."

I couldn't get used to the tight jumpsuits, or the long frosted finger-nails. They posed a risk on the inflatable kayaks.

We sat on the floor around the coffee table. "There's too much cheese on this," Gina said, pulling a piece out of the box, a string of cheese trailing across the table to her paper plate. "I love it," Dixie said.

"Me too," Pu said.

"You should've ordered a salad," I said.

"Boooo," Dixie said.

"Boooo," Pu said.

They looked at each other and giggled.

"You guys sound like a couple of school girls," I said.

Pu laughed and threw her hand over her mouth. After the accident on the bridge, she had never again attended school.

"We don't sound anything like the gals in my high school," Dixie said. "Mouths worse than sailors, and s-l-u-t-s to boot."

"Who's that?" Pu said.

"Nothing you need to know about," I said.

131

"Bet you weren't as bad as us," Gina said.

"Oh, you're on," Dixie said to Gina. "In Lafayette..." she dabbed the corners of her mouth, "in Lafayette we were so bad we used to set fires in the girl's bathroom."

"You call that bad?" Gina said. "Here, we used to take our Tampax and..." she glanced at Pu, then whispered the rest of the story into Dixie's ear.

Dixie put down her pizza slice. "You win, cowboy. Now that, that's bad."

Gina nodded, "Yup."

"Tell me," Pu said.

"Sweet Pea, there are some things not fit for the ears of angels."

Pu grinned, in love with Dixie. I didn't like it. Given Uncle's record, I predicted Dixie would be on a plane back to Las Vegas or Louisiana by the end of the year—like wife number five and wife number four. We never heard from them again.

"Now, about this hotel," Dixie said, reaching for an anchovy. She popped it in her mouth. Pu did the same, then her faced tightened. Her mouth fell open.

"Did that surprise you, Sweet Pea? He's a salty little devil." She held a napkin under Pu's mouth, "Go ahead and spit out that nasty thing."

"Drink something, Pu," I said. "In fact, could you do me a favor and bring in the Cokes?"

Pu stood, hands on her hips. "Moani, you forgot the magic word."

"Please."

"Please, what?"

"Please bring our drinks."

"I think you've got a great idea," Dixie said to me. "I loved it up there on the Big Island. Ka-ha-la? It's beautiful country. And I'll be your first guest."

"You were up there?"

"I didn't tell you?" Dixie nodded and chewed, her napkin in front of her mouth. "Sam and I went up—was it the day before? He said he wanted to see what the fuss was about."

"Why didn't he tell me he was going up?" Why didn't he invite me along? Hear my ideas about the place?

Pu returned carrying a tray, glasses with ice and cans of Coke. "Put the tray on the table first, Pu, before sitting on the floor."

"Mo-a-ni, I can do it myself."

132

"Of course you can," Dixie said.

Pu knelt, cracked open a can, held the glass at an angle and poured. She handed the glass to Dixie.

"Thank you, Sweet Pea, just like a pro." Dixie sipped. "Oh, that is nice. Just what I needed."

Pu rocked on her knees.

"Could I have some?" I said to Pu.

"What do you say?" Pu said.

I grabbed a can and cracked the top.

"Moani. I have to give some to Gina first. A guest is always first."

"That's right, Sweet Pea. Now where did you learn to be a hostess with the mostess? Sounds like you're ready to run your sister's hotel."

Gina laughed, "That's a good one."

"I could," Pu said.

"Of course you could," Dixie said.

Pu looked at Gina, triumphant.

WHILE THEY ATE ice cream I emptied the drugstore bag on the floor in front of the coffee table, inside three pregnancy kits. "Pu, remember what we talked about?" I said. "If you're having a baby—"

"Jesus..."

"Then we need to find out for sure."

"Jesus..."

I handed Pu a wide mouth plastic cup.

"Oh what a wonderful child."

"I want you in the bathroom aiming into this cup."

"Where'd that song come from?" Dixie said. "I know that song." Her tangerine helmet of hair had flattened at the end of the day.

Pu reached for another cookie.

"That's your tenth cookie, Pu."

"She could be eating for two now," Dixie said.

"We don't know anything yet," I said.

"Something happened," Gina said. "Else she wouldn't be going on about it."

"Finish the cookie, then hit the toilet," I said.

"Moani, leave me alone." Pu moved closer to the TV. She was watching *The Sound of Music* again.

"Hey, I can't see," Gina said.

"Pu," I pointed to the bathroom.

"When I have my baby, you can't tell me what to do anymore. Because then I'm the mommy and you can't tell mommies what to do." She turned to the TV.

"Pu, the bathroom. Now."

She stomped down the hall to the bathroom.

The pregnancy tests consisted of dipsticks activated by Pu's pee. I gave one dipstick to Gina, one to Dixie and kept one for myself.

Pu returned carrying a cup of her warm pee. I dipped first, hoping for a minus instead of a plus.

But there it was: Positive.

"Positive," Gina said, looking at her stick.

"Ditto," Dixie said.

Pu leaned against Dixie's shoulder and smiled.

"Pu, who you been partying with?" Gina smirked.

"We're not talking about a party here," I said.

Gina dropped her eyes.

Pu smiled at me. "I told you, Moani."

"Pu, this isn't a game."

"Told-you. Told-you," she sang.

"Stop it, Pu."

"Stop-it-Pu."

"I mean it, Pu."

"I-mean-it-Pu."

"Shut up, Pu!"

Her face fell. She put her fingers to her mouth.

"How could you be so stupid?" I said. Her face began breaking apart. "I want to know who did it."

"Whoa, Moani," Gina said. She put down the can of beer.

"I hate you," Pu told me.

"Now come on you two," Dixie said. "You need each other."

"You're jealous," Pu said.

"You little bitch." I could've punched her.

"Pu, go to your room." Gina knew.

"A baby," I said. "In the middle of everything."

"I'm having a baby and you can't."

"I don't want one."

"Go on, Pu," Gina said. "Go to your room. I'll help you run the bath."

"Yes you do," Pu told me. "Everyone wants a baby."

"I don't want a baby. And I don't want you having a baby. How the hell will you take care of a baby?"

Pu dropped her voice. "You help me."

"No, I won't help you," I said. *"I'll* be the one taking care of your baby. *I'll* be the one raising it. If anything, you'll be the one helping me. How's that fair?"

"We'll all help, Moani," Dixie said.

"Excuse me," I told Dixie. "I don't need your—"

"You could teach my baby to swim," Pu said.

For a moment I imagined the little one's chest in my hands as I held her on the surface of the water. "God, Pu, how could you do this? How am I supposed to build a hotel and take care of a baby?"

"Nobody cares about a hotel," Pu said.

"I care."

"The man said he would help."

"Who, Pu? Who did this to you?"

Dixie and Gina stared at Pu.

"My boyfriend," Pu said.

"Your boyfriend said he would help?" Gina said.

Pu cried and rubbed her eyes. "No. Not him."

"Who, Sweet Pea? Who said he would help you?"

"The man that called," Pu said.

I stood up and began pacing.

"Come on, Moani," Gina said. "Let's take a walk."

"The man—" Pu said.

"Pu, if you tell one more lie..."

"The man said he would help," Pu said.

"When, Sweet Pea?"

"Today—"

"What did he say?" Dixie asked.

"Said, 'Could I speak to Moani.' I said, 'She's not here.'"

"Then what did he say?"

"Said, 'Could I leave a message?' I said, 'OK.'"

"Then did he leave a message?" I said. "A number?"

"Yeah."

"You wrote it down?"

"Yeah. I put it there." Pu pointed to the telephone. At the telephone table I found Pu's block handwriting on the note pad. "Did he say his name?" I said.

Pu shook her head.

"You didn't ask?" I said.

Pu began crying again.

"Now she was doing so well," Dixie said to me. "There was no call for that."

"Just a minute," I said. "I don't need you telling me how to talk to my sister."

"Well, you could've fooled me," Dixie said, staring me down with her made-up eyes.

I knelt beside Pu. "Did he say anything else?"

"Yeah. Said it's a Maui number so you gotta go 8-0-8."

At first I didn't understand. I thought I was on the trail of the son-of-a-bitch who knocked up Pu. But instead, I'd found Lydia's grandson.

THAT NIGHT I saw my mother in a dream. She sat in the front of the car driving, while I sat in the back seat.

"Remember, Moani?" she told me in the dream. "Remember *Sleeping Beauty*?"

In real life, she had taken us to see the movie four times.

She said, "What's the song the dogs sing when they're eating spaghetti?"

"That was *Lady and the Tramp*, Mama."

By then we had seen it twice.

"How did it go, Moani? I keep forgetting."

1921, Kohala
Sam

Let me tell you how easy it was to break into the girls' school. They put the dorm rooms above the classrooms and never locked the classroom doors. Once I was in the classroom, I was only steps away from the stairs. Once I was on the stairs I was only steps away from Patience's room. I used to lay on her bed waiting for her to finish lunch. She always brought me something to eat.

That day, I was waiting in her room when I heard footsteps coming up the stairs. I checked my watch. It was too early for Patience, who wasn't the type to skip dessert. Quick, I rolled off the bed and watched from underneath. The door opened. I knew those shoes. I sat up. "Lydie."

"Sam."

"What're you doing here?"

She held a pile of white towels. "Me? What are *you* doing here?"

"I gotta spell it out for you?"

"You better get out of here," she said, putting a towel on Patience's bureau.

"I don't feel so good," I said, sitting on the bed. "Think I better see the nurse."

"You're gonna get in trouble."

"Tell the nurse to hurry." I held my stomach.

"You're gonna get Patience in trouble."

"Tell the nurse I need plenny medicine." I fell back on Patience's bed.

Lydie sat on the bed next to me. "I need to ask you about something. I met someone."

"That's your question?"

"Shut up," she said, pushing me.

"Fine with me." I locked my lips and crossed my arms over my chest.

"It's important."

But I wasn't allowed to talk, on Miss Lydie's order.

She punched me in the shoulder. I held out to her the key which would unlock my lips, but she hit my hand away. "Come on."

I covered my eyes with my hands. Now I was the deaf, dumb and blind monkey.

"Sam."

I opened my eyes and held out the key again.

This time she put her finger on my lips and turned.

"Finally," I said.

"This's serious."

Now I was the professor. I sat up, crossed my legs and held my chin in my hand.

"Something almost happened, but it didn't happen, and I'm not sure how it'll happen."

I lay back on Patience's pillow. "The fuck you talking about, Lydie?"

"That."

I sat up. "Who!?"

"Shhh..."

"First of all, I'll kill him."

"Shhh..."

"Tell me who."

"Where's he gonna put it?" Lydie said.

I covered my mouth, but I couldn't stop from laughing and fell back on the bed again.

"You dog."

I rolled over and laughed into Patience's pillow.

"I hate you."

I turned back over. "You know where it doesn't go, right?"

She punched me again.

"You know where you bleed?"

Another punch.

"That's your target."

"But how will it fit?" she asked.

Poor Lydie. Who else could she talk to? Mama? That was a good one. Her school friends? No, no, and double no. Those gossips would spread Lydie's business all over the District. I told her, "You gotta find it for yourself first."

Lydie tried to punch me again, but I grabbed her hand and put it in her lap. "Try," I said. I rolled on my side, facing away from her and toward the window. "I won't watch."

"That's nasty."

"How else you gonna know, unless you test yourself first?"

I heard her skirt rustle, then everything was quiet. I turned around and found Lydie's back facing me—her hand in her lap. I pulled her down beside me on Patience's bed—and so what? We always slept together, until we were six or seven. Until Mama caught me showing Lydie my little stiffy.

I asked her, "Did you find it?"

"It's too small. How's he gonna fit?"

"It's gonna stretch," I said, remembering her little girl's pussy—and how the folds of skin opened to a bright pink bud. Lydie sat up on Patience's bed and looked back at me. "Sam, how do you kiss her?"

"What? Patience?"

She nodded.

I sat up. "Like this." I kissed Lydie's cheek.

"Tell me if I do it right," Lydie said, and kissed my lips.

"Harder."

She pressed her lips against mine.

138

"Like this," I said and pushed my tongue in her mouth.

Lydie pulled away and wiped her mouth. "I don't like that."

"I won't do it again." I kissed her cheek. I kissed her lips, red and soft.

"Sam, did the first time hurt Patience?"

"She didn't cry." In fact, the first time I fucked Patience she closed her eyes and rocked her hips.

"Sam," Lydie said. "Show me."

1985, Honolulu
Sarah

My girl Silvie placed a tray on the coffee table. "Granny? Are you up?" she said. "Time for lunch."

I looked out onto the *lanai* and saw no shadows. The sun was directly overhead, but I could not remember the morning passing. I looked at the tray she had prepared. Some kind of sandwich, pudding, milk.

"Did I eat breakfast?" I asked her.

"Yes, Granny. Remember? You wanted a glass of sherry?"

"No, no. You're lying again." I drink coffee and juice at breakfast. "Take this away, I'm not hungry."

"Please, Granny," she said. She sat beside me, cut the sandwich into quarters and held a corner to my mouth. "Just a little."

I opened my mouth.

She pushed the corner in. "That's it, Granny. Now a sip of milk." She put the straw to my lips.

"It's too cold."

"I heated it, Granny—just how you like."

"I take my sherry at 4:00," I said. "At 4:00, not 3:00. At 4:00." And one glass of sherry. Not two glasses, not three.

"Don't cry, Granny. We'll have our sherry at 4:00. Let's try one more bite."

I have taken my sherry at 4:00 since my days at Trinity. In the afternoon, when the girls practiced down on the playing field, I would shut my office door, kick off my shoes and prop my feet up on the desk. I sat like that for half an hour, sipping and forgetting about those spoiled brats.

They had all the options money could buy, but how they squandered them! All they talked about was clothes, hair, shopping though they had the best teaching staff in the islands. The best library. When a telephone call from my desk could have put them at Mt. Holyoke or Smith or Barnard. I warned them, "Do not assume that money will realize the dream, but only that, used wisely, it may assist the endeavor." They politely listened, hands in their laps and ankles crossed. But they returned to their parents' oceanfront homes during the Christmas and Easter breaks. They returned to sweet-sixteen birthday cars, and their own private telephone lines.

There was one girl in particular—Kelly or Kimberly or some such name—whose parents took her to Tokyo for an abortion. Of course when I learned about the trip I had no choice but to end the girl's Trinity career. I told the trustees at the specially convened meeting that with or without her parents' consent it sent the wrong message.

Those old goats were ready to surrender to the demands of the girl's wealthy parents, who threw money at the school so that their daughter could graduate with her class and obtain a Trinity diploma. "Think of the girl's future," one of the trustees said.

"With all due respect," I answered, "I doubt that we are interested in the young lady per se, but rather with the school's purse."

They shuffled their feet under the table.

"No donation from her parents will repair the loss in reputation Trinity will suffer by engaging in such pandering."

"Oh, pandering is not—"

"No doubt the school's short-term financial health is important. But as headmistress I am charged with caring for this institution's long-term educational goals. That means excellence in all areas, and demanding the same of the our young ladies."

There. That sent the old goats back to the hills. They followed my recommendation of dismissal. It served the young lady right. She received failing marks as to discretion. Calling her stupid was not out of order. She had bragged about the trip, as if it were a vacation. A vacation! You can bet the parents were behind the attitude: a casual disregard for the consequences of one's behavior. Last I heard the parents had shipped her off to a finishing school in Virginia.

Lydia did not have Tokyo or Virginia.

Since a sudden departure would have sparked suspicion, her mother Julia waited until the end of the school year before shipping her off. The

140

Kohala gossips entertained themselves by speculating about where Julia had sent Lydia for the birth. Some said to Julia's own mother—the Hilo native and one-time common-law wife of an American vagrant who had washed up on our shores. There were thousands in those days, crawling over the islands like ants. Julia's mother was said to have given birth to five children in as many years, but as it went with the Hawaiian, Julia was the only child to survive. Her father dabbled in farming and store-keeping, then left the Islands. He deserted his wife and half-caste daughter Julia, who grew into a young woman no less comely than the half-caste princess, Ka'iulani. Julia caught the attention of the Kaluhi family, who belonged to Kohala *ali'i*—the chiefly class. They understood the value in pairing their ne'er-do-well son with the light-skinned commoner who spoke and wrote English better than the American vagrants.

Other gossips said that Julia's mother was dead, and that she must have sent Lydia to live with one of Lipo's relations. Still others said she sent Lydia to a Catholic home for unwed mothers in Honolulu. But I could not believe that. Catholics? Not Julia. There was a report that Julia had taken Lydia to the valley on the other side of Pololū. Charlie Moku had been seen descending the trail into Pololū, a sack of provisions slung on his back. Thirty minutes later he had been seen crossing the black sand beach at the mouth of the valley, walking to the trail leading up and out of that valley, over the rise and into Honokāne—where Lydia purportedly waited. Of all the stories, I wished this last one to be true. I wanted to believe that Lydia awaited her child's birth in the valley beyond the valley. I wanted to believe that the boy Charles visited her each day, undaunted by their predicament. That he possessed the strength to ford streams and climb mountains to reach his beloved, whom he nestled in his arms each afternoon while she napped.

Mine was a schoolgirl's dream. It had nothing to do with Lydia's actual predicament, suddenly before me at the end of that summer when I least expected it. Everett and I were returning to Kohala from Honolulu. The inter-island steamer stopped in Lahaina at dusk, with passengers departing and boarding before the steamer crossed the channel for the Big Island. I sat beside Everett on deck through the unloading and loading of luggage and cargo.

He tried to sleep, but he was so miserable he could not. He sickened easily on any boat, and became especially nauseous during stops like that. He endured the sea's pitch with his eyes closed, his hands clasped tightly across his chest. After the passengers had boarded and twilight came, I whispered to Everett, "I'm going to the railing for a bit."

He did not answer.

"It might do you some good—to have the wind in your face." I enjoyed the ship's pitch and roll. It settled my stomach and calmed my nerves.

He turned away, tucking his face into the blanket. At the railing I saw Lydia's brother, Sam, on the ship's deck not twenty feet away. I could not understand why this boy of fifteen years was traveling alone, and in first class. Where did he get the money? I approached, then stopped.

Sam leaned over the rail and waved at a figure on the Mla Wharf. I could not tell if it was a boy or a girl, a man or a woman. The figure leaned against the wall at the dock's edge and waved to Sam as our boat pulled away. Then the figure walked down the dock to a pyramid of lamplight. Of course: Sam had come to see his sister Lydia.

Her steps were slow, her enormous belly pulling her forward. Under the lamplight she reached beneath her stomach. She stepped back, as if the baby had just kicked her. Then she waved with one hand at Sam, while the other supported her child.

Mean, rough Sam Kaluhi gripped the railing and cried. As we pulled away from the dock, he climbed the railing and waved. I thought he might even jump ship and swim back to her, but he simply watched and cried. Exiled Lydia stepped out from the shelter of the lamplight, then walked down Māla Wharf and disappeared into the dark Lahaina streets.

1985, Honolulu
Moani

Before dressing the next morning I checked our answering machine, hoping Charlie Moku had returned my call while we slept. But there was nothing. I called my office answering machine. No such luck. I called his Maui number. Now the telephone company said they had disconnected his line. I called again thinking I had misdialed, but received the same message. I called information for a street address. They told me none had ever been listed with the disconnected number.

I walked down the hall to Pu's room. "You up?" I said, pushing open the door.

Dressed, she sat on the bed, the telephone receiver to her ear. "Hello?" she said. "It's me."

"Pu, are you ready?"

"Mo-a-ni..."

"Who're you talking to?"

"You not dressed yet," she said. I had packed her bag the night before.

"How do you feel this morning?"

"We gonna get late."

"Feel like you might throw up, Pu?"

"Then I won't go swimming."

"Try and eat something while we're at home."

"We gonna miss the plane, again," Pu said. "We gonna miss Dixie."

Dixie was supposed to have slept over with us the night before. We would all go to the airport together for the Wednesday morning departure to Moloka'i. But Uncle had called after the pregnancy dipsticks. He said that since Dixie was leaving for five days, he wanted her for the night.

The sky was pale blue in the east, no clouds. The wind was calm. Our flight left Honolulu for Moloka'i at 7:30. We stopped at a coffee shop for breakfast. "Pancakes," Pu told the waitress, pointing to the menu and the glossy photograph of a stack, a melting butter ball and syrup running over the side.

"How about some eggs?" I said. "I'm making pancakes tomorrow morning at the campsite."

Pu tapped the glistening butter ball.

"How about an egg on the side of that?"

"I don't like eggs," Pu said.

"Since when?"

"Since I'm having a baby."

The waitress's eyes dropped to Pu's stomach. If anything, she was losing weight.

"Eggs and sausage for me," I told the waitress. Then to Pu, "Maybe we could share?" I wanted her to eat protein.

"No way, José."

"How about a glass of milk?"

"Moani, leave me alone."

She ate everything on her plate, and two of my sausages.

"Moani, you better pay," Pu said. "We gonna be late."

"You don't feel sick?"

She sat back in the booth and thought about it. "Nope. Don't think so."

"Very good, Pu."

"Very-good-Pu."

"Would you do me a favor?" I said.

"Would-you-do-me-a-favor."

"During the trip— "

"During-the-trip."

"Don't repeat, OK? It's really annoying."

"Moani's-really-annoying." She put her hand over her mouth and laughed.

The coffee shop sold rolls and buns. I bought three dozen. Pu held the bakery boxes on her lap in the car. Henry and John were at the airport, Henry with the group at the departure gate, John down on the tarmac with the airline baggage manager and all our gear: eight deflated tandem kayaks, twenty paddles, air mattresses, life jackets, an air pump and a backup air pump, a camp stove, three large ice chests with our food, a water filter, fifteen dry bags containing everyone's personal gear, the medical kit, a grill and Dutch oven.

"Good morning," I said to the kayakers.

"Morning," they mumbled.

"It's a beautiful morning. The weather service tells me we can expect the same for the next five days."

The group of ten stood together with their arms across their chests, wearing reef walker sandals, sports bras and plastic visors. "I know it's a bummer to adjourn the launch date two days in a row," I said, "but it was worth it to take advantage of the upcoming forecast. By the way, if you didn't have breakfast we picked up some goodies."

They looked at the bakery boxes.

"It's important to eat," I said. "Lots of physical activity ahead. Everyone's met my assistant Puanani?" Pu wore her new sunglasses inside the terminal. I had attached an elastic band to the frame so she wouldn't lose them. She arranged the bakery boxes on the empty seats. The group gathered.

"Help yourself to coffee or juice at the concession," I said.

"Tell them you're with my company and they won't charge you."

One of the nurses looked into the boxes. "You know how to tempt a girl." She was short and chubby, and had a good body for kayaking. It was a storehouse of energy. Clients like her paddled slow and steady for four, five hours. They were the first ones up in the morning, lighting the campfire and putting on the coffee.

"Most of my clients report a weight loss after our trips," I told her. "So eat up."

"Well, sticky buns are my favorite."

Henry was already finishing one and grabbing another.

It was 6:45. "We won't be eating again until we're ready to launch around 12:00, 1:00. It's a good idea to eat something now, even if you're not hungry."

"Yoo hoo." Everyone turned. It was Dixie run-walking toward us, Uncle trailing behind carrying her bag.

The biggest health risk in the kayak business was sunburn. This meant that Dixie had no business spending even two minutes in the sun, let alone four hours in a kayak, five days in a row. But she had dressed for the trip exactly as I had urged, with leggings that covered her knees, and an oversize long sleeve blouse with a wide collar to protect the back of her neck, and cuffs that covered her freckled hands. If I'd planned on staying in the business, I would have taken a picture of Dixie and sent it to all prospective clients: This is how you dress for a four-hour kayak trip under the Pacific sun.

"Thank goodness," she said, her hand to her chest. "I thought we would miss the flight."

"Dixie," Pu said.

"How're you doing this morning, Sweet Pea?"

"You look different," Pu said.

No kidding. Dixie wasn't wearing a smudge of make up.

"Ready to go swimming with the sharks?" Uncle said to Pu.

Pu's face fell. The nurse stopped chewing the sticky bun.

"Oh, Sam," Dixie said.

"I never seen no shark where we going," Henry said.

"Never," I said.

"Yeah, right," Uncle said, reaching for a sweet roll. He shoved half the roll in his mouth. One more bite and it was gone.

"Moani, is it true?" Pu said.

"Do me a favor?" Uncle said to me, his eyes narrowing. "Make sure my wife don't drown."

"Sam, for goodness sake," Dixie said. She told the nurses, "He doesn't mean anything."

Oh yes he does. He'd wreck the entire excursion if he could, just because he couldn't go.

"Not to mention my Puanani," Uncle said.

He saw the others returning with coffee. The lawyers and nurses' husbands compared the gear they had bought for the trip: waterproof cameras, watches and compasses. Uncle marched off to the concession.

"I'm so sorry," I said to the nurse.

"Who is that?" the nurse said.

"He's been terrible this morning," Dixie said.

"Why's Uncle mad?" Pu said.

"He's your uncle?" the nurse said.

"He's jealous that I'm going away for a few days," Dixie said, dropping her voice and leaning against me. Without the goop, her eyes were quiet and serene. Without the paint her lips were thin and direct.

"Moani, are there sharks?" Pu asked.

The honeymooners drew near.

"Sweet Pea, your uncle is just an old fibber sometimes. Pay him no mind, you understand?"

Pu nodded.

"He's jealous that we'll be having the time of lives, while he's shut up in an office working."

"Amen," Henry said.

"Sharks in Hawaiian waters are rare," I added for the benefit of the honeymooners and nurse. "They're a lot more nervous about us. By the way, I want to introduce a last-minute registrant who'll be joining us on the trip. She's a family friend."

"No," Pu said. "She's more than a friend."

Dixie took Pu's hand. "You're just a cup of gold, now aren't you?"

"Yup," Pu smiled from behind the sunglasses.

WE MADE GREAT time that morning. By noon we had arrived at our launch site on Moloka'i, unloaded the kayaks from the trailer, inflated them and loaded the heavy gear. Before launching, I laid out our lunch, bread and cold cuts, grapes and cookies and juices.

We were a party of fifteen, total. Pu and Dixie, and my second- and third-in-command, John and Henry. There were the four lawyers; the two nurses and their husbands; the honeymooners; and me.

The lawyers waited while Dixie and Pu, the nurses and the honeymooners made their sandwiches. They sat together with their heads bowed before eating.

"What they doing?" Pu said.

"Praying, Pu. You saw the nuns do it."

"Not like that."

"Here you go, Sweet Pea," Dixie said. She took one of Pu's hands and closed her eyes, "Good food, good grief, thanks God, let's eat."

The nurses, honeymoon-girl and Dixie cleaned up after lunch. It was a good sign. When the women worked together, it shaped the group. The women became the center of camp activity, and the men secured the perimeter.

After lunch we gathered at the shore in front of the kayaks. The group wore life jackets and held paddles in their hands. "I know we practiced back in Honolulu," I said. "But before we paddle out of the bay and into the open ocean," I pointed with the paddle toward the mouth of the bay, "I'd like you to pair up, and take a spin around the bay first."

Once they were in the kayaks, I described a series of commands they might hear me call from the shore—paddle left, paddle right—and how they should respond. A reef lay in the middle of the bay beneath two feet of water with waves breaking over the surface. "In case you haven't noticed the surf breaking in the middle of the bay, take a look now. You want to stay away from the breakers. John? Want to add anything?"

"Yeah. Don't go by the breakers."

We pushed them away from the shore and out into the water. Now John, Henry and I watched them paddle. Honeymoon-guy aimed straight for the reef.

I grabbed the bullhorn. "Attention, Rick and Shari, paddle left. Attention. Rick—" I turned to Henry, "What's his last name?"

"Pa-ga-something."

"Attention Rick. Paddle left immediately."

But he continued paddling right, into a wave breaking over the reef.

"Moani, look what he's doing," Pu said.

The wave hit the honeymooners' kayak on the starboard side and flipped them over.

I heard one of the nurses say, "Oh my God." She and her husband began paddling toward the honeymooners.

"Hold your position," I ordered. "Do not enter the break zone. We will be there immediately." John was already swimming out.

"Didn't you just tell him to stay clear?" Dixie said.

"This's a first," Henry said. "A capsize in the first five minutes."

"The first five minutes of a five-day trip," I said.

Pu laughed.

"Pu, it's not funny," I said.

"But the girl—the girl's hair—"

Out on the reef John turned the kayak upright, found the paddles, and caught their dry bag before it floated into another wave set breaking at the far end of reef. He lifted them both into the kayak, then hauled them ashore, dragging the bow onto the sand.

"You guys OK?" I asked.

"I guess so," Shari said. One of her earrings was missing.

John handed Rick his sunglasses which had fallen off when they capsized.

"It happens on every trip," I said, "with experienced kayakers or novices. Someone always capsizes. That's the bad news. The good news is that it happened here, in a sheltered bay, so we don't have to worry about it anymore."

Rick's jaw clenched and unclenched. He threw me a look, like it was my fault.

When everyone was back on shore, I said, "For today I want to make some changes in the pairing. Rich—"

"Rick."

"Rick, I'm paring you with John. Shari, I want you to paddle with Henry."

"I'm staying with Shari," Rick said—all attitude now that he'd fucked up.

"This is a temporary arrangement," I said. "For now, you need to trust my judgment. OK." Big smile. "We're shoving off in ten minutes." I held up ten fingers. "Use the facilities if you have to." There was a thick row of hedges in the back. "We'll be in the water four to five hours. The trade winds are with us today, that's good. It'll make the paddling easier. Our pace will be set by you two," I said, pointing to one of the nurses and her husband. I liked their paddle strategy, slow and steady.

"You will be our point guard today. Under no circumstances will any kayak paddle ahead of the point guard. John? Anything to add?"

"Yeah. Under no circumstances does anyone paddle ahead of the point guard," John said. "Henry, you want to add something?"

Henry was eating another sandwich. He swallowed and said, "Don't paddle ahead."

"Any questions?" I asked.

One of the lawyers raised his hand. "Could we paddle ahead?"

They laughed.

Henry held up the marine radio. "If you're really in a rush and can't follow the rules that's fine. We'll call our backup to take you out."

"We're in the wilderness now," I said. "Slow and steady is the rule of the day. And we stay together at all costs. OK." Another smile. "Usually people want to take a group shot before we launch."

They began wiping their camera lenses, setting dials and buttons. Dixie held up a small mirror, dropped her sunglasses to the tip of her nose and examined her eyes.

Henry put his arm around Rick's shoulder and drew him away from the group. John and I followed, John holding a kayak paddle.

When we were out of earshot from the others I said to Rick, "Didn't you hear me warn about the reef?" Before he could answer I stepped closer. "What were you thinking, paddling over there?"

He smiled.

"That wasn't funny," I said.

He smirked.

"You think that was funny? You guys capsizing?"

His faced dropped. "Hey, back off." He looked to John and Henry.

"Listen," I said. "I'm this close to dumping your ass."

"Whoa..." He tried to walk away, but John and Henry blocked him.

"You think I'm fucking around?"

He looked at Henry.

"She's not fucking around," Henry said.

Rick said, "Shari was leaning—"

"Don't blame Shari!"

"Calm down. Relax." He used his tough-guy voice. Then he smiled, looking from John to Henry again. "It was no big deal. We're fine."

"Wrong. You're the man. You're in control of the kayak. You paddled toward the reef when I told you not to. Then you paddled into the reef when I was on the bullhorn ordering you to paddle left."

John handed Rick the paddle.

"When I say paddle left, what does that mean?"

Rick stood there holding the paddle, acting like he was pissed off, but he was scared now. John and Henry weren't going to back him up against me.

"Paddle left means you stroke left."

John lifted the paddle in Rick's hands and pulled down sharply on the left-hand side. Rick tried to keep his balance.

"Not right, and not into the fucking waves."

Rick faced me again. His mouth and eyes had fallen.

Good. I had his attention now. "For the next five days when I give orders, you follow. You follow because out there when you paddle into rocks and reef, we gotta save your ass."

John and Henry stepped closer to him. Both were a head taller, Henry a good seventy pounds heavier. John at least fifty. They were expert watermen and lifeguards, but the idea was to prevent disaster in the first place.

"If we have to save your ass, that means we're all at risk because you think you're special. I don't like that."

"Ricky?" It was Shari. She held their camera.

"Tell her to wait with the group," I said.

"Be right there," he said.

"What did I just say!?"

Now he looked confused.

"What did I say?"

He looked at Henry.

Henry said, "She said for you to tell Shari, 'Wait-With-The-Group.'"

Rick called to her, "Wait with the group."

"No more shit from you," I said. "If you wanted to go on a honey-moon, you should've gone to Kaua'i like everyone else. Lock yourself in a room and fuck your brains out. Bad enough you drag her out here—then you capsize your kayak."

Now he wouldn't look at me.

"One more stunt and I'm kicking your ass outta here."

Henry burped while staring at him.

Rick walked ahead to Shari. She wrapped her arm around his waist. "Everything all right?" He pulled away from her.

"Did you have to burp in his face?" I said to Henry. He rubbed his belly and burped again.

For the photo I squatted in the front of the group—pleased actually. On the whole, I liked them—the lawyers, the nurses. Pu had kept down her breakfast and lunch. Dixie was quiet without all the frosting. And I wasn't too worried about Rick anymore. I had made my point with him, so why not enjoy one of my last kayak runs?

At the shore I tucked Dixie into the bow, one of the lawyers into the stern. She had smeared a white paste over her nose, and strapped a wide-brim visor over her forehead. "Moani? Suppose I need to, you know, visit the little girls' room."

I stood up and addressed the group. "Folks..."

They were busy settling into the kayaks.

John put his fingers in his mouth and whistled. They looked up.

"Folks, if you need to relieve yourselves, raise your paddle first to get our attention and we'll stop and wait for you. Just slip over the side of the kayak. Otherwise if you catch a cramp or get tired, or just want to slip over the side of the kayak and cool off for a few minutes, let us know. John, you want to add anything?"

"Yeah, don't feel shy about needing to stop. The last thing you want to do is stop drinking water because you're embarrassed to make a pit stop. That's how you get dehydrated."

Henry had opened the cookies. He pointed to John, his mouth full of crumbs. "What they said... Just tell us."

Dixie told me, "Guess I'm a little nervous. I was never the outdoorsy type."

"Could've fooled me."

"Oh Moani... I feel like giving you a little hug."

What can I say? Kayaks do things to people. She wrapped her arms around my neck and whispered in my ear, "You're a good kid, you know that?"

"Hey young lady," her partner said. "I'll have none of that aboard my ship."

Dixie wiggled her fingers at him.

I checked on Shari at the bow of Henry's kayak. "How're you doing?"

"OK, I guess."

I figured she would discover the missing earing that night. "Once we get out of the bay, onto the open ocean... Well, wait till you see the view of the coastline from the kayak. You'll be glad you came."

"I hope so," she said.

Rick sat at the bow of John's kayak. I squatted beside him. "Did you get some fresh water up here?" Each person had two liters.

He wouldn't answer.

"Wait till you see the dinner I've got lined up: salmon steaks, Caesar salad and *crème brûlée*."

Now he made eye contact, dropped his head and smiled.

"True. I figured out how to make it with a small blowtorch over the campfire." I had planned on serving the *brûlée* tomorrow night, but under the circumstances...

"Moani." Pu sat in the front of my kayak, the paddle on her lap.

"Your life jacket strapped on, Pu?" I checked the buckles.

She wore her camera on a cord around her neck. Her teeth chattered. Her face was white. "You feel OK?"

She nodded.

If seasickness set in, it was usually in the first hour, as people became accustomed to sitting low in the water and riding the pitch of the kayak right to left. I kept my fingers crossed, given the flat sea beyond the bay. There wasn't a whitecap in sight.

I launched everyone, then returned to Pu. "Well, here goes nothing," I said, and shoved the kayak into the water, then slipped into the stern. "For now, Pu, don't bother paddling," I said. "I'll pull us ahead and we'll drop into the middle of the group. Once we're clear of the bay, if you want, you can help."

"I help."

"Sure you will, Pu." We glided through the clear turquoise water.

"Moani."

"Yeah?"

"We're—we're going."

We left a tapered wake behind us. I paddled to the rear of the group, catching up with John and Rick's kayak.

"Hi," Pu said to them.

John smiled. Rick paddled harder.

I paddled up to one of the nurses and her husband, in front of John and Rick. "How're you doing?"

Big smiles. "I can't believe we're finally here." To our left, blue green cliffs rose one thousand feet over the bay's entrance. "It's so beautiful," the nurse said, sitting in the front, her camera poised while her husband paddled.

"I'm paddling ahead of you," I told them. "John will bring up the rear."

I paddled alongside one of the lawyers. "Sorry you're alone for today's paddle. We'll rearrange for tomorrow."

"My God, this's beautiful." The blue-green cliffs reflected off his sunglasses.

"Let me know if you want to stop to take pictures," I said.

"See Roger up ahead?" he said. "He's on camera duty today. We're taking turns so all of us don't have to be thinking cameras all day."

"You lawyers."

He was the oldest of the lawyers. I knew he wouldn't mind the solo paddle.

"I'll swing in front of you and take the position in the middle of the group."

He lowered his right paddle blade to slow his glide.

"Beautiful," I said. "You've got John two kayaks back. I'm right here ahead of you. We've got you covered."

The sea was calm. I glided in front of him as we entered the mouth of the bay, the turquoise water shifting to cobalt. Usually we struggled at that point, with the current flowing into the mouth of the bay. But that day, with the sea flat, the current guided us out of the bay, into the sea lane that ran along the northeast coast. The trade winds were at our backs. The conditions were as close to perfect as I had ever known.

"OK, Pu. If you want to help you could paddle now."

She lifted her paddle and dipped the right blade in the water.

"That's it, Pu. Now stroke. Now the other side."

She dipped the left blade in the water, her fingers loose around the paddle.

"Get a good grip on it, Pu." We carried five extra paddles with us. Each year I lost up to twenty-five. The sea floor was littered with yellow paddles, 'Lost Paradise' stenciled on the blade.

A white tropic bird drifted on the wind current rising from the bay. It swooped down to the water, then fluttered its long, tapered wings against the breeze and hovered above us. "Look, Moani." Pu rested the paddle on her lap.

I made wide clean strokes, pulling Pu and me through the blue black waters. I felt as if I could paddle forever. "Sing me a song, Pu."

She dropped her head from following the bird, now drifting upward, back toward the cliffs. "Guess what, Moani?"

"What, Pu?"

"I can't think of any songs."

THERE WERE NO sandy beaches along that coast. Our campsite for the first two nights was a rock and pebble beach at the base of a cliff. There, fishermen had built a lean-to shelter the length of a three-car garage, consisting of two rock terrace floors, the high one for sleeping and

153

the low one for sitting and eating. For use of the shelter I had hauled in supplies for them on an earlier boat run, fresh water, firewood and charcoal.

After securing the kayaks and unloading the gear, Dixie helped Pu into dry clothes while I built a fire and cooked our dinner. I wrapped potatoes in foil, grilled salmon steaks, and made a lemon-butter sauce. A lawyer made a Caesar salad.

"Oh my God," one of the nurses said. She was returning from the outdoor shower with the other nurse. Both wore towels around their heads. "I saw the five-day menu, but didn't think you could pull it off."

I pointed to the custard dishes. "That's the *brûlée*. After dinner I'm serving it with the cappuccino."

"This's a twist on a wilderness experience," a lawyer said. "Hey, Roger, make sure and get a shot of this."

I squatted beside my grill for the picture. The group ate well, but quietly. They helped to clean up, then made their beds from the air mattresses and blankets. It was the same with every group for the past sixteen years. They passed out the first night. The next night they would stay up later, and the following night even later.

Pu lay next to me, and Dixie beside her. Dixie had propped a flashlight against her chest and was reading a paperback book. The surf washed up the rock and pebble shore. The nurses and their husbands made their beds outside the shelter, beneath the starlight which washed the night sky gray.

"Moani."

"What, Pu?" I kept my eyes shut.

"Moani."

I opened my eyes and found Pu's black eyes glistening in the dark. Dixie had turned off the flashlight. I closed my eyes again.

"Moani."

I opened my eyes.

"Stay with me."

"I'm tired, Pu."

A minute later, "Moani."

"Please, Pu, let me sleep."

"Moani, I'm gonna name my baby after you."

"Oh, Pu..."

"Can I?"

"What, Pu?"

"Name my baby after you?"

"Yes, Pu. That would be fine."

At 2:00 in the morning I woke up. I found the plastic potty bowl and squatted behind the shelter, then crossed the slippery rocks to throw it in the sea. Back under the shelter, I saw that Dixie's bed was empty. I stepped out from under the shelter. The nurses and their husbands were huddled beneath the stars. Dixie wasn't with them. Then, down at the shore, I saw the beam of a flashlight. I grabbed our high-beam and picked my way over the slippery rocks. It was Dixie.

"Do you know how dangerous it is out here?" I said. "Suppose you twisted an ankle?"

She looked at me—Dixie and her quiet eyes I couldn't get used to. "Sorry, Moani."

I began walking back, shining the flashlight ahead of us on the rocks. "I thought you said you weren't the outdoor type."

"Didn't mean to worry you."

Then I heard a rock turn behind us. I held up the flashlight and there was Henry standing in the dark, his hand in front of his eyes against the high-beam.

"Just getting some air," he said.

Not much surprised me, but I didn't expect to discover Dixie and Henry that night. They were returning from the dark side of the beach.

"Would you two do me a favor? Get your air, or whatever you're doing, during the day when you won't fall and break your neck." I walked ahead, then turned to Henry. "You should know better."

Beneath the shelter I lay beside Pu again. A minute later Dixie lay down on the other side, her back to us.

"Moani," Pu whispered.

I turned to her.

"Why was Dixie walking with Henry?" Her sleepy breath washed over my face.

"You saw them together?"

"Before dinner," Pu said.

"She needed some air," I said. "Now try to sleep."

Pu nestled against me. "Dixie couldn't sleep," she said. "Cause Henry said he's gonna help her."

155

1921, Kohala
Sam

I fucked and fought all over Kohala. Gentle was never my style. But everything was different that day, Lydie sitting next to me on Patience's bed and asking about things she wasn't suppose to ask about. "Who you got plans for, Lydie?"

"Promise you won't be mad?" she said.

"Tell me."

"You have to promise."

"OK already."

"Say it," she said.

Ho! "I promise. I promise."

"You saw him," she said.

I saw him?

"I was talking to him on Sunday."

I couldn't think of anyone. "I only saw you talking to Charlie Moku." Lydie smiled.

"No! Come on, Lydie. Him?"

"He's nice to me."

"That dumb Hawaiian?"

Her smile fell.

"He can only talk about fish and fishing?" I said.

"He talks about other things."

"Why him," I said, "when you could have any boy in the District?"

"You don't understand."

"Try me."

"I told you, he's sweet to me."

"Oh yeah? That's what you call sweet? When a boy's trying to fuck you?"

"Ever think I might be the one?" she said.

At first she caught me off guard, but I came up with a good answer for that. "If you're the one, then I still blame him. He made you want it."

"Sam, you're such a dope." She fell back on Patience's bed, arms crossed over her chest.

Fine with me. Now I was the dope. "Duh. I don't know how for do nothing." I fell back on the bed beside her.

She turned and punched me in the shoulder. "Come on."

"I'm just one dumb *kanak*."

Lydie grabbed my shoulder, "Sam..."

I looked at Lydie, all confused. "Who you?"

Another punch.

I looked around Patience's room. "Where we?"

"Stop it."

I grabbed Lydie's hand. "I'm scared."

Lydie grabbed both my hands and rolled on top of me. "You're so mean."

"If you say so." Now I was mean. Now I was a tiger. I pushed Lydie off and rolled on top of her.

"What do I do when I'm with him, Sam?"

"Don't do nothing. He's gonna know what to do." Maybe. But hopefully Charlie Moku fucked as dumb as he looked, and I didn't have to worry about anything.

I pushed my groin into Lydie's crotch.

"That doesn't hurt."

"You gotta lift your legs higher."

Lydie lifted her knees

"Wrap them around my back."

Lydie wrapped them around my middle. "It doesn't feel bad."

"Gonna be different without your skirt."

"Let's try."

Whoa.

"I need to know." She pulled down her bloomers. There was her bare pussy—the brown slit was covered with soft black fur. I began pushing in.

"It hurts, Sam."

"It only hurts in the beginning."

"Sam, you're getting sweaty."

I pulled it out and pushed it back in.

"Sam, won't I get pregnant?"

"I'm gonna pull out before it happens."

"Let me up, Sam," Lydie said. "I've felt enough."

"Just a second."

"It's hot in here."

A little more.

"Let me up now."

Just a little more.

"Sam..."

I felt her punching my back, but I was in the land of no return. I grabbed her hands and held them down. She tried to pull in her legs, but I pushed them further apart with my knees. Then the door opened.

"Oh my God," Patience said.

"Oh my God," Lydie said.

I felt the cool air from the hallway on my sweating ass. "Shut the door," I said to Patience, but she ran down the stairs, leaving the door wide open. Then I heard more footsteps climbing the stairs.

"They're coming back from lunch," Lydie said, trying to kick me off.

Quick, I jumped up, ran to the door and slammed it shut. When I turned back to Lydie, she was staring at my stiff, dripping prick. I pulled up my pants, one drop bleeding through. I picked up Lydie's bloomers. "I meant to get off," I said, handing them to her. "I was trying."

She stepped into them.

"Don't be mad," I said and sat in front of her on the bed.

"Is that what Charlie will do?"

Yeah. Fucking is fucking.

Then we heard the girls outside in the hallway, walking and talking.

"How will you get out?" Lydie whispered.

"Let's fix your hair," I said.

"Patience will tell," Lydie said.

"Patience's going back to Kona," I said, trying to tighten the ribbon around her hair. Then I decided that Patience could never set foot in Kohala District again. In fact, I wanted her off the island. She had to move to Honolulu and lose her way back home.

"It wasn't her fault," Lydie said.

"Makes no difference. She still gotta go."

"I'll talk to her," Lydie said. "Maybe she didn't see that it was me." Lydie walked to the door and looked at the bed. "Maybe she couldn't tell because you were covering my face." I followed her to the door and looked back at the bed. Not a chance. It was a small room and we both looked at the door when Patience opened it. No doubt about it—Patience saw me fucking my sister.

"I'll find her," Lydie said.

"No, I'm gonna wait here for her." I lay on the bed, my hands underneath my head.

"Be nice to her, Sam."

"What're you doing now, Lydie?"

"I'm finishing laundry duty."

"When are they feeding you lunch?"

"You're thinking about food?" Lydie said, picking up the pile of towels. "After what just happened?" She opened the door, checked the hallway then stepped out, closing the door behind her. I listened to her footsteps going from room to room, leaving a towel in each.

I turned over and pressed my face into Patience's pillow. I could smell Lydie's hair. Then I heard her footsteps returning to Patience's door.

Come back!

But Lydie kept walking down the hallway.

I closed my eyes and saw her in my mind's eye lying next to me. I opened my eyes and she was gone. I closed them again and found her black pearl eyes shining at me. When I opened my eyes again, the one o'clock sun slapped me in the face. So I locked shut my eyes for the rest of the day. I could live in the darkness as long as I had Lydie.

The next thing I knew, someone was shaking my shoulder. I opened my eyes to a dark room. Outside the sky was pink.

"You have to get out of here," Patience said.

I closed my eyes and pulled her down onto the bed. She pushed against me, but I held her fast. In the dark Patience was Lydie. "You're so beautiful," I told her.

"We'll get in big trouble," Patience said.

"I've always loved you," I said.

Her body relaxed. Now, in the dark, my Lydie lay with me again. I stroked her cheek down to her chin. I stroked her lips. "I would do anything for you."

Her hair was full and soft. I tucked my knee into her crotch. "Let's never leave here."

"I won't tell anyone what I saw," Patience said.

"You're my princess," I said. "If anyone touches you, you tell me." I rolled on top of her and kissed her. "I could never love anyone more."

1922, Kohala
Sarah

I used to try and sleep. But when I closed my eyes, instead of finding the soothing darkness I craved, I would find myself walking along the cane-haul road at night holding a single lantern. Its gold light reflected off the wall of green leaves until I came upon a gap in the wall, where the sugarcane had been crushed. The half-clothed body of a young woman lay across the crushed cane. Before I could go to her, she would stand up and walk to the middle of the cane-haul road, then turn to face me.

"Will you remember me as I am now?" Lydia would say, her hair wild, her blouse soaked in blood.

My dear child...

"Or only as you wish to remember me?"

TWO NIGHTS AFTER Lydia's funeral, I was awakened by heavy footsteps in the manse. They began as a dull march from the kitchen, intensifying as they approached the front parlor, then the hallway outside our bedroom door. It was my brother Daniel, who entered his bedroom next to ours and slammed shut the door behind him.

Through our bedroom wall, I heard him flip the light switch. A sliver of light escaped his room at the ceiling and streaked across our bedroom ceiling. I heard him yank open a bureau drawer. His bedsprings squeaked. He grunted and his boots dropped to the floor. I heard him mumbling, and fumbling with his things. Then the ray of light across the ceiling disappeared.

Then Daniel's bedroom door flew open, hitting the wall. He stomped down the hallway, through the dining room, the kitchen and out into the yard. I heard him whistle for the horse. The saddle leather crunched beneath his weight. I turned to Everett, but he remained asleep beneath the blanket, drawing in the thick midnight air, then blowing it out across his cherry lips.

The next day, I waited until my camp girl folded the last of the laundry. After she left and the house was empty, I opened Daniel's bedroom door and walked to the middle of his neat, quiet room. I did not know what I was looking for, but began searching. I rolled open the desk top. The surface was empty. A box of pencils lay in the top drawer next to a pen case. A box of never-used stationary lay in the side drawer, 'Daniel Steven Christian' printed across the letter sheets and note cards. At the bureau I opened a drawer. There his clothes lay, clean, pressed and folded. I sat on his bed, the bed springs squeaking like the night before. The mattress gave way, and the bedspread draped over my foot. I kicked it off, then saw that it lay across the bed unevenly. I began to straighten it and suddenly knew. The answer lay beneath the bed.

I lifted the bedspread and saw a wood crate. Lydia's schoolbag lay inside, limp and smudged, casually imparting the devastating truth. Her bag was soft and full. It may have contained her clothing. It may have contained Daniel's clothing. I didn't look. Instead, I checked the time: Father and Everett would not return for hours. I took Lydia's bag to the old wood-burning stove out behind the tool shed. The yard boy used it to burn trash. I filled it with charcoal and lit the fire. When the coals were blue in the middle, I broke up a crate and threw in the wood. I waited until the flames filled the oven, then threw in Lydia's schoolbag. There was a mountain apple tree in the back. I picked three and ate them while listening to her bag burn.

THAT NIGHT DAG Olson called us. "Come quickly," he said.

"Whatever for, at"—I checked the clock—"9:30?"

He stammered, "You brother. You come."

Everett and I drove to the store. In the back room we found Daniel lying in his cot, with Sam Kaluhi kneeling next to him and holding a knife to his neck.

"What in God's name?" Everett rushed toward Sam.

"Wait," I said.

But Sam sliced off Daniel's earlobe—Daniel screaming through the rag stuffed in his mouth.

"He thinks he can get away with it," Sam cried. Everett's eyes leapt from Sam to Daniel to Olson, who held a rifle on Sam. "What on earth is this boy talking about?" Everett said. He took a step toward Sam. "I know you're upset," Everett said to him.

"You don't know shit."

"Lousy *kanak*," Olson muttered. He cocked the rifle.

Sam drew the knife along Daniel's right cheek. A stream of blood oozed out, running down his jaw and neck. Daniel's eyes rolled back in his head. Olson's eyes widened and his grip slackened. "Say something else to me," Sam told Olson, the knife poised on the left cheek.

Then there was a blow against the door. It flew open. Father was on the other side. He scanned the room, then told Olson, "Put that down."

Olson dropped the rifle.

Father marched to the cot where Daniel lay. He told Sam, "Give me that knife."

Sam looked up at him, waving the knife. He cried, "He killed Lydie."

Father grabbed it and delivered a backhand blow to Sam's face, who fell to the floor. "They'll be no more killing in this District," Father said. He pulled the rag from Daniel's mouth.

"I didn't—" Daniel began.

Father smashed his fist into Daniel's face. Then he cut the rope at Daniel's wrists and ankles, grabbed him by the bloody collar and lifted him against the wall.

Face to face with Father, Daniel burst into laughter and began singing, *"There's a wideness in God's mercy—"*

"You," Father cried.

"Like the wideness of the sea."

Father struck Daniel again, blood from his ear splattering onto my white sleeve. Daniel crumpled to Father's feet.

Father lifted him again.

"Stop." Everett tried to push the two apart, but Father shoved him aside with one hand, all the while holding Daniel with the other.

Daniel's eye was swollen. A stream of blood ran from his ear down his neck, soaking his shirt. Still yet, he smirked and baited Father. "Ever notice," he said, "that *haole* girls have pink ones—"

"God help me," Father cried.

Daniel laughed. "But on Hawaiian girls..."

Father threw him into the wall. I heard something crack and Daniel crumbled to the floor.

"You killed him!"

1922, Kohala
Sam

Day after we buried Lydie, Eddie-Boy Kauka came to me. He opened his hand, as big as his feet. In the middle lay Gramps's coins. "Where you got these?" I said.

"Some buddha-head lost his bet at the cockfight down at the camp."

I took a coin and held it to my nose. I could smell the rooster scratching the dirt. I held it to my ear and heard Lydie's murderer grabbing the coins, then letting them fall to the bottom of his pocket. "Show me who," I told Eddie-Boy.

He took me down to the camp. We found the Japani, who told us Daniel Christian used the coins to pay his wife for laundry service. After the camp, we went to Olson's store in Hāwī. In the back there was a room where Daniel Christian slept. It wasn't locked and we walked right in.

"Looks like a girl's room," Eddie-Boy said, knocking over the books on the shelf, and pulling clothes off the hook on the wall. At Daniel's cot he picked up the pillow and sniffed it.

"The fuck you doing, Eddie-Boy?"

He laughed, threw the pillow back on the cot and kicked it over. That's when we saw a box under the cot, and inside lay Lydie's schoolbag.

"How did he get this?" Eddie-Boy said.

"How do you think?"

"But—"

"Yeah, that's exactly what it means," I said. Inside the bag we found Lydie's clothes, the baby blanket and Daniel Christian's red shirt, now stained brown. "You know what that is, Eddie-Boy?"

He nodded, looking at the stain. "That's his big mistake."

"That's the mistake of his life." I shoved the shirt back in the bag. I turned the cot upright, put the bag in the box and kicked it under the cot.

"What we gonna do, Sam?"

"First, I'm gonna make him piss like a girl."

Eddie-Boy smiled. "Always wanted to see a *haole* piss."

In Olson's store, I stole a small knife and ball of twine. The next night, I went back to the store alone. There was no sense in dragging Eddie-Boy along—he had enough problems. I pushed open the door and there was Daniel Christian lying on his cot smoking. "You killed Lydie," I said.

"Prove it," he said and took a long drag on the cigarette. I could smell the whiskey on his breath and clothes. I could see it in his pickled eyes. I yanked him off the cot and kicked it aside, but the box was gone. He started laughing.

"Where is it?"

He kept laughing, even as I dragged him on the cot, and tied his hands and feet to the side. "I've gotten rid of all the evidence. You know what the law says: innocent until *proven* guilty."

"You think I give a shit about the law?"

Daniel stopped laughing.

"I already tried you. I already convicted you."

Daniel turned his face to the door going into the store office.

"Olson," he said. Weak.

"The only thing I hate more than a stupid, drunk Hawaiian, is a stupid, drunk *haole*." I slapped him, shoved a rag in his mouth and took out the knife that came in its own box. "I wonder what that means?" I said, holding up the box. "Pa-ring? Oh, like this picture? For cutting the skin off an apple?"

Now he was squirming.

"What? You scared?"

His eyes changed: Fuck you.

I laughed. "I'm ready to cut off your balls, and you're throwing me dirty looks?" I pulled one of his fingers out of the fist he made and sliced across the middle of his nail.

His eyes came all teary.

"Come on. We're just having fun."

A tear rolled down his cheek.

"You scared?"

He looked back at the office door.

"You gotta nod: Yes I'm scared of you."

He nodded.

"You think my sister Lydie was scared of you?"

He looked at the door.

"I asked you one question, *haole*. Was my sister scared of you?"

He nodded.

"Now, think about this question before you answer: Do you think my sister was more scared of you than you are of me right now?"

He nodded.

I punched his face. "You're the dumbest *haole* I ever met. You couldn't save your own two balls if you tried. Let's try again: Think she was more scared?"

Again he nodded.

Again I punched him. This time I heard a crack—and too bad. The party was over, but he opened his eyes.

"Good boy," I told him. "You're strong—I can tell. We're gonna play all night long."

Then there was knocking on the other side of the office door.

It was the store owner, Olson. "Daniel?" he said.

I pretended I was Daniel, "Yeah, sleeping."

"I'm lonely, Daniel."

"The fuck?" I whispered to Daniel.

"I open smoke oysters and German beer," Olsen said.

"No..." I looked at Daniel.

"I miss you."

"You're taking it up the ass?" I said. "That's how you like it?"

"Hal-looo..." Olson said.

"Yeah. Must be," I said. "Otherwise, why would he keep a drunk on the payroll?"

"Can I come in?" Olson said.

"No!"

But Olson opened the door. His white shirt was unbuttoned and the shirttail hung down to his knees. "Where are you?" he said, until he saw me. He slammed shut the office door, and locked it from the other side. I heard him run into the store, then back through the office.

The door flew open. Olson pointed a rifle at me. "You touch him," he said. "I kill you."

I grabbed Daniel's head and pulled it to one side, jabbing the knife tip into the skin behind his ear. "Shoot if you like," I told Olson, "but I'm taking your boy with me."

"You just don't move," he said.

He ran back into the office. I heard him on the telephone. "He kill you brother."

So now the Christians were coming, and I had a choice. Number one, I could go. Number two, I could stay and let Reverend Christian know that his end was near. All his talk about saving our souls was just that, talk. All along, they'd been planning to murder my sister. Ten to one, Bernie was next. I decided to stay put. I wanted to see Reverend Christian's face when he realized that his gig was up. First Sarah and the son-in-law came, the two having the nerve to act all surprised. All innocent. I didn't buy it for a second, not in the district where Sarah taught half the girls, and her husband preached to everyone else. They must've heard, they must've seen, they must've known that Daniel had been hunting Lydie.

Then Reverend Christian came, and I never knew that puny old goat was so strong. He threw me to the side and picked up the cot with Daniel tied to it. He threw the whole thing into the wall. Then he told Sarah, "Send your brother somewhere. I don't care where, just get rid of him."

"Pack his things tonight," Reverend Christian told Olson. "I'll send for them in the morning."

"Punish this boy," Olson said, pointing the rifle at me.

"I'll take Samuel home," Reverend Christian said. "He's overwhelmed by his sister's death."

"It wasn't death," I said. "He murdered Lydie."

"He's trying to put blame wherever he can," Reverend Christian said.

"He comes my store again, I kill him," Olson said. "Lousy *kanak.*"

Alone outside with Reverend Christian, he grabbed a fistful of my hair. "What do you want?"

Looked him straight in the eye. "The way I figure, the last thing my sister saw was your boy murdering her."

He smacked my head and my face went numb. I told him, "You hit good, Reverend."

He hit me again and I saw white lights. My body felt warm and my feet tingled.

"An eye for an eye," I told him. "But since I don't want your stinking son or your pig-face daughter, better you give me everything else you got."

He hit me on the other side of my face, sharp and clean.

"You hit just like Papa did," I said, wiping the blood from my nose. "I want your new car, your house, the church, the school." Another smack.

My belly tightened. Chicken-skin crawled over my ass. "The way I figure it, you got a problem. If I point my finger at Daniel, it's all over for you."

"You'll never prove anything."

"I don't need to. Everyone knows your boy's to blame—the way he was hunting Lydie out in the open. The way he thought he could do whatever he wanted. Anything wrong with Daniel is your fault."

"I'll kill you," he said.

"You don't have the balls."

"You ungrateful..."

"You should've dumped him with the sharks a long time ago."

SARAH SENT DANIEL to a hotel on the Hāmākua side of the Hilo bridge. Before leaving Kohala to find him, me and Eddie-Boy visited the Moku place. But Charlie was gone, Mrs. Moku told us. "You folks haven't seen him?"

"Come with us," I told her. "You're entitled to the first crack on your son's behalf."

Ho! That lady cried.

Back outside their house I told Eddie-Boy, "What did I say?"

"Try go easy, once in a while," he said.

166

"Go easy? Lydie's rotting on the hillside and I'm supposed to go easy?"

We found the hotel—room number 8. Daniel opened the door, like he was waiting for someone—but not us, that was for sure. He ran from the door, across the bed to the window. But he couldn't get away from me. Besides being stupid, Daniel Christian was clumsy and weak. I grabbed him at the window and hauled him back onto the bed—Daniel punching like a girl. "Did you think I would forget about you?" I said. "We've got some unfinished business."

We trussed him up, good and tight. "What's that lesson your father's always talking about?" I said. "An eye for an eye? Something like that?"

Eddie-Boy had the best ideas, especially when I told him about Olson and Daniel. He took a piece of pipe and went to the other end. I stayed up front, talking sweet into Daniel's ear. "Sing, Daniel. Pretend you're with your fat boy Olson. Here"—I kissed his cheek. "Turn you on? You getting hot?"

That night we wiped the smile off his face. For the rest of his short life, he couldn't piss or shit. And most important, his raping, murdering days were over. The way I figured it, we revenged Lydie and served the community interest, all in one night.

Then I had business with Reverend Christian. First of all, he had to pay because he made Daniel the way he was. Second, he had to pay because he expected me to keep my mouth shut about Daniel and that didn't come free. Reverend Christian's new car? Mine. When I heard he was buying land in Kamuela, I waited for the sale and drove to the manse.

"Knock, knock." I looked through their screen door. "Is the Reverend in?"

Sarah threw down her mending and stomped away. She knew I was the reason her brother was dying in Hilo, and that she couldn't say anything about it.

Reverend Christian acted all surprised when he saw me.

"I heard you got something that belongs to me," I said.

"You get out of here," he said.

"Remember your teaching, Reverend. Blessed are the poor."

"I'll call the sheriff," he said, opening the screen door.

"Let's see how you like being Hawaiian."

He smacked my face.

Oh yeah. My dick was pointing straight up. "You do that good, Reverend."

WHEN REVEREND CHRISTIAN had a stroke I claimed full responsibility. Then the son-in-law split, and I had nothing to do with that one. You just look at some *wahines*, and you know you're looking at the Sahara Desert for a pussy. After I'd been living in Honolulu for a couple of years, I heard Sarah moved to Honolulu too. I heard she found a job at Trinity Girls School and that was just fine with me. I had my business; she had her school. For twenty—thirty years, it was live-and-let-live between us.

Then Moani's mother drove off the bridge—my niece Haunani picking up where Papa left off. He drowned in three inches of water; Haunani drowned in 20 feet. She left behind Puanani, who now had scrambled eggs for a brain, and it looked like Moani might follow her. Each time I went to the hospital, Moani kept coloring in the coloring book, her finger turning white from holding the crayon so tight. She wouldn't say hello, goodbye—nothing. The doctor called it post traumatic stress. He said Moani was pretending what happened didn't happen. He said she could come around in days, or years.

One day I went to visit, but Moani wasn't in her hospital room. I found the nurse who was all excited. She led me down the hallway, saying Moani had walked to the play room by herself. In the play room, I had to cover my ears because that was how loud those kids were. I told the nurse, "I thought they were suppose to be sick?"

She laughed like I was joking.

Then I saw Moani, sitting at a table by the window, crayons in front of her—the little mouth working so hard. "Look Moani," the nurse said. "Your uncle's here."

Moani looked up, then turned her paper so I could see. "I made a tree," she said.

The nurse was teary. "She made a tree."

I shrugged.

"She wants you to know that she made a new tree."

OK.

"She's telling us that she's back."

"All that in a tree, huh?"

The nurse nodded.

I called Bernie. "The doctor said the sooner we bring her home the better."

"Not yet," Bernie said.

"What do you mean, 'not yet'?"

"I can't take her."

"You're the grandmother. You gotta take care of your daughter's daughter."

"No, I'm just not ready," Bernie said—one foot stuck in Haunani's grave.

And me? By then I was working on wife number four. What the hell did I know about raising a little girl? That's when I remembered Sarah Christian.

I drove to Trinity School and asked to see Sarah. "Will she know what this is in reference to?" the lady said. She sat at a desk outside a set of double wooden doors.

"Just tell her Sam Kaluhi's outside."

Sarah's office smelled like an ashtray. She sat behind a wood desk the size of my dining room table. "What do you want?" she said. Her face looked like a smashed cigarette butt.

"Where's your manners? No, 'Hello'? No, 'How you been'?"

She stared at me with her cigarette butt eyes and said, "I'll ask you once more, what do you want?"

I sat on one of the chairs in front of her desk. "Might as well get right to the point, myself. I need a favor."

"I don't owe you any favors."

"Sounds like you're forgetting where you come from, Sarah. Remember how my sister Lydie looked in the sugarcane field? Remember who did that to her?"

"What does that have to do with anything?"

"I got a niece, great-niece actually. Her name's Moani. I want her in your school. I want you to take care of her. She saw her mother and sister drown, so be extra nice to her."

"I won't have this."

"Tomorrow we're coming. No admission test, no interview—none of that shit. Just sign her in. And like I said, everybody be nice."

"I won't let you hound me like this."

"What're you smoking? Two, three packs a day?"

"I'd like you to leave—now."

"Fine. My business here is done. Remember, do like I say, otherwise tomorrow I'm gonna call the papers, radio and TV. Everybody's gonna hear about Trinity's head nun—"

"I'm not a nun."

"Everyone's gonna hear about your brother and the dirty secret you hid all these years. Wonder whatever happened to him?"

"I'll resign before I let you force me to do anything."

"No matter to me. Resign. Take a long trip to China. As long as you do what I say. How do you think this will look in the papers: Trinity nun involved in murder."

"You're the one who murdered. You killed my brother."

"First of all, prove it. Second, so fucking what? Everybody knows I'm a prick. I never tried to be different from who I am. But you, acting like mother superior. It looks like you've got a big stake in this place."

"I won't stand for this."

"We're coming tomorrow morning. Remember, everyone needs to be real nice to her. You gotta let Moani know you love her."

The next morning, while driving Moani to Trinity, I explained to her that I was enrolling her in a boarding school because her grandmother couldn't take care of her.

"Why not?" she said.

"Cause Bernie's weak."

"Oh."

"And there's nobody else to take care of you."

"Nobody?"

Nobody. All the babies were buried on that hillside in North Kohala. "It's not your fault. We just got dealt a crap hand. Sometimes it goes like that."

Walking up the school steps, I told Moani, "They're all waiting for you. I talked to them already and made them promise to be nice to you. Anytime they get mean, you call me."

At the office, the secretary told us that Sarah was gone for the day, but she'd left papers for me to sign. The first one was Moani's application, stamped, 'Admit'. I knew Sarah wasn't stupid.

The secretary showed me where to sign, promising to pay Trinity a pile of money every year to house and educate my niece. Fine, and better them than me. I wasn't stupid either.

"Moani? Is that you?" the secretary said. She walked around to the front of her desk and took Moani's hand. "There are some girls just your age who would love to meet you. They're having lunch now. Why don't we join them?"

Moani walked away holding the lady's hand without looking back at me. She was smart that way. Why make things harder? Within the week

Sarah announced her retirement. The newspapers praised her for "outstanding service to Hawaii." They called her "an educator of the first order," and published her picture, *leis* up to her nose. Big smile.

THAT WAS WHAT I did for Moani, and more. I paid the Trinity tuition and boarding fees. I paid for all the uniforms and books, pocket money and anything else she wanted. After that, she went to college and nobody was prouder than me. She was like my own daughter.

When she wanted to come home for Christmas and summer, I sent her the plane fare and picked her up at the airport. When she wanted to go to Europe with her friends, I told her, "Good. Go look at those paintings—the ladies with one eye here, one tit there. Go listen to those folks screaming on stage. Get some high-class *haole* culture in your bones."

I couldn't believe it when she said she wanted to come home, with only one more semester left to finish. She told me she was taking a break. "Doesn't sound like a break to me," I told her.

She promised to go back, but I knew better. Still, I kept my mouth shut.

She came home and I bought her an apartment. When she wanted to open a business I was right behind her with seed money, plus my accountant and lawyer—I paid all the fees. It's not easy starting your own business. It takes guts. Once you start your business, it's even harder to make it work. But she did it. Moani made money—good money.

She wanted to buy her own condo with her own money? I thought, this's what it's all about. Teaching them to stand on their own. She wanted to pull Puanani out of St. Teresa's? I supported her, even against Bernie. "Her heart's in the right place," I told Bernie. "Let's give it a try."

She put Puanani to work. "It's good for her," she told me. "She'll make her own friends—her own money." I thought, look how smart this girl is.

It never bothered me that Moani didn't get married again. It's more trouble than it's worth. It never bothered me that Moani didn't have kids. They're loud and they stink half the time. See? That was what I did for Moani. I would've given her double that. I would've given her triple that. She and Puanani were all we had left.

OK. There was also Lydie's daughter Angelina and her son. But I had a big problem with that girl because maybe she was my own kid. Even though I promised Lydie I wouldn't shoot my load in her that day, all you need is one drop. After Lydie died, I went to Maui to find her baby. Listen to this: Angelina called me Papa right off the bat. Now why was that? Worse yet, she looked like two Kaluhis put together, with the same bow in the middle of her lip, and the same birthmark above her right knee. And I couldn't see one ounce of Charlie Moku in her features. Even though Daniel Christian cut her throat, Lydie was in the field that day—running away to Maui to find her baby—because of what I did.

The only solution was to forget about what happened, and that meant forgetting about the baby. I told the Maui lady, Gladys, "I'm gonna send you money once a year, but I got a couple of conditions: don't ever call me; and don't ever come to see me. And from now on the baby's name is Angelina." That was the name Lydie picked the day she ran away.

"How much money are we talking about?" she said. "And if you're giving first names, then you better come up with a last name too."

"Moku," I said. "That's the baby's last name, and here's the story of her birth." I told Gladys to tell Angelina that she was adopted because her mother and father died.

That story worked for twenty years, until Gladys was about to die and made some kind of deathbed confession to Angelina, who called me. She said she didn't want money or trouble, just the truth. Was Lydia Kaluhi her mother? Did she come from the valley of the Light in the Darkness?

I told her I didn't know a Gladys, or a Lydie, or a dark valley, and I hung up the phone. Just because Gladys caught a case of the blabs in her final hour, didn't mean I had to change my life, and ruin my peace and happiness.

Now Moani was trying to ruin it. She started asking about Lydie and about Lydie's baby. The first time I told her, *pau kl.* She played dumb, but she knew what I meant. The second time she came to my office demanding money for her hotel scheme and answers about Sarah Christian. Again I told her, enough. Finished. Listen, when you can write a check like the one I gave Moani that day, you're entitled to call the shots. But even after I gave her two warnings, even after I gave her a loan for five hundred thousand dollars, she kept at it. According to Puanani, Moani had called Angelina's son Charles. According to Puanani, Charles had called Moani. I had no idea how those two found each other in the first place. Now that they were together, I had to be practical. The situation was beyond my control.

Still, I held the purse strings. If Moani wanted to defy me, fine, but she had to pay the consequences. I called my bank and asked for the manager. "Remember the check I wrote the other day and gave to my niece?"

"Of course, yes," he said.

Goddamn right he remembers. Nobody else in Honolulu could write a check like that.

"How can I help you with that?" he said.

"What's the status?"

"Hold for a moment." Then, he came back, "It looks like your niece just deposited it."

"So no funds have been transferred yet?"

"No."

"Cancel it."

"Cancel the check?" I could hear his glasses sliding down his greasy nose.

"Do it now, while I'm on the phone."

"Right away, Mr. Kaluhi. Hold for a minute."

When he came back I said, "Done?"

"The check is canceled, Mr. Kaluhi."

Next, I called the real estate agent. It was time to discuss the purchase of certain land on the Big Island, North Kohala District.

1985, Moloka'i
Moani

Sea spray chilled our camp that morning. We all wore sweat shirts or windbreakers while sipping tea and coffee. I heard the outboard motor long before the boat appeared. The mechanical hum agitated the crisp morning air. The boat appeared off the western point, cut its engine, then glided into the bay. The nurses sat up. The lawyers stood.

I was tending banana pancakes while watching Dixie. She sat beside Pu sipping coffee and wouldn't look at Henry. Henry squatted beside me at the camp stove frying sausages and wouldn't look at Dixie.

"Who's that, Moani?" Pu said.

I recognized Spooks and his wife Doreen. We had shared camp with his family before. Spooks' three sons jostled with each other at the boat's edge. His young daughter peered over the side of the boat wearing an oversize life vest.

"Some old friends, Pu," I said.

I asked Dixie to watch the pancakes and sausage. With Henry and John, I walked down to the shore. John shoved one of the kayaks into the water and paddled out to help Spooks unload gear. His boys jumped overboard, then bobbed to the surface. They screeched and crawled over each other in the water, their cries echoing off the cliff walls.

One of the nurses had an eight-year-old son back in San Francisco. She watched the boys, smiling. Two of the lawyers began sipping their coffee again, watching John ferry to shore Spooks' gear, Doreen and the girl. The other two walked down to the shore, and helped John and Doreen haul the gear up to the shelter.

I returned to the shelter. "Folks, we've got company. I'd like you to consolidate your gear, move it to one side, and reserve space for Spooks and his family."

"But we were here first," Rick the honeymooner said.

"There's plenty of room," I said.

"Do they own the land?" Rick said.

I folded our sleeping bags and moved our things to the far corner of the shelter, hoping Rick would follow my example. Doreen hauled their food and ice chest next to our makeshift kitchen. The girl looked at the pancakes I had stacked beside the griddle.

I told Doreen, "I've got thirty here and more on the way."

"You sure?" Doreen said.

I made a plate for the girl. She sat with the plate on her lap, syrup spilling over the sides of the stack. She stuffed her mouth with pancake, held it in with her fingers and chewed. The boys ran across the slippery rocks at the shore line to the griddle. I made plates for them then mixed more pancake batter.

"I don't like this," Rick said.

"What's the problem?" one of the lawyers said. "There's plenty."

"That ain't the point," Rick said.

The boys stopped eating.

"What's happening?" Spooks said, walking up from the shore, his fists swinging.

"I didn't pay to feed other people's kids," Rick said.

"Fine then." Spooks grabbed one of the boys' plates and threw it at Rick's feet. The girl began crying.

"You got a problem?" Spooks said to Rick—Rick easily outweighing him.

"It's just that..."

"What, *haole*? What's your problem?" Spooks said. Next thing I knew it was fucking *haole* this, fucking *haole* that.

John and Henry gave Spooks a chance to get it out of his system, then stepped between the two before they threw blows at each other. I radioed my emergency boat, then told Rick's bride Shari, "Sorry, but it's in everyone's interest that you and Rick leave the trip. We'll probably be sharing the next camp with people too."

Her chin trembled. She still wore only one earing from the capsizing the day before.

"I've radioed for our emergency lift out. It should be here in an hour." Then I decided, this was my last trip ever. John and Henry could command the five remaining trips during the summer season. I didn't care what the engineers said, I was dumping Lost Paradise and buying the old school in Kohala.

Now Shari began crying.

"It's better to cut your losses now. You'll be back in Waikīkī this afternoon. Still have some honeymoon time for yourselves."

"OK."

"Guess you should pull your gear together. Try to eat some breakfast."

"No, thank you."

We finished breakfast, then Rick decided to take a dip. Fine, I thought. Give the camp some breathing space. But he swam out beyond the mouth of the bay. John and Henry watched, shaking their heads. We'd seen this before. When guys fucked up on the kayak trips—capsized, lost a paddle, fell down—to cope with the embarrassment they became macho and hostile. They did dumb stuff like swimming into waters they had never swum in before.

John held the bullhorn, ready to call him in. Then I saw the tip of a shark's fin moving slowly from the west mouth of the bay. I grabbed the bullhorn from John. "Attention," I called to Rick. "Stop swimming."

He kept swimming.

"Attention, Rick. Do not move."

John and Henry shoved a kayak in the water and began paddling out. When Rick saw them he waved, until he saw the fin. Now he began wildly swimming toward John and Henry. The shark zeroed in, butting Rick in the side and spinning him over. He screamed. Then Shari screamed. The little girl cried. Rick surfaced, thrashing.

John and Henry grabbed him by the arm pits and hauled him into the kayak. I saw two hands, two feet.

"I want to get out of here," Shari said, crying.

John and Henry paddled in, Rick lying across the kayak, shit streaming out of his trunks. On the shore we pulled off the trunks, cleaned him in the water, then hauled him up to the shelter and lay him on one of the air mattresses. I covered him with the blankets. He just stared ahead while a nurse took his pulse. "His heart's racing," she said.

"Boys." Spooks called to his sons hovering over and staring at Rick. "Come over here."

Rick's face had turned gray, his pupils dilated.

"Do you have any kind of sedative?" one nurse asked.

"He's going into shock," the other said.

I began massaging Rick's right foot, Henry the left. Then I realized that I would have to ride out with Rick and Shari on the emergency boat. Once we returned to Honolulu, I wanted to make sure Rick spent the night in a hospital. If I left, then Pu would have to leave too. Dixie could stay with Henry if she wanted. Go ahead and cheat on Uncle. Who knew what else was going on?

"Look at the color returning to his face," one of the nurses said.

We began working the tendons above the ankle. The calf, the knees. Henry worked his thighs. "Think this'll be my last season. Been thinking about it for awhile. It's got nothing to do with today."

"Moani's making a hotel," Pu said.

"You're in the hotel business?" the lawyer said.

"That would be a mistake," another lawyer said. "I mean, leaving this business. You're good at it."

"Without you and your crew," a lawyer said, "he would've been a goner."

Without me and my crew we wouldn't be out here dodging sharks and reefs—torching *brûlée* over the campfire. Why not just eat in a restaurant already?

Then Rick rolled over and vomited. It was a good sign. His vitals were back.

"I'm gonna throw up too," Pu said.

"No you're not, Pu."

"But—"

"Just because he throws up, doesn't mean you have to," I said.

"Oh."

BACK IN HONOLULU Rick insisted that he was fine—and maybe he was. If he was going to have a heart attack, it would've happened in the water, or when we hauled him ashore. Still, I wanted him in the hospital overnight for my own protection. We stood at the baggage claim, Rick refusing to go to the hospital, or sit in the wheel chair the airline had provided.

"If you don't sit down and shut up," Shari said, "I'm on the next plane back to Philly."

Dixie had returned with us. "I give them a year at the most," she whispered to me.

"You give them a year?" I said.

Pu and I finally walked into our condo at 3:30 p.m. I listened to the telephone messages from the past two days while sorting through our gear on the living room floor. Pu loaded laundry in the washer off the kitchen.

"This's CJ Moku," the message said.

I ran to the answering machine and turned up the volume.

"Just wanted to say hi. Been having some phone trouble, so don't mind us." He whispered to a child, "Say hello."

"Hello," the child said.

Pu walked in from the kitchen. "Do you think that man's gonna be OK?"

"Pu, I'm trying to listen."

"That's my youngest," CJ Moku said. He called to another. "OK, looks like she's mad at me today. Probably been talking to her mother again. So—yeah. That's about it. Just to say hi. My phone service should be up and running again soon. You know how that one goes."

The child said something.

"That's true," CJ Moku said. "OK. You there? Yeah. Good idea. We gonna leave a friend's number."

I grabbed the pen.

He repeated the number twice. "You can leave a message for us there. We'll get it sooner or later. Eh, why not visit Maui sometime? Plenty room with us. Nothing fancy, but, you know, it's home."

"Who's that?" Pu said.

"Remember that man we talked about?"

"He threw up?"

"No, not him. That message is from the man who's our cousin."

Pu's teeth chattered. "Uncle said we can't talk to him."

What? "When?"

"He told me not to tell," Pu said. "Because, because—"

"Wait, Pu. When did Uncle say this?"

"He told me that if you did, if you did... Uncle told me to tell him if you did."

"Pu, you've been spying on me?"

"Uncle told me."

"Well, Pu, I've got to call."

"But Uncle—"

"Tell Uncle if you want," I said.

"But we have to do what Uncle says."

I picked up the phone.

"Moani, you not supposed to."

I dialed the number CJ Moku left me.

"Moani, you gonna get in trouble."

No one answered at the number CJ Moku had left.

Then our telephone rang.

"Uh oh," Pu said. "It's Uncle."

I picked up the phone.

"Oh, Moani, you're there. I thought you were on an trip this week."

Pu said, "Told you, told you."

"It's Ben at the bank, Moani."

"We ran into a problem," I said. "A sick kayaker."

"Well, I hope nothing serious."

"Why call me at home when you thought I wouldn't be here?"

"Well, Moani," he laughed. "I really didn't think you'd be there now."

"I noticed."

"Moani, we've run into a slight problem."

"Slight problems are not problems."

"That's very good. I'll have to remember that one."

"Talk to me."

"I don't know how to tell you this," he said. "But the upshot is that your Uncle stopped payment on that check you deposited."

"When?"

"Yesterday."

"I deposited that check last week. Those funds should've cleared within two days."

"Actually, you deposited the check near the close of business on Tuesday. Under bank policy..."

Blah, blah, blah. "Fine, I don't need his check," I said. "I'll extend my credit line."

"Sorry, Moani."

"I've never drawn down on it before."

"Your uncle asked that I cancel the credit," he said.

"He can't do that. It's my account."

"Your Uncle has been our customer—"

I hung up and looked around our living room. I knew what I had to do: I would sell the condo. When was the last time we used the gym downstairs? And that stupid waterfall in the lobby... I looked at our gear across the living room floor: I would continue kayaking for another year to raise the money. I could open lines of credit somewhere else.

I called the engineer and architect. We were supposed to inspect the property together the following week, after I returned from the Moloka'i trip. They both said they could meet tomorrow at the airport.

I called our babysitter Gina, but she had made plans through the week anticipating that we would be away. I called Dixie. "Are you busy tomorrow? I need someone to stay with Pu."

"We'll go shopping," Dixie said. "Make it a girls' day and buy baby clothes." Just what I needed to hear. I told Pu I would be away tomorrow and that Dixie would babysit.

"I want to go with you," she said.

"Pu, the last time we went to the school, you wanted to leave."

"No. I want to go with you."

"You said it was too dirty."

"No I did-n't."

"Sorry, Pu. Tomorrow's strictly work. We'll be walking in dusty basements. Through spiders webs. Gotta find out if she's in good enough shape to buy."

Her teeth chattered. "I'll be good."

IN THE EARLY morning flight to Kona the attendant brought us guava juice. "Isn't that nice?" Dixie told Pu. "What a wonderful taste." Instead of a girls' day buying baby clothes with Pu, Dixie had agreed to come along and babysit Pu while I walked through the old school with the engineer and architect.

Pu hated guava juice, but drank hers for Dixie, then finished mine because I hated guava juice too.

The engineer and architect sat across the aisle from us. As the plane descended to Kona, Dixie pulled a mirror and lipstick from her purse. Now that she had returned to civilization, the goop was back in full force. Pu watched her apply the lipstick.

"Would you like some?" she said to Pu. "It's"—Dixie turned over the tube—"guava. Isn't that funny?"

I rented a van. Just as we left the airport Pu said, "Uh oh, Moani."

"Better pull over fast," Dixie said. She pushed open the door and helped Pu out to the road. Pu vomited the guava juice.

"You always bring sick people along on business trips?" the architect said to me.

"For your information," Dixie told him, "she needs to stay with family right now."

"Is she OK?" the engineer asked me.

"Just a bit of morning sickness."

"She's pregnant?" the architect said.

Dixie helped Pu back in the van. She told the architect, "Welcome to the real world, hot shot." She was supposed to babysit Pu while I walked through the buildings with the engineer, and discussed restoration with the architect.

"Sorry, Moani."

"You did good, Pu. If it happens again, just give me a warning. I'll pull over."

"OK," she said. Her t-shirt hung off her shoulders. Her face had thinned.

"How about a song, Pu?" I fiddled with the radio.

"No singing," she said, laying her head against the window.

STANDING IN FRONT of the old school, Dixie said, "I just love it up here. I told Sam we'd be your first guests."

The engineer smiled, looking at the building. "See?" I said to him. "Would this make a great hotel or what?"

"Let's not jump ahead. Let's see what kind of shape she's in."

"How will we do this?" I said. "Walk through each building together?"

"Check all the supports," he nodded. "Weather damage. Infestation." He held a notepad. There was a flashlight tucked in the waistband of his pants. "Do you know how old she is?"

"Turn-of-the century," the architect said. "You can tell by the window sills."

We entered the main room on the ground floor. "Look at that," the architect said, walking to the piano. "Must be over one hundred years old."

The engineer pushed each support beam and stomped on the floor. He knocked on the walls and listened. He squatted over a dark spot on the floor, then studied the ceiling directly overhead. He walked up the staircase. I heard him stomping and knocking against the floor and walls on the second floor. He called down to me. "You got a ladder around here?"

Then the piano rang out a melody, but in out-of-tune keys. I turned to find Dixie sitting on the piano bench with Pu beside her. "Ragtime," Dixie said. "I can imagine the girls walking through this room in long flowing skirts."

The architect was sketching in his pad. He looked up and nodded. "I can see it."

"This's what they would've played," Dixie said.

"That's what they *wanted* to play," the architect said. "You can bet the folks who ran this place wouldn't have approved. Their idea of music was church hymns and Christmas carols."

"Looks like we've got a self-appointed expert on this trip," Dixie said.

"But keep playing," the architect said. "It's nice to hear live piano."

Dixie left the piano bench.

Pu hit the same key again and again. The architect's jaw clenched and unclenched.

"I'm gonna work here," Pu said.

"Really?" the architect said.

"I'm gonna be the hostess with the mostess."

"Is that right?" he said. "Before or after the baby?"

I decided to fire him once we returned to Honolulu.

I had bought sandwiches and drinks in Hāwī before driving up the valley to the school. After inspecting both buildings we sat on the porch and ate.

"You might have yourself a hotel here," the engineer said.

"The buildings are in good shape, especially given their age. You'll need to shore up the foundation. Invest in weather protection. Siding. Fumigate."

Then Pu threw up again.

"I thought that was only supposed to happen in the morning," the architect said.

"Your mama was doing the same thing thirty years ago, hot shot," Dixie said.

"My wife couldn't keep anything down the first couple months," the engineer said. "She lost twelve pounds and we had to put her in the hospital."

"Try a little juice, Pu," I said.

She sipped half the can.

"Good job, Sweet Pea. I'll pack some crackers in my purse for the ride back."

"Give her a week," the engineer said. "If she's still not keeping down her meals, then better visit the doctor." And eventually we had to face the examination table again. Maybe if Dixie went with us.

1985, Kohala
Sam

I bought the school and church, cash. I recorded the deed, then took Dixie back up to Kohala to watch the show. The crane was already in place, standing next to the classroom building, the wrecking ball hanging from the top.

"You can't be serious," she said.

I didn't say nothing because there was nothing to say. Now, I just needed to make a couple of points. First of all, she was getting too close to Moani and Puanani. She needed to understand that she was on the wrong path. There was only one path in my family, and it led to me.

Second, something happened on the kayak trip. She came home different. Now she was quiet and distracted. She didn't listen to me when she should've been listening to me, and I only had one thing to say about that. Whatever happened, she'd better come home soon, or else Daddy was gonna lock the doors.

"Sam, please don't do this," she said. "Those two have their hearts set on this place."

I blew the car horn. The crane operator waved to me.

"Sam, wait. Moani will make this work."

"Of course she's gonna make it work." She got that from me—and that wasn't the point.

"She wants this place so bad," Dixie said. "It'll be a home for herself, Pu, the baby—"

"The hell you talking about?"

Dixie looked all frightened. "It's Pu. She's, well, she's pregnant."

"You're fucking kidding me."

She nodded. "We tested her."

"Puanani's hāpai?"

She nodded.

"Puanani's having a baby?"

"It's true," she said.

"This's Moani's fault. That damn girl. I knew she couldn't take care of Puanani."

"It's not her fault."

"It's gotta be someone's fault."

"Sometimes things just happen."

"Nothing just happens," I said. "If Moani was taking care of Puanani, this never would've happen."

The crane operator was watching me. I raised my arm outside the car window and dropped it. "Do it," I said.

"Please, Sam," Dixie grabbed my arm. "This's all wrong."

"It's my property, and that means I can do what I want."

"Your property?"

The crane operator turned the carriage and let the wrecking ball swing. It hit the second floor, knocking out a window.

"Oh God," Dixie said. She looked so pretty, a tear falling down her cheek.

I took her hand, soft and white—all the little freckles dancing over her knuckles. "Just some old buildings," I said.

She pulled away her hand. "Why did you bring me here?"

"I've got a point to make."

"The only point you're making is that you're a son-of-a-bitch."

It happened fast, like the time before. My hand flew up and smacked her across her mouth. She acted all surprised, staring ahead, her hand over her mouth. Then the wrecking ball made a second swipe, knocking in the wall on the third floor. I knew I was looking at Patience's room. I yelled to the crane operator, "Tear down this place. Don't wait for my signal anymore."

183

The wrecking ball fell into the roof. My prick began sitting up. I took Dixie's hand and kissed the freckles. "You're with me now, nobody else. See what I can do?" I said. I reached up and drew a circle around her nipple. "I can do anything I want." I dropped my finger to her crotch and made a nice slow circle just above the drop-off.

She opened her legs.

"Good girl." I pulled her knees apart. In the valley she was damp and hot. "That's it." I ran my finger up and down the seam, nice and tight and ready to rip apart.

"This's my island," I told her. "My family." I kissed her ear, while running my finger up and down the seam.

"Oh—"

"Yeah. You belong to me now. You didn't know that, did you?"

1985, Honolulu
Moani

I NEVER WENT to hospitals because I never got sick. The one where my grandmother had taken Pu looked like a hotel, what with the gift shop in the lobby and splashy flower print on the couches.

The woman at the front desk said Pu was in the special surgery wing, but in special surgery they said try maternity. In maternity the nurse said Pu was in obstetrics and gynecology. There, a man said that my grandmother admitted Pu that afternoon for an abortion.

"Did they do it yet?"

He checked a chart. "Not yet. Is there a problem?"

I had to be careful. Even though Pu lived with me, Uncle was her legal guardian. Under his authority, he could commit Pu to the hospital, order an abortion. "No problem," I said. "I just wanted to offer some moral support."

"And you are?"

"Her sister."

"She's down the hall, sitting with your grandmother. The doctor should be back in"—he checked the clock on the wall—"say, an hour."

In the waiting room, Pu sat on a couch rocking back and forth, *"'Tis a gift to come down where we ought to be."*

Our grandmother sat on another couch, clutching her purse across her stomach.

"What you doing here?" she said when she saw me.

"And when we find ourselves in the place just right..."

"Why go behind my back like this?" I said.

"'Twill be in the valley of love and delight."

"You're the one responsible for all of this," she said.

"Does Pu know what'll happen here?"

"How did you know we were here?"

Dixie had learned of the plan and called me.

"Moani," Pu said. "Grandma said it's time to take out the baby."

"Dixie told you," our grandmother said.

I said to Pu, "She didn't bring you here to have the baby."

"She told me it's time," Pu said.

"Damn whore I gotta share my house with," our grandmother said.

"You didn't tell Pu what's going to happen?"

"Fat frosted bitch."

"Tell Pu why you brought her here," I said.

Our grandmother looked at Pu. "Puanani, some things are just for the best."

Pu's teeth chattered. Then she said to me, "You jealous. I'm having the baby and you not."

"You need to understand why you're here, Pu," I said.

"Grandma doesn't want you to have the baby. She brought you here—"

"Uncle brought us," Pu said. "And you in trouble."

"Pu, listen to me..."

"No."

"They want to get rid of the baby."

"No."

"That's why you're here. The doctor's going to kill the baby."

"Don't say that," our grandmother said.

"Kill the baby?"

"There's no baby in there," our grandmother said. "Nothing but a lump with a tail. We just gonna put everything back the way it should be."

"Kill my baby?"

"This's your fault, Moani," our grandmother said. Her fingers were long and she'd painted the nails pink. She pointed her forefinger at me.

"We're holding you responsible. She's living with you. It's your watch. Now she's pregnant. After this, we're putting her back in St. Teresa's."

"No way," I said.

"At least we'll know she's safe there, instead of that other place. All day she's around guys worse off than her. No wonder this happened."

The nurse came to the waiting area. His name tag said Calvin. "The doctor's back early," he said. "We're ready to prep the patient."

Pu's mouth fell. She didn't trust the situation now. Good.

"Puanani?" the nurse said. "Is that you?"

"Yeah."

"You ready to get this taken care of?"

"I'm having my baby now?" Pu said.

The nurse glanced at our grandmother, then at me. "No one explained to her?"

"Doesn't look like it," I said.

"Well, that's not good. The hospital has procedures. Unless she's declared incompetent, she has to understand the nature of the procedure and consent to it."

"I'm having a baby."

"Oh, she's incompetent," our grandmother said. "We got the papers to prove it. We're the legal guardians. We decide."

"I'm sorry," the nurse said, looking at the chart. "I see no such determination in our records." He sat next to Pu. "Puanani? Do you know where you are?"

"My baby's gonna be Moani."

"Puanani, do you know where you are?"

"The hospital."

"Good. Do you know why you're here?"

"To have the baby."

"No." He shook his head then took Pu's hand. "The reason you're here today is to end your pregnancy. You're not going to have a baby today."

"Later I'm having the baby?"

"No. The reason why you're here today is to get rid of the baby growing in your tummy." He put his hand on her stomach, then looked at the chart. "And I see a hysterectomy is also planned. Does she know about this?"

I looked at our grandmother. "I can't believe you guys."

"Might as well, while they're in there," she said. "Don't want to go through this again."

"I'm sorry," the nurse said to our grandmother. "I have to refer this to our legal department."

"That's fine," I said. "I think it's time for us to go."

"Are you her guardian?" the nurse asked.

"I'm her sister. She lives with me."

"The legal guardian?"

"No. My uncle and grandmother are. They told her she's having the baby today."

"I never said that," our grandmother said.

"You didn't tell her the truth."

"The truth is that she got knocked up, and that's your fault."

"Moani's gonna teach my baby to swim."

I took Pu's hand. "We're leaving."

"You can't just take her," the nurse said.

"That's right," our grandmother said.

"I'd like the doctor to see her first, then someone from our legal department should see her."

"Don't you dare, Moani," our grandmother said. "I'll be damned if this retard is giving birth to one more retard in the family."

"Excuse me," Calvin said, "but that's not how it works."

"If you walk out of here with Pu," our grandmother said, "then we're coming after you with the sheriff. That's in our rights as guardian."

"Later I'm having the baby?" Pu asked me.

"Looks like it, Pu," I said, walking away from our grandmother and the nurse.

I heard our grandmother ask Calvin, "Where's your phone?"

OUR GRANDMOTHER WAS quick. There were two police cars at my company headquarters. I drove past.

"Uh oh," Pu said. "You didn't turn."

"Let's go home, Pu."

"Uncle made the police find me?"

"I can't believe he's doing this."

"I can," Pu said. "Cause Uncle's mean. Uncle's a sonna bitch."

"Hey, you never talk like that."

"You do. You say that."

"I never said that in front of you."

187

"But that's what you think."

"You don't know what I'm thinking," I said.

"I can see what you think."

"You can't."

"I can because your mouth looks funny," Pu said. "And that's when I know."

Inside our condo I locked the doors.

"We're in trouble, right Moani?"

"Yeah, Pu. We're going to disappear for a little while." We walked down the hall to her bedroom. I opened her closet. "Where's your suitcase?"

Pu sat on the bed.

I clapped my hands and she jumped. "I want to leave here in five minutes."

"Is Dixie coming with us?" Pu said, pulling the suitcase out from under her shoes.

"She'll stay with Uncle."

"She's pretty."

"I suppose." I opened her underwear drawer.

"I wish I looked like her."

"No, Pu. You don't want orange hair."

"Is Gina coming?"

"Don't think so."

"Then who's gonna watch me?"

"We'll figure it out as we go, Pu. Don't worry." I grabbed handfuls of her panties and stuffed them into a duffle bag. Pu looked in her closet. It was packed with *mu'umu'us* Uncle had bought her each birthday and Christmas, the tags still hanging from the arm holes.

"Take the things that are biggest on you, Pu."

"Where we going, Moani?"

We would leave Honolulu. I was leaning toward finding a place on the Big Island—in Kamuela maybe—where I could leave Pu while renovating the Kohala property. "Remember the school we visited?"

"We have to live there?"

"No, not yet."

"But—who gonna watch me?"

"Hurry, Pu, you'll need lots of clothes. Make sure and take some sweaters."

"The man said he would take care of me," Pu said.

"Who?"

"The man who called."

"The man on Maui?" On second thought, maybe we'd go to Maui. Uncle would surely look for us on the Big Island.

"And I been there too."

"Pu, when did you go there?"

"In my dream I went there. In my dream I was swimming and swimming. Then I stepped on the sand and there was a man."

"Hurry, Pu."

"Guess what the man said?"

"We need to leave soon," I said, running out of her room.

"Guess what the man said?"

In the bathroom I began sweeping the bottles on the counter into a knapsack.

She yelled down the hall to me, *"Yo soy un hombre sincero, de donde crece las palmas..."*

"Pu—"

"Y antes de morirme quiero..."

"Shut up and pack!"

"Echar mis versos del alma."

In my room I grabbed shorts and t-shirts out of my bureau drawers; then I called the Maui number CJ Moku had left, but no one answered.

At the airport ticket counter I considered my options. CJ Moku was the only family Pu and I had left, but I had never met him. We stepped out of the ticket line. I told Pu to wait with the bags, then called the Maui number again, but there was still no answer.

At the ticket counter I bought two tickets for Maui, one way.

I DIDN'T BELIEVE in luck. The way to succeed was through planning, execution and hard work. My rule of thumb was: expect the worst. Then I would be prepared for it. So when I saw the man walking toward us in the Maui airport, 7:00 in the evening, I expected the worst: he was one of Uncle's thugs come to kidnap Pu. Drag her back to Honolulu, rip out her insides, then dump her back in St. Teresa's.

I was carrying Pu's knapsack over one shoulder. In my hand I pulled along the suitcase with her shoes, our clothes. As the man approached, I grabbed Pu's arm. "Keep walking, Pu."

"Are you Moani?" he said.

If he touched us, I would scream.

189

"She's Moani. I'm Pu."

"CJ Moku," he said, touching his chest. "Long time no see." A girl and boy skipped up behind him.

I wasn't expecting the fair skin and green eyes. "You're Lydia's son?"

"Grandson," he said. "I never knew her. My mother never knew her. But that's what she told me."

A noisy gang of tourists passed.

"The Big Chief called me," he said.

"You talked to Uncle?"

"After my mother died, he came to visit." CJ began laughing. "You should've seen his face when he saw my lettuce crop behind my house, my house without paint, and realized I was the poor relation. He walked around my house, shaking his head. Said, 'Least let me pay for a paint job.'"

"Moani—Moani—"

"I told him, what's that gonna cost me?" CJ laughed. "Ho! That guy's got a nasty temper."

"Moani—"

"He called me today. He told me be on the look out for you two."

"How did he know we were coming here?" I thought of Dixie, but she didn't know that we had fled Honolulu for Maui.

"Moani—"

"Pu, did you tell Uncle we were coming to Maui?"

"Uncle said—Uncle said—"

"When?" We'd been together since the hospital.

"He told me to call him when I see you," CJ Moku said. "He told me anything I wanted, I could have. But I never took a dime from that son-of-a-bitch." His hand flew to his mouth.

"Dad!" the girl cried.

The boy spun around.

"You owe us a quarter," the girl told him.

"A quarter!" the boy held out his hand.

"Sheee." He reached in his pocket.

Pu told him, "I'm having a baby."

He paused, then said, "Might as well. Otherwise the family's just you and me. And these two robbers—hitched a ride to the airport with me tonight."

The girl gasped. "I think that's another quarter, Dad."

"What did I say?"

She spelled, "R-o-b-b-e-r."

"That ain't a bad word: Robber."

"That's two quarters now."

"You believe these two?" he told me. "And at first they were such nice babies."

"Uncle tried to kill my baby," Pu said.

The children quieted.

"You stay with me, cousin," CJ Moku said. "My house, my land. Nobody gonna hurt nobody, anymore."

1986, Maui
Moani

I always liked the feel of the paddle in my hand, pushing back the water and pulling forward the kayak. I liked sitting low in the water, the kayak gliding over the surface. I loved seeing the wave roll away from the kayak's bow, leaving a wake behind me. I loved days like this off the south shore of Maui. The island of Kaho'olawe lay across the channel. The sky was clear, the wind gentle and at our backs. There were whitecaps in the sea channel, but nothing to worry about as we paddled inside the protected bay.

I had the baby with me. As soon as she saw the kayak she had begun babbling. She was eight months old.

"Oh look at her," the tourist lady said, the mother of two boys. One boy sat with CJ in one kayak, the other with their mother in another kayak. I paddled the third with the baby, Bernie. The lady was recently divorced, she had told me over the phone from Chicago. "The kids and I just need a break from everything."

Now, sitting beneath the bright Maui sun, the lady said, "She loves this, doesn't she?"

Bernie looked at the lady while gnawing on the strap of her baby-size life vest.

"Since she was six months old," I said, and the day Pu had plopped her in the kayak between my legs.

"Tell me her name again," the lady said and I told her. We called her Bernie, short for Bernice. I had been against it. Let's face it, I told Pu after she gave birth, Grandma tried to get rid of the baby. But Pu had said that one day Grandma would be glad to have the baby.

"Aren't you worried that, you know, knock on wood"—the lady rapped the side of the kayak—"but what if you capsize? Or, God forbid, but what about sharks?"

The bay where I led family kayak excursions was protected by a reef at the mouth. At its deepest the bay was only eight feet. The water was piss warm and perfect for Bernie. It was perfect for my newest client base, families with children looking for tropical adventure beyond the hotel swimming pool.

We paddled near the mouth of the bay. "I saw a dolphin pod earlier today," I told the lady.

"Really?" she said.

Frankly, no. It was the wrong time of day, the wrong location. But tourists wanted to see dolphins, especially parents like my lady desperate for paradise.

I told her, "So if we just stay put for a little while, maybe they'll come back."

At best we might see a turtle pop his head above the surface.

"I have a tuna sandwich," the lady told me.

"OK."

"I mean, maybe we could use it for the dolphins."

"You want to bait the dolphins?"

"Not like hunting or anything. But don't you think they'll come around if we toss some food in the water?"

CJ paddled closer. "Really a bad idea. It's bad for the dolphins, the water, the reef."

Bernie stood when she saw him. I tried to bend her at the waist, pushing her locked legs out in front of her but she twisted her body right and left, then threw herself overboard.

"Oh my God!" the lady said.

CJ waited for her to surface between our kayaks, then scooped her out of the water.

I maneuvered my kayak along side CJ's while telling the lady, "Throwing trash in the water is against the law." CJ's kayak was unstable now, with both Bernie and one of the lady's boys aboard. I helped him slide from CJ's kayak into mine.

"Oh, it's not trash. Just a tidbit." The lady pulled a sandwich out of her fanny pack. She opened the wrapper and broke off pieces for the boys. "Break it up and feed the dolphins," she told them.

I had never been a tourist, actually, but times like this I told myself I needed to go on a vacation, maybe to one of the resorts in Bali. It seemed like everyone was going there. I needed to find out if the same thing would happen to me: I pay top dollar for a week in paradise and, therefore, believe I can do whatever I want. Wear stupid outfits. Waste food. Offend the natives.

Poor CJ. For nine months he had been helping with the kayaks on Fridays and weekends when he could leave his lettuce crop. He had no patience for the tourists, no sympathy for the families fleeing the Chicago winter for the Maui sunshine. From the beginning he'd called all their children "brats," the fathers assholes, and generally ignored the women. He looked at the lady, shook his head in disgust and paddled back to shore with Bernie. There Pu waited with the restaurant-prepared box lunches for the lady and her kids.

"Wait a second. Doesn't he have our camera?" the lady said. "He's supposed to take pictures of us kayaking with the dolphins."

Be cool, be nice, I told myself for the millionth time in my kayak career. Play this right and she'll send all her friends to me on Maui. This could be a new client base: Kayaking Through Divorce. Or, Kayaking Through the Tears. Or how about, Paddling Your Own Kayak.

"I've got my waterproof camera right here," I told her. I held it up and focused. "Say kayak."

I BOUGHT THE new fleet of kayaks with money from the sale of Lost Paradise—the money I had intended to use in the Kohala purchase.

A month after settling in with CJ, I flew back to Honolulu to close the sale with the kid from New Zealand and sign the sales contract on the Kohala property. The kid bought the headquarters and all the gear. Since he needed a place to live he bought our condo.

With the money transferred, I went to the real estate agent. "It's always so cold in your office," I told him.

"I sold that property six weeks ago," he said.

No. "You were supposed to call me."

"That's kind of hard when you didn't leave a working number."

"I had the message service. You promised to call if there were counter offers."

"We had a surprise buyer. I couldn't turn down his offer."

"Who?" No one knew about the property, so far away from usual resort areas.

"You know Sam Kaluhi?"

I walked to the window. There was a ficus tree in the corner. Dried leaves covered the carpet beneath it.

"Moani?"

"That's why your plant's dying—because it's so cold in here."

"He offered five percent over the seller's price."

"I was ready to move on it."

"Actually, you weren't. You kept saying you were, but you weren't."

"You knew what the property meant to me. You knew my plan."

"Let me give you some advice, Moani. Don't take business personally."

"How else am I supposed to take it?"

"You expect the seller to turn down five percent?" He looked at me for a moment, then his expression changed as if he suddenly understood the situation. "Wait. Are you in the same Kaluhi family?"

"What did he give you to keep your mouth shut? Four, five thousand?" I said. "Cash, right?"

"I resent your implication."

"That's interference with a contract." I thought I knew about business law. "I could sue you. I could subpoena your bank records."

He sat up. "We never offered you an exclusive contract on that property."

"What's he planning on doing with the land?" But I knew. Uncle intended to steal my idea, renovate the old school and open another hotel.

"He leveled the place, from what I've heard."

I didn't believe it. Uncle was vengeful, but in the end always pragmatic. I couldn't imagine him letting an asset just sit.

"He'll probably keep the land vacant."

"My uncle? I doubt it."

"He's your uncle?"

"Unless he can squeeze a dollar from something he's not interested."

"Your kidding, right?"

"Do I look like I'm kidding?"

"Your uncle stole the deal from you?"

"Yes. We're that happy Hawaiian family you're always hearing about."

The next morning I flew to the Big Island. I had to see it for myself. As soon as I turned off the smooth, paved highway onto the old road leading up to the school, I knew it was true. Uncle had destroyed the place. The quiet in the forest told me so.

The old church was gone; only a square of dirt remained, surrounded by grass. I parked alongside it. The dimensions seemed too small for a church now. The nearby forest creaked. Soon it would reclaim the empty ground. Vines had already begun creeping toward it.

I drove up the valley road, over the bridge and dry stream, then stopped. The posts that had held up the entrance gate were gone. The gate lay in the bush, smashing the mock orange hedge. The site where the dormitory and classroom building once stood was now a flat, empty plot. There was another empty plot where the dining hall had stood. Another for the chapel, the garage and laundry buildings.

There wasn't a scrap of wood left. Uncle had even ripped out the mango tree that stood in front of the building. I knelt and studied the empty depression where the building had been. Ten thousand worker ants scurried across the red dirt. A team hauled a beetle carcass to the corner.

1986, Honolulu
Sarah

EVERYONE SAID I was lucky to have a bungalow rather than one of the apartments in the high rise. The bungalows were larger and had porches. They leased for twice the rent of apartments and there was a waiting list. You see? Even at the end of life, one still compared circumstances. There would always be something better. There would always be someone with more. Such silly talk. This was one reason I didn't eat in the dining room; I didn't care that I paid for it.

I was never enamored of this place. No one was, although many pretended. I suppose that was a useful philosophy in this facility landscaped with ginger and gardenia: pretending that death was not lurking under our beds. It worked well when hosting the grandchildren, painting watercolors in the art studio and attending the symphony on one's good days.

Yet I had never deluded myself that this place was anything more than a well-appointed depot, where we waited for death to come for us. It was not that I was afraid to die. I was not afraid. It was just that I was not yet ready. I was not ready because I did not want my dream of paradise to die. It was a dream so beautiful I had become its slave. My life was to service this dream of our beloved home in Kohala and all that might have been. I never tired of it, hour after hour reflecting upon it, seeing it in my mind's eye, all the while laying on the couch in my bungalow.

My body, however, had a mind of its own. To be specific, it was my lungs which were failing me. On Friday they were going to move me from the bungalow to the hospital facility. Today was my last day.

Finally Silvie arrived. She thought I could not hear. She thought I could not see. She opened my bungalow door and walked in like I was a nobody and not worth the common courtesy of knocking, just because I'm old. Just because the end is near. She began poking through my cupboards.

"Who's there?" I said, lying on the couch.

"Oh, Granny. Looked like you was sleeping."

I corrected her, "It looked like you *were* sleeping."

"What, Granny?"

I said nothing more. What difference would it make?

"Gotta start organizing the kitchen stuff, Granny. The movers is coming after lunch."

"The movers *are* coming after lunch."

It was more like she was stealing. Yesterday she sorted through the bedroom and bathroom closets, carrying out bags of towels, sheets and bedding—the barefoot little thief, feet like a frying pan. At first she came to me with each bundle, asking whether it should go to charity or storage.

Storage? I had asked. Storage for what? I would not be returning to the bungalow.

Silly girl. She began crying. It was that way with the Hawaiian, especially that one. I'd seen her crying over television commercials.

How did it happen that she was the only one I had left? She was the granddaughter of my nephew's second wife—my nephew who was one of my brother Daniel's bastards. Many my age had no one. I suppose I should have been grateful for her.

Well, there were two more. My visitors. One was the Trinity girl, who kept coming to see me. I did not know why as I refused to answer her questions, this niece of Sam Kaluhi. Who did she think she was, demanding that I provide her with information?

Then after months of absence, last week she came back to me with a man, or boy. To begin with, she offered no excuse for her absence, which is, by the way, typical of those spoiled Trinity girls. Then she said she wanted me to meet someone. Imagine the audacity! Thinking that she had the right to change my world? Thinking she could bring a stranger to my home and force an encounter. My body had become a sack of hollow bones. My eyes were dim, my ears muddy. My tongue was exhausted after the millions of words spoken. But my mind was as crisp as ever. It had to be, what with a Trinity girl in my home. Lose your focus, drop your guard for a moment, and they would own you.

The man, the boy, knelt before me. Everyone seemed so young. At first I couldn't believe my eyes. It was as if Charles Moku was kneeling before me, asking permission to marry the girl Lydia Kaluhi. I suppose I gasped, or tried to pull away from him. I heard him say, "Didn't mean to frighten you. Sorry."

Well you had better be sorry—all the trouble the two of you caused. The entire school scouring the Kohala hillside searching for Lydia. Why couldn't the two of you have followed our orders? *Why couldn't you people behave yourselves?* Didn't we give you the best of ourselves? Couldn't you see that we were only trying to help?

"Granny?"

I tried to see. Was that Silvie? The Trinity girl?

"He wanted to ask you about his grandmother, Lydia."

Wanted or wants? For Godsake, speak with clarity.

I heard their words, melting together like crayons left in the sun. The colors had become useless lumps of wax, void of purpose. It was infuriating that a Trinity girl could not do better. Where was her pride? Where was the leadership?

"Lydia," I heard them say the name again.

Lydia. There was so much I could have told them, searching for history. As if my recounting those days could possibly provide them with an understanding of Lydia, her family, our school and church. Kohala. As if my words could give form and dimension to my memory.

Were I inclined, were the powers of speech still mine, I would have told them to go to Kohala. I would have gone with them, if they wanted. I would have shown them Girls' School Road in the early morning, when the doves were calling. I hear them clearly nowadays. I would have shown them the Girls' School. We could wait until the afternoon bell tolled. Look, there walks Lydia through the school gate. See how she waits until she thinks no one can see her, then begins running down the road and into Kohala forest. Look, there in the clearing stands the boy Charles, waiting beneath the shimmering green canopy. Lydia runs into the clearing and stops. He smiles, stands and reaches for her schoolbag. Could they possibly understand that there was no more perfect moment? I couldn't risk it.

197

If things had been different I would have told them to see for themselves the world that gave birth to our memories. The journey would be worth all their efforts and all their losses. Loss of family. Yes, I was sure the girl's uncle Sam Kaluhi was in all of this, but on the opposite shore. He watched their movements, pacing back and forth along the sand, anxious and furious that they were attempting a crossing. Sam could not stop their advance upon the truth we had buried and guarded all these years. The girl and boy had come to claim it. The belief in paradise, and the demand to know why it had been obliterated. The quest had reached out and grabbed them.

When the girl Moani realized I would not speak to her, she brought the boy, as if he would make a difference. The two of them wore such pained yet determined expressions on their faces. The tenacious pursuit of questions without answers. They seemed young, yet simultaneously old. Supremely confident, yet full of doubt. Twenty years ago, I would have laughed. But now I see that it goes like that, a maddening swirl of yes and no.

My loyalties, however, lay elsewhere. Even at Lydia's sacrifice. Again the knife slashed; the ground drank. I saw her murder repeatedly those final days in the bungalow when the girl and boy demanded to hear the story. Oh that attitude! How much I wanted to strangle it, red with jealousy. How much I wanted to help them, fearless children I never had.

As for Sam and I, there was pain no matter my response to the girl and boy. If I provided the answers to their questions, I would hurt him because I would subvert him. If I said nothing I would still hurt him, because I would hurt his own blood.

When I left Trinity, destroying Sam Kaluhi would have brought great satisfaction. But another generation passed and I was not the same. Sam's pain. My pain. There was no distinction any longer. I saw the faintest glimmer of this realization when he came to my office that morning, his young, frightened niece in tow. A thin margin of pink light surrounded his brown-black pupils, revealing behind them a soul soaked in anguish. Still yet.

My voice rose to match his. But in spirit it was the same as his eyes: beneath my studied timbre that made Trinity famous, my voice betrayed its first hairline crack, the first inkling of a bud now before me in full bloom. My dream of returning home. Back to the green valleys past Pololū, past Honoke'ā. In the valley of the valleys, my arms about trees, my feet clutching smooth black pebbles in a stream, I should like to weep for a long time.

Sam wanted to go there too. Yes, I was sure of it. He thought about it every day. Those green valleys that gave us life never left our memory. Or the sound of water rushing over smooth rocks in the stream bed. And Kohala Mountain. No matter where I stood, it saw me. It saw us, there being no difference any longer. We were, Sam and I, the same now.

The niece named Moani, the boy she brought to me, both have this knowledge, although they are not yet aware of it. It lies in their guts waiting for them to discover it: the knowledge that another girl, the one we left behind in the sugarcane field that night, has walked alongside us each day of our lives. And that we are, after all, children of Lydia's memory.

Acknowledgments

The author gratefully acknowledges the authors and/or sources of the following previously published material which appears in this book:

SONGS: excerpt from "Aloha 'Oe", copyright 1884 by Queen Lili'uokalani (1838–1917); excerpt from "Be Thou My Vision", traditional Irish, translation copyright 1905 by Mary E. Byrne (1880–1931); excerpt from "Buffalo Gals", circa 1844 by Cool White; excerpt from "Clementine", copyright 1884 by Percy Montross; excerpt from "Danny Boy", copyright 1913 by Fred W. Weatherly (1848–1929); excerpt from "Holy, Holy, Holy", 1826 by Reginald Heber (1783–1826); excerpt from "Jesus Oh What a Wonderful Child", traditional; excerpt from "Simple Gifts", 1848 by Joseph Brackett, Jr. (1797–1882); excerpt from "There's a Wideness in God's Mercy", by Frederick William Faber (1814–1863); excerpt from "Waltzing Matilda", copyright 1903 by Andrew Barton (Banjo) Patterson (1864–1941).

POEM: excerpt from 'Versos Sencillos', by José Martí (1853 –1895).

BIBLICAL VERSE: excerpts from The Book of Psalm, chapter 23, verses 4 and 6, chapter 27, verse 7, New King James Version.